THE
HAUNTED FOREST TOUR

JAMES A. MOORE JEFF STRAND

Copyright © 2007 James A. Moore and Jeff Strand

Cover design by Lynne Hansen
www.LynneHansenDesign.com

All rights reserved.

This book is a work of fiction. Names, characters, places, and incidents are either products of the author's imagination or are used fictitiously. Any resemblance to actual events, locales, or persons, living or dead, is entirely coincidental. No part of this publication may be reproduced or transmitted in any form or by any means, electronic or mechanical, without written permission from the author.

For more information about this book, visit JamesAMoore.com and JeffStrand.com.

ISBN-13: 978-1977529992
ISBN-10: 1977529992

ACKNOWLEDGMENTS

Thanks to Paul Miller, Matt Bechtel, and Bob Booth.

PROLOGUE

Mike Fradella had finished off three beers after work, which didn't seem like quite enough to make him hallucinate the pine tree growing through his front porch. In the desert town of Cromay, New Mexico, he wouldn't have expected to see a ten-foot-tall pine tree growing *anywhere*, much less right next to his porch swing.

He got out of his car and stared at the tree for a long moment. It didn't go away.

This had to be a prank. Mike was pretty sure none of his buddies had done it, since their style of humor was more the "pull my finger" variety than anything this elaborate. It was also destructive—they hadn't merely placed the tree on his porch, they'd pried up some of the boards to make it look like the tree had sprouted right through the wood.

Kids, maybe?

They'd never really been a problem before, except for the mouth on Agatha Donald's son. Mike wouldn't mind seeing that little brat get his mouth washed out with sandpaper-wrapped soap, that was for sure. But Agatha's son was only six and unlikely to have engineered this particular project, and an out-of-the-way place like

Cromay didn't see many visitors, especially where Mike lived, five miles out of town and a half-mile from the nearest neighbor. Still, *somebody* had done it.

Mike walked up the steps. The punks had gone to an enormous amount of trouble, because it really did look like a tree had just grown right through his porch. He'd been at work all day, and then the bar for another hour, so the pranksters would've had time to pull off something like this, but why? Why wreck his front porch for a joke, and then not even hang around to see his reaction?

Or was he being secretly filmed for one of those dumb-ass reality shows? *Extreme Makeover: Destruction Edition.*

He sure hoped his homeowner's insurance would cover this kind of thing.

Mike ran his hand along the tree trunk. It was definitely real.

He went inside and called the sheriff.

***

"That's very...odd," said Sheriff Nelson.

"I know! Who do you think did it? Crackheads?"

Sheriff Nelson shook his head and scratched at the gray stubble on his chin. "Crackheads would've left the job half-finished. And this is too elaborate to be the work of kids, even college kids from out of town. I feel a bit silly asking you this, Mike, but is it possible that you hired professionals to plant a tree in your front yard and just miscommunicated the location?"

"No, it's not possible! What kind of idiot do you think I am?"

"Don't take offense. Like I said, I felt silly even asking, but we both would've felt sillier if that turned out to be the case. You have to admit, there aren't a lot of logical motives for this kind of vandalism." Sheriff Nelson crouched down on the porch, turned on his flashlight, and shone it down into the gap. "I'll be damned."

"What?"

"Take a look."

Mike crouched down next to Sheriff Nelson. The sheriff moved the flashlight beam in a small circle. "See those roots? This wasn't recently planted."

"Well, it sure wasn't here this morning!"

Sheriff Nelson stood up and dusted off his knees. "Mike, I feel kind of silly asking you this question as well, but you wouldn't happen to be trying to pull one over on me, would you?"

"Of course not!"

"I didn't think so. Again, I felt foolish even asking, but a professional has to cover all of his bases. I don't know. The best theory I've got is that this here tree grew right through your front porch."

"In ten hours?"

The sheriff nodded. "It's an acceleration from the norm, that's for sure."

"It's a freak show! I mean, what kind of tree grows that fast? What kind of pine tree grows right through somebody's front porch out here in the desert?"

Sheriff Nelson shrugged. "I may have to call in a botanist for this one."

"Botanist? Call a magician! This is insane, Sheriff! The insurance company will never believe that some radioactive mutant tree broke my porch. Even if this thing were a cactus it wouldn't make sense. I'm gonna be doing overtime for the next three months to pay for this!"

"Now, now, don't worry about the insurance company. I'll file a full report. Their claim investigator won't be able to argue with the evidence right in front of them..." He trailed off, staring into the distance.

"What?"

"Was that tree there before?"

Mike looked where the sheriff was pointing. About five hundred feet away, in the open desert, was another pine tree. This one was about twice the height of the one protruding from his porch.

"No," he said.

"Then it's very peculiar."

"Maybe it was there and I just didn't notice."

"Now, Mike, neither one of us is prone to being an idiot, and I think it's safe to say that we're both observant enough that at least one of us would have noticed it," said Sheriff Nelson. "I'm definitely going to get an expert out here. Don't they have a lot of pines in New Jersey?"

"Sheriff!" Mike frantically pointed at a spot in the middle of the dirt road. A thick tree trunk burst from the ground, sprouting branches as it grew. Mike and Sheriff Nelson stood there and gaped as the tree rose fifty feet high within thirty seconds.

"I...I'm dropping the prank theory," Mike said.

Two more trees popped up in the distance. Sheriff Nelson grabbed his walkie-talkie and pushed the button on the side. "Francine? You there?"

The sound of splintering wood, breaking glass, and a large object being overturned made Mike flinch. A moment later, a tree burst through the top of his house, stretching past the roof high into the air.

"Francine, I need you *now!*" Sheriff Nelson shouted into the walkie-talkie.

It's Armageddon, thought Mike. *End of the world and that kind of stuff.*

The front of Mike's car began to rise. As he and the sheriff watched helplessly, it rose almost completely upright and then toppled over onto its side.

"Let's get the hell out of here!" Sheriff Nelson shouted. He and Mike sprinted over to the sheriff's vehicle as a second tree burst through Mike's front porch, taking the swing with it. Mike threw open the passenger-side door and got inside the car, slamming the door shut behind him. He instinctively reached for the seat belt, then immediately decided that he very well might need to leap from the vehicle at some point.

Sheriff Nelson thrust the key into the ignition and started the engine. Mike cried out in surprise as a tree appeared right next to his window, the branches scraping across the glass as they rose. As more and more trees sprouted from the ground, they sped out of the driveway and down the road.

"Sheriff, what's going on?" Mike wailed.

"I couldn't explain the one piddly little tree on your porch! What makes you think I can explain this?" Sheriff Nelson swerved to avoid a tree that burst through the center of the road.

They raced the five miles into town, with Mike clenching his teeth so tightly that he thought they might explode into white powder. Trees continued to pop out of the ground on all sides of them, and Mike's heart gave a jolt as one scraped the rear bumper.

Finally they made it to Main Street, the only paved road in Cromay. It was pure chaos. People screamed and ran for non-existent safety as tree after tree appeared, breaking through shops and homes.

If this wasn't literally the end of the world, it was pretty damn close.

Seventy-eight year-old Mrs. Tunstall pushed her husband, who'd been confined to a wheelchair six years ago, at a full sprint, a sight that would have been comical under other circumstances. The tip of a tree caught the wheelchair under the front wheel, abruptly jerking it upward. Mrs. Tunstall wailed as the handles popped out of her grasp, with Mr. Tunstall clutching the sides for dear life to avoid tumbling out. He managed to hold on until he was about five stories high, and then he slipped out of the wheelchair, bellowing as he plummeted onto the sidewalk in front of his wife.

Mike winced, slammed his fist over his mouth, and turned away. The sight on the other side was no better, as Hugh the video store clerk dropped from the air onto the copper statue of John Cromay, the town's founder.

"Sheriff! Thank God!" cried Craig Zebsmith, who'd been one of Mike's drinking partners after work. Sheriff Nelson rolled down his window as Craig rushed over to the car. "You've gotta get me out of here! You've gotta—"

A tree popped up right in front of Craig, catching him under the jaw and snapping his head backward in a mist of blood. The rising tree quickly hid the rest of the grisly sight.

"There's gotta be someplace we can get these people that's safe!" Sheriff Nelson said. "These trees can't break through *everything*, can they?"

The copper statue toppled over, landing on top of Video Store Hugh's mangled body.

"Let's just get out of here!" Mike insisted.

Sheriff Nelson looked as if he wanted to make some sort of heroic, selfless statement...but then he slammed on the accelerator and they sped down the street. Mike watched in horror as a tree burst through a pump at the gas station, spraying fuel everywhere.

"Aw...crap!" Sheriff Nelson slammed on the brakes as a pair of trees broke through the pavement directly in front of them, blocking the road. He put the car into reverse and looked back over his shoulder as they rocketed backwards—

"*Watch out!*"

—smacking into a man who ran out into the road behind them. He disappeared behind the vehicle too quickly for Mike to see who it was. Sheriff Nelson slammed on the brakes again.

"Don't stop!"

"I'm not going to just leave him there!"

"Pretty soon there won't be any road left!"

A tree popped up underneath the sheriff's car, knocking it onto its side. Safety glass from the windshield sprayed over both of them, and Mike dropped onto Sheriff Nelson with a loud grunt. The sheriff cried out in pain.

We're dead, we're so dead, Mike thought as he scrambled through the front windshield. He shook the glass off his hands and reached back inside for the sheriff.

"You broke my damn arm!" Sheriff Nelson shouted.

"C'mon, c'mon, let's go!" Mike grabbed the sheriff's good arm and tried to pull him to safety.

A tree came through the ground directly beneath the sheriff, bursting right through his chest. Mike screamed and frantically scooted away as the expanding tree ripped the car in half.

Mike got to his feet, stumbled a bit, and blindly ran down the street, barely even noticing as some branches slashed across his cheek. This was *not* the way he'd planned to die. He hadn't exactly given a lot of thought to the ways he might want to perish, but killer trees were definitely not on the list.

"Mike!"

He spun around. It was Jo-Anne Sanes, vigorously waving to him from the doorway of Jo-Anne's Sweets, her candy shop. Mike wasn't a big candy eater, but he and Jo-Anne were both divorced, and he stopped by every once in a while for some harmless flirting. She stepped out of the way as he rushed inside, colliding with the gumball machine and sending it crashing to the floor. Multi-colored gumballs rolled everywhere.

"We won't be safe here," he blurted out as she pulled the glass door closed.

"We might be. Those things can't cover the entire town, can they?"

"I don't know. They seem to be doing a pretty good job."

The glass front of the store shattered as something exploded. It sounded like it came from the gas station.

Mike took Jo-Anne's hand. "We should run for it."

"No," she said, pulling away. "We need to hunker down someplace safe! This'll all stop, I know it!"

A tree burst through the floor of the shop, displacing an entire shelf of candy jars. A second tree followed almost immediately after, popping up directly beneath Jo-Anne and lifting her to the ceiling.

The tree easily broke through the roof. Jo-Anne did not. Her body hit the floor, landing on broken glass,

Atomic Fireballs, and sour gummi worms.

Mike ran out of the shop, barely able to breathe. The trees were almost forest-thick now, and the shrieks of Cromay residents were like rusty nails through his eardrums.

A rising tree tore across his back. He stumbled forward into another one. Branches sprouted beneath his feet, lifting him up, and he instinctively hugged the tree as tightly as he could.

He quickly rose into the air. More branches sprouted from the tree, slashing across his arms and legs. One branch ripped right through his left forearm, and he could do nothing but close his eyes and scream as he went up and up and up...

Finally, the ride stopped. He waited for a moment, completely unmoving, and then forced himself to open his eyes.

From this vantage point, hundreds of feet in the air, he could see trees rising for miles. There was an end to it, though—they seemed to be forming a perfect circle.

The top branches wobbled in the wind, and he held on more tightly.

He took a deep breath, closed his eyes again, and wrenched his arm free. His scream of agony echoed across the brand-new forest.

The branch beneath his feet seemed to be relatively sturdy, so he manipulated himself into a position where he could apply pressure to his injured arm while still holding on. As long as he didn't bleed to death, he could stay up here until they sent a helicopter or something. A forest sprouting up in the middle of the desert would certainly attract quick attention, right?

He was starting to feel light-headed already. Hopefully

it was just from being up so high and not from blood loss.

Be strong...you've gotta be strong. Wait this out and you'll be okay, and you'll have one hell of a story to tell on the talk shows. Movie deal, book deal, merchandising...you'll be rich. Just wait it out. Don't bleed to death.

The branches beneath him rustled.

A clawed hand wrapped around his ankle.

Mike screamed for the last time as he was pulled off his perch.

CHAPTER ONE

We'll discuss this on Monday...

It was the adult equivalent of "wait until your father gets home." And just as Christopher Brummit's mother had used that technique to extend the misery of upcoming punishments, Mr. Tylerson was going to purposely make him sweat all weekend. There was no reason they couldn't meet this afternoon and get it over with, but the sadistic bastard wanted him to suffer, unable to eat or sleep, stomach churning, headache pounding, wondering if he'd still have a job when he wandered into the office Monday morning.

Christopher had been putting in seventy and eighty-hour weeks for the past several months. He wasn't the only one. The lack of a life outside of work was a source of masochistic pride for his co-workers; hell, it was practically a competition to see who could put in the longest workweek. Simply working eight-to-five was unheard of. Lunch breaks were for the weak. If you weren't a slave to Novellon, Inc., then you weren't a team player.

Christopher did his work without complaint. Since his divorce a year ago, he really didn't have a life outside of work anyway, unless you counted Netflix. But the long hours and non-stop pressure were wearing him down, and he finally made a mistake.

A big one.

Well, technically, a small one. A single typo in a spreadsheet. But it was a typo that made Mr. Tylerson "look like an ass" in front of the board of directors.

"Would you like to explain to me how this happened?" Mr. Tylerson had asked, tossing the flawed spreadsheet across his luxurious desk. His face—already naturally ruddy—was so red that Christopher worried that his pores might start seeping blood.

"I didn't have time to double-check it."

"What do you mean, you didn't have time to double-check it?"

"You needed it quickly, before the meeting, remember? Normally I would double-check all of the formulas, but I didn't get a chance."

Mr. Tylerson gave him a disgusted look. "I don't want excuses."

"You asked how this happened. I'm trying to explain."

"No, you're trying to pass the buck. This is a business. Things move fast in the world of business. We don't have the luxury of spending hours double-checking things that should have been done right the first time. We need to be at the top of our game every minute of every day. Otherwise there are consequences. We'll discuss this on Monday."

Christopher wanted to protest, and he also wanted to knock out a half-dozen of his employer's teeth. He did neither. Instead, he got up and left Mr. Tylerson's office without a word.

A couple of his co-workers gave him sympathetic

looks as he returned to his cubicle. Novellon had pettiness and backstabbing galore, but Christopher was well liked, and everybody knew that a disciplinary meeting with Mr. Tylerson was serious business.

I'm gonna lose my job.

Would that really be such a bad thing?

Yes.

Maybe not if he'd quit or been laid off, but in this crappy job market, getting fired would be disastrous. He was thirty-eight years old and didn't want to have to start over with a whole new career.

He struggled to work for the rest of the day, then went home and threw up.

* * *

Christopher lay on his bed on top of the blankets, still in his work clothes. Maybe that's how he'd spend Halloween weekend: lie in bed, stare at the ceiling, and count the time in quarter-second intervals until Mr. Tylerson saw fit to reveal his fate.

His mother had told him weeks ago not to make any plans for this weekend, insisting that she had "an amazing, wonderful, thrilling surprise" that he'd just *looooove*, but Christopher didn't feel up to anything more amazing, wonderful, and thrilling than lying here and getting in a lot of quality moping-around time.

The phone rang. He briefly considered letting it go to voice mail, but his mom wasn't big on leaving messages and would keep calling until a live person answered.

"Hello?" he answered, still lying flat.

"Christopher? You sound mopey."

"I'm not mopey."

"Good. Are you ready for your surprise?"

"Yeah."

"That didn't sound very enthusiastic. Are you feeling okay?"

"I'm fine. I'm just tired."

"Too tired for...The Haunted Forest Tour?"

Christopher immediately sat up. "What?"

"Oooh, *now* you're not so mopey, are you?"

"You got tickets to the Haunted Forest Tour?"

"Not just the Haunted Forest Tour. The *Halloween* Haunted Forest Tour. It's the deepest any tour group has ever gone into the forest."

"Are you kidding? How'd you get those? I thought they weren't available to the general public."

"What makes you think I'm the general public?"

"Seriously, how'd you get them?"

"I won them. Did you know that at one point *The Texas Chainsaw Massacre* was going to be called *Headcheese*?"

"No."

"I did. That's how I got the tickets."

"How are we going to get there?"

"Well, since I'm not up for a twenty-three-hour drive, I bought us plane tickets. Our flight leaves tomorrow at seven. Sorry you don't get to sleep in."

Christopher couldn't believe this. He'd been interested in the Haunted Forest Tour ever since it opened a year ago. Screw Mr. Tylerson and his *We'll discuss this on Monday* crap. Screw lying around wallowing in self-pity. He'd worry about his potential for becoming an unemployed loser after the tour.

"How much were the plane tickets?" he asked.

"None of your business."

"Then let me pay for the hotel."

"How about you finally pay back that fifty cents you borrowed when you were six?"

"Never!"

"I'm paying for everything," she assured him. "The downside is that you have to spend an entire weekend with your mother. It'll be fun. You need some fun in your life."

You couldn't be more right. "Well, thanks!"

"So what were you moping about? Bad day at work?"

"Eh, the usual. Just waiting for the aspirin to kick in."

"I won't keep you, honey. Hurry up and get packed. We've got a great weekend ahead of us!"

"Thanks, Mom. I really appreciate this."

"That's what mothers are for. Happy Halloween!"

Christopher hung up the phone. Wow. His mom had actually made everything all better.

He got up and went to his closet. He would've done a load of laundry if he'd known he was leaving town for the weekend, but he could scavenge something wearable.

Four years ago, scientists were beyond baffled by the events at Cromay, New Mexico. An entire forest sprouted out of nowhere, engulfing the desert town and killing a presumed two hundred and seventy-three people. The tales shared by those who escaped were unbelievable, but yet difficult to contradict considering that there was now a forest out in the desert that hadn't been there the day before.

Christopher and his ex-wife, Samantha, had watched the nightly news with fascination. Rescue teams went into the forest to search for survivors and never returned. The forest was too thick to explore from overhead, but news crews in helicopters were able to capture footage of eerie glows within the trees.

Mark J. Cardin, Jr., a hotshot reporter for Fox News, was grabbed by...*something* while doing a live newscast. Something big. His blood covered the camera lens, making it difficult to figure out exactly what happened after that, but neither Mark nor his cameraman ever returned.

"The Haunted Forest" continued to make nightly headlines. There was a lot of debate over whether it was truly "haunted" or merely populated by unidentified creatures, but the name stuck. The Internet was filled with conspiracy theories, the most common of which was that the United States government had developed a high-tech tree growth hormone that had gotten out of control, and that the creatures in the forest were being bred as super-soldiers.

The Haunted Forest eventually faded from the news headlines until a year ago, when H.F. Enterprises announced the Haunted Forest Tour. They'd installed track that, while it didn't go deep into the forest, did circle the entire perimeter. The trams were reinforced and, according to the advertisements, "impervious to damage by any creature or ghost."

The tours were a smash hit, making countless millions of dollars for H.F. Enterprises. Any type of photography or video recording was strictly forbidden, but tour patrons reported sightings of all manner of bizarre and frightening creatures. One elderly woman died of a heart attack when a fanged creature scraped at the window next to her seat. The resulting lawsuit was settled out of court. But beyond that, H.F. Enterprises proudly boasted of its "100% safety record! Nobody has ever been eaten on one of our tours, and nobody ever will!"

Christopher had really wanted to go, but that was right around the time of his divorce. There was no infidelity or any other single destructive event involved. Rather, it was twelve years of gradually accumulating annoyance with each other that finally exploded. Samantha flew to California to "find herself," while Christopher worked, watched television, and ignored his mother's advice to go out and try to meet people.

Then H.F. Enterprises had announced the newest incarnation of the Haunted Forest Tour. This one cut right through the center of the forest, with "shocking sights that will absolutely blow your mind!" The tour was set to open on Halloween, and he hadn't realized that it was possible for non-millionaires to get tickets.

Christopher was almost giddy.

Scratch that. He was *completely* giddy.

* * *

He was slightly less giddy when the alarm went off at four-thirty. Even during one of his sixteen-hour days at Novellon, he got to sleep in later than this. But a hot shower and Godzilla-sized cup of coffee put him back in an excited frame of mind.

His mother stood outside waiting for him as he pulled into the parking lot of her apartment complex. Mindy Brummit looked at least ten years younger than her real age of fifty-seven. In fact, the only time Christopher had seen his mother looking her true age was at his father's funeral.

He parked and got out of the car. Not surprisingly, she'd packed three large suitcases for a two-day trip.

He gave her a tight hug. "You know, they only let you

check two pieces of luggage."

"Two each. How many suitcases did you bring?"

"One."

"See? Problem solved."

Christopher unlocked the trunk. His mother had curly red hair that she insisted was her natural color. Of course, she'd insisted that last month's brunette shade was her natural color, along with the bleached blonde look of last year. She wore a blue and green Hawaiian shirt, shorts, and sunglasses, a strong contrast to the slacks and white dress shirt that Christopher was wearing.

"At least you didn't wear a tie," she said, reaching up to adjust his collar.

Though she was a small woman, she was anything but frail. Christopher often joked that she could beat the crap out of him in a bar fight, but he secretly wasn't entirely certain that it was a joke. She worked full time as a receptionist at a law firm, and devoted her spare time to gardening, gourmet cooking, pottery, bicycling, swimming, "power-knitting" (racing against her friends to complete a sweater in the fastest time), and karate.

How'd she end up with such a boring son? he wondered.

He put her suitcases—which weighed approximately eight thousand pounds each, or so he told her—in the back of the car, and they left for the airport.

"Thanks, Mom," he said. "I really appreciate this."

"Remember that when it's time for my nursing home. I want the place where they *don't* harvest your internal organs in the middle of the night. At least not the important ones."

"Gotcha."

"Are you ready to be scared out of your wits?"

"Absolutely!"

CHAPTER TWO

The air was crisp, with just a hint of autumn that would probably fade away as the sun rose higher. It was a perfect day for a picnic. Less perfect for a terrifying tour through a monster-ridden forest, but that was okay. Mark Harper knew that the tourists would still get their money's worth, big-time. They always did.

The people arriving on the tour bus all looked excited, even the older ones. After all, how often did you get a chance to see monsters in a safe environment? Or any environment? Though Mark's involvement with H.F. Enterprises was entirely on the scientific research end, rather than the spook show end, he thoroughly enjoyed the idea of the Haunted Forest Tour and occasionally took a ride himself just to see their reactions.

A large banner read *"Welcome to the First Annual Haunted Forest Halloween Tour"* in bright orange letters on a slime-green field. The official logo of H.F. Enterprises was on each corner of the banner, as if anyone would suddenly forget where they were.

Below the banner were stacks of T-shirts, posters, coffee mugs, snow globes, monster-shaped candy, Christmas tree ornaments, ball caps, key chains, jewelry, watches, press-on tattoos, ties, sunglasses, refrigerator magnets, monster masks, and countless other examples of overpriced crap available for your purchasing ecstasy. Mark Harper had tried the Haunted Forest taffy once. *Once.*

Behind the banner and the displays of souvenirs was the actual office of H.F. Enterprises, a four-story affair. The large windows were reflective and cast back slightly distorted images of the various people who walked in front of them as well as the cerulean sky and just a few puffy white clouds. The forest itself, about half a mile away, was a dark, jagged shadow along the lowest edge of the glass.

Mark looked at his own reflection in the glass and straightened his tie. He also finger-combed his hair because, as always, he wanted to look his best for the woman walking up the stairs behind him.

Hannah Chambers was not his lover. She was his coworker and damned good at her job. Mark was a happily married man who just happened to think—in a purely platonic, non-sleazy manner—that his co-worker was one of the sexiest women alive. He did not speak of these things with her, or with his wife Chloe. That would be bad. Extremely bad.

He loved Chloe and would never be unfaithful to her.

Unless he ever got really, really drunk or accidentally swallowed a few Viagra tablets and even then, the only way he would ever go through with it was if Hannah put him in a situation where he absolutely couldn't refuse. Perhaps it was a matter of life or death, or possibly somebody's honor was at stake, or maybe she was under such incredible stress that if she didn't find a release she'd have a heart attack, and he couldn't very well let somebody this important to the workings of H.F. Enterprises have a heart attack...

Mostly they just flirted, and then Mark did his best not to think of the situations in which he would willingly cheat on his wife with his peer. He could only count a few of them (if you included only broad generalities), which wasn't so bad. And he'd probably never go through with them even if those situations presented themselves, because he was happily married. To Chloe. The love of his life.

It was best that way, really, but he still always wanted to make sure he looked his best for Hannah.

He turned away from the window before she could see him looking at himself and smiled as she moved past a crowd of tourists. There was a little tyke begging his mom for an *I Survived The Halloween Haunted Forest Tour* T-shirt, complete with a smiling one-eyed ghoul illustration. There were no smiling one-eyed ghouls in the Haunted Forest, of course. Not as far as Mark knew at any rate, and if anyone would know, it would be him or Hannah. It was their jobs to know.

Hannah moved closer and smiled. "Can you believe this crowd?"

"Can you believe how many of them are buying the taffy?"

She laughed and rolled her blue eyes, flipping her blond hair back from her forehead. She wore a little makeup, but only a little. She didn't need it. She also didn't necessarily need all of those clothes, since she would look perfectly stylish and professional in only a-

Chloe. He made himself remember his wife and look away from Hannah before he could stare at her ample chest. Chloe had a great body too. Just in a different way.

Really.

The problem with Hannah was that she was just as smart and witty as she was attractive. Mark's infatuation was totally understandable, and totally within the bounds of what was acceptable in a morally sound marriage. Though it would have been easier if Hannah had a big leaking wart on her nose.

Hannah stood up a little straighter, and that was enough warning for Mark. Two seconds later, he saw Booth coming in their direction. Most of the big guys at the H.F. Enterprises preferred to go by their first names, but Martin Booth preferred to go by "Booth." Not Mr. Booth. Just Booth.

"How are ya, guys?" Booth smiled as he walked past, looking spry and happy. His dark hair was perfect, and the matching mustache and goatee were trimmed close to his face. That he was happy was a relief, because Mark had seen the man angry, and it was enough to create a whole row of ulcers.

"Couldn't be much better." Mark smiled and tried to look relaxed. Booth owned the company, yet had little to do with the actual running of it. In fact, Mark rarely saw the man. Seeing him out here, acting all chipper, was just plain weird.

Booth patted his shoulder. "Glad to hear it. Big day today, yes indeed. Should be interesting to see what everyone has to say about the new extended tour."

Mark and Hannah had both traveled the new route several times and were still impressed by it. Hannah nodded emphatically, and Mark noticed Booth's eyes checking her out. He managed to avoid bristling at the visual undressing. First, it wasn't his concern, since he was a happily married man who was completely devoted to his wife Chloe and would never cheat, and second, Hannah would probably club him over the head if he acted like a teenaged boyfriend around her.

Booth smiled again, obviously enjoying the mental image he had drawn up of Hannah's nakedness. Mark wondered how closely it matched his own. And how closely his own image matched the real one. "Well, I'm gonna go make sure everything's set up properly," Booth told them. "You guys be on your best behavior, okay? The press is swarming this place. Oh, and Happy Halloween."

He headed on his way without waiting for a response.

Mark watched him go and from the corner of his eye he saw Hannah watching as well. Her eyes weren't aimed at the back of his head, but substantially lower.

She caught him looking and smiled. "What?" She blushed a little. "He's got a nice butt."

"Can't say I ever noticed."

"It's firm and shapely and probably inflexible to the touch, just the way I like them." Hannah punched him playfully in the arm. "Anyway, let's get inside. It's lecture time again!"

* * *

"Can I have one, Aunt Jean?"

Tommy Walker looked up at his aunt and put on his most effective wide-eyed expression. It didn't take much work, because he already had wide eyes and a face that bordered on pretty. At least that was what his uncle always said. His uncle always said weird things like that. Aunt Jean said it was because he worked in Hollywood and liked to find new ways to look at things. Mommy always said it was because Uncle Perry was a pervert.

He had no idea what a pervert was, and Mommy wouldn't tell him, but he figured it had to be something funny, because Mommy always laughed when she said it.

He liked hearing Mommy laugh. It didn't happen all that often.

Aunt Jean looked at the Day-Glo shirt in his hands and shook her head, but she was smiling when she did it. It seemed like there were a zillion things he wanted at the stands around them, from the neat shirts to the candy and even the books with pictures. He was in six-year-old heaven.

"Maybe when we're done with the tour, okay, honey?"

Tommy frowned. He already knew enough of his aunt's code to understand that meant he wasn't going to get the shirt.

Uncle Perry was nearby on his phone, talking to somebody in a loud, angry voice. Tommy knew that he was working on a deal, and it was supposed to have been finished two weeks ago, but things hadn't worked out right. Tommy didn't completely understand what was going on, but Uncle Perry was pretty mad about it, and Aunt Jean was mad that he was talking on the phone during their vacation.

He hoped that Uncle Perry's deal didn't make them miss the tram. He wanted to see the monsters. Real ones, not like the ones in *Harry Potter*. He was a little scared, but Aunt Jean was there with him and she always protected him. Even when Mommy and Daddy yelled at each other, it was Aunt Jean who came over to take him to her place to sleep for the night. He spent a lot of time with his aunt.

Sometimes Uncle Perry was there, too, but a lot of

times he was out of town and making movies. Tommy set down the T-shirt and pointed to the candy bars.

"Can I have one of those?"

Aunt Jean looked at the array of Haunted Forest Tour confections and sighed. "Okay, but just one. We have lunch after the tour and we don't want to spoil it."

Uncle Perry closed up his phone and walked back over to them. "Stupid. Stupid, stupid people. God, I hate stupid people."

"Did he back out?"

"He's trying to. Stupid idiot moron jerk."

As Aunt Jean sighed, Tommy tried not to pout. He definitely wasn't going to get a T-shirt after the tour.

* * *

Mark stood at the podium and watched Hannah as she stacked her papers together. She brought the same papers with her every time they did the lecture, but she never referred to them. He sometimes suspected they were there strictly for show and merely contained half-finished Sudoku puzzles, but either way, watching her shuffle them around and then put them back into a neat stack was always fun. Her body had the most interesting way of shaking when it came time to get the messy heap into an orderly shape.

Chloe. Right. Back to work.

The group came in as a mob, and he could tell that the auditorium was going to fill up quickly. That sounded impressive as hell, but the room only had 160 seats, enough for exactly four tram cars' worth of people.

There was a sign that very clearly stated that Monster Biology 101 was not for the squeamish and was not recommended for younger children.

The thing about cryptozoology was that it was mostly speculative. The thing about the Haunted Forest cryptozoologists was that they got to do a shitload more hands-on work than any of their peers. Mark smiled when he thought about that. He and Hannah were the envy of damned near everyone working in their specialty. They got to play with monsters.

Well, the dead ones. He wasn't so keen on the idea of actually trying to dissect a live one. People lost fingers and throats that way.

He checked his remote control to make sure it was on as the crowd settled in. Then he looked over at Hannah. She was straightening her skirt and looking at the crowd. For one moment he allowed himself a daydream, in which he got to play with her skirt the same way.

Chloe. Right. Back to work.

"Happy Halloween everyone!" His voice came through the PA system without any extra feedback. The microphone never had feedback. It was actually kind of unnatural and disturbing.

The audience gave an enthusiastic "Happy Halloween" right back.

"Welcome to the Haunted Forest Tour! Actually, welcome to what I like to call Monster Behavior and Biology 101. My name is Dr. Mark Harper. I'm one of those obnoxious people who put Dr. in front of their names without being medical doctors. The lovely lady to my left is Dr. Hannah Chambers, who is equally obnoxious. We're both cryptozoologists. We get paid to study unusual life forms and to discover them whenever possible. Now, most of the people in our line of work might run across a new form of fish or even get lucky enough to catch a glimpse of a Sasquatch if they spend their entire lives hunting for it. Technically, cryptozoology is a new science, but really it's just the name that has changed. There have been people looking for new types of life as long as there have been people, and there have been people for a long time."

That line never got a laugh, but Mark was going to continue to use it until it did.

"The difference for us is that we get to work here, right at the edge of the Haunted Forest."

Hannah stepped forward with a dazzling smile. "What that means is we get paid a very mediocre salary to find out about everything in there." Several people chuckled. A few of the men looked at Hannah with decided interest. "We've had a few delicious encounters with the things in the Haunted Forest, and we're going to show you a few slides of the things we've encountered. But, again, we do not recommend this part of the tour for anyone who is squeamish, and we also don't suggest that any children sit through the presentation."

Hannah looked out into the audience, first at where a tyke sat with his mother and father and then where a couple of preteens could be seen. The people took the hint and the little kid left with his mother and father. One of the preteens stayed, but the other left with her father.

"The reason for my warning is that a big part of what Mark and I do is perform autopsies on the creatures that live in the Haunted Forest."

Mark smiled as he stepped back up to the microphone. "I'm sure you'll all be disappointed to hear that we won't be performing an autopsy in front of you." The audience groaned in mock disappointment.

"Unless any of you volunteer to lie on the table, of

course," said Hannah.

I'd love to have you lie on the table, thought Mark, which was the same thing he thought every time she used that joke.

Hannah's joke earned a few chuckles from the audience. It was easy to work with them, because they were there to be amused. They were hyped as hell and excited about the trip they were about to take.

Given what they had paid to be here, keeping the visitors happy was extremely important.

It was also a good chance for Mike and Hannah to strut their stuff.

Mike stepped back and let Hannah do the talking. She took care of the main speech, and they took turns handling the questions afterward.

"We've been investigating the Haunted Forest since shortly after it first showed up. That's right, long before we allowed a tour into the dark and scary woods, we started investigating and cataloguing everything we could find. And believe me, there's been a lot to find."

Hannah pointed to Mike and he flicked the ON switch for the projection screen. The first image showed up, an extreme close-up of an ogre's mouth, all of the teeth in full display. The gums were black, and the huge teeth were put into perspective by a ruler that clearly showed the smallest of them was over four inches in length.

They'd had the fortune to run across a decomposing ogre a couple of years back. The body was still in cold storage, and from time to time, just to scare himself, he read over the autopsy notes and reexamined the facts. Muscular density was four times what it was for a human being, and the bones were almost as dense as petrified wood. A creature that should have already weighed in at close to a thousand pounds, the ogre corpse was closer to a ton. When you counted in the missing limbs and decomposition of the body, that was pretty damned scary. When you added in that the corpse belonged to an adolescent ogre, it was terrifying.

The good news was that they had never run across a living ogre. Mark suppressed a pleasant shiver at the thought.

Mark and Hannah continued the half-hour presentation, stopping on several occasions to answer questions even though they usually asked people to hold their questions until the end. It was one of the most excited, interested crowds they'd ever had.

It was going to be one fun Halloween.

CHAPTER THREE

"Ladies and gentlemen, welcome to the Haunted Forest Tour!"

Christopher and Mindy sat near the back of the tram. It held about forty people total, with only two people per row so that everybody got a window seat. They'd boarded after passing through a metal detector, an X-ray machine, and receiving a generous pat-down search. "Biggest thrill I've had in years," his mother had said with a grin.

"My name is Barbara, and I'll be your tour guide today," said the perky young brunette in the park ranger uniform. She stood up front, speaking into a microphone. "I'm so glad you could be here for this special Halloween event. Is everybody excited?"

The crowd indicated that, yes, indeed, they were quite excited.

"Good. Now what I want everybody to do is knock on your window. Go ahead. Knock on it."

Christopher knocked on his window as instructed.

"The reason I asked you to do that is not because we want somebody to answer the window." Barbara waited for polite laughter. "No, I wanted you to see that the windows are very solid. They may look like glass, but they're actually made out of a very special kind of plastic with a long scientific name. The creatures in the Haunted Forest are far from domesticated, and some may come right up to the tram, but rest assured, they can't get in to eat you."

Most of the tourists laughed.

"Also, the bottom of the tram is a giant electronic magnet that our driver can turn on with the flick of a switch. If he does that, not even a team of charging rhinos could knock us off the track. And since you're all wearing your seat belts, you can enjoy the rhino attack in safety and relative comfort. Are there any questions or concerns about your safety while onboard? Good."

The young boy seated in front of Christopher, who was probably about six years old, looked as if he had plenty of questions or concerns about his safety while onboard, but his father winked at him and ruffled his hair.

"It's important to remember that this is a real forest," said Barbara, "and we've only just begun to explore it. There are no animatronic animals out here. This means that your tour will be—say it with me—unpredictable. Your driver will be focusing on driving, and though I'll be watching for interesting sights, I only have two eyes. Therefore, it's your job to not be shy and to let the rest of us know if you see something. Just raise your hand and we'll stop the tram. Another tram will be following about half an hour behind us, so we can't hang out forever, but we do want to make sure that all of you get a chance to see the fascinating sights within this forest. Are there any questions?"

A man raised his hand. "What if we don't see

anything?"

"Well, then we'll be forced to erase the memory of each and every one of you to ensure that you don't tell anybody about your disappointing experience. No, of course I'm only kidding. Believe me, the forest is well inhabited, and I guarantee that you'll see things you never imagined. I would like to take this opportunity to warn you that some of the sights may be disturbing. These aren't all cute fuzzy little animals. Some of them may be quite frightening. But it's Halloween, and that's why you're here, right?"

"Hell yeah!" said Mindy.

"Heck yeah is right," said Barbara. "So fasten your seatbelts, unfasten your imagination, ask the person next to you for permission to grab them if things get scary, and get ready to experience the awesome sights of...the Halloween Haunted Forest Tour!"

The lights illuminating the inside of the tram suddenly turned red. "Mood lighting," Barbara explained. "We do that just to put you in a spooky mood. Is everybody in a spooky mood? Good." The lights went back to normal.

Christopher grinned as the tram began to move. The next batch of tourists waved them goodbye. The tram left the small station and glided slowly and silently along the tracks. It was a beautiful, sunny day, and the Haunted Forest loomed ahead.

"If you want to wimp out, I'm sorry to inform you that your last opportunity for cowardice expired, oh, about fifteen seconds ago," Barbara informed the group. "If you wish to close your eyes and hide under the seats, please be aware that there's not enough room under there for even the tiniest of children, and that we cannot guarantee your comfort. And now, ladies and gentlemen, we're about to leave the world that you know and love behind in five...four...three..."

Christopher almost wanted to giggle. He didn't, though.

"...two...and...*one!*"

The tram entered the path cut in the forest and was immediately cast into darkness. Not total darkness, more like gloom, but there was definitely very little hint of the beautiful, sunny day. Christopher peered out his window and strained to see what was out there.

"Though light does get through the trees, it's not enough to give you an optimal viewing experience," Barbara explained. "So we have to bring our own."

Bright lights on the side of the tram turned on, illuminating the forest all around them. The tram slowly moved along the track. The forest looked pretty normal so far, but—

"Look at that!" said his mom, nudging him harder than necessary. "In the tree!"

Several of the other tourists looked where she was pointing. There was some sort of furry brown creature, about twice the size of a squirrel, perched on a low branch, eating what looked like a bird. The creature had large fangs and paid no attention to the tram.

"Oh, yes, what you see there is a Laura. You may think that's an unusual name for a creature like that, but an amusing piece of trivia is that many of the people who discovered creatures in the Haunted Forest were allowed to name them. The Lauras were in fact named after the ex-wife of the person who discovered them. I'm sure that's not the way she wanted to achieve immortality, but that's the way it goes."

The Laura stuffed the bird's feet into its mouth. Mindy

grimaced.

"Yes, we've already seen one of the grisly aspects of the forest. Hopefully there won't be too many of those, but you never know what's going to happen...on Halloween!"

At this point, Christopher had to admit that he was ready for Barbara to speak a bit less frequently. So he tried to tune her out and watch for cool stuff outside.

There was a definite flash of movement behind one of the larger trees, but he couldn't tell what it was.

The tram continued moving deeper into the forest, and Christopher realized that he was starting to develop a nervous knot in his stomach. The tour was exciting as hell, but at the same time, the forest was almost creepy in a *bad* way. He wasn't into any of that "negative energy" crap, yet he couldn't quite get over the feeling that, yes, this place was giving off negative energy.

"Oooh! Oooh! Oooh!" said the little kid in front of Christopher. "What's that? What's that?"

"That looks like a ghost!" said his father. He raised his hand. "Is that a ghost?"

Barbara glanced out the window. "I don't see it, point it out."

"It's gone now."

"Well, we'll stop the tram and see if it comes back." The tram came to a gentle stop. "The Haunted Forest does contain some spectral activity. You wouldn't expect to be able to see a ghost in our bright lights, but actually they show up just fine."

"Are these the ghosts of the people who died when the forest appeared?" the man asked.

Barbara shrugged. "Like so many things about the Haunted Forest, that's a mystery. But it would not surprise me if the spirits of the people who were killed on that bizarre and memorable night were not at rest."

"Can they get through the windows?" asked the little boy.

"No, they sure can't."

"Why not?"

"We put ghost spray on the windows."

"Oh."

Barbara grinned at the other tourists as if sharing a private joke. Christopher thought the little boy had brought up a darn good point. How *did* they keep the ghosts out?

They waited for about three minutes, but the ghost did not return. The tram slid back into motion.

The delighted tourists saw several other creatures as they moved through the forest: a humanoid whose face was ninety percent teeth, a beetle the size of a small dog, bat-like things with glowing red eyes, and a wolf with bloody fur.

"We're now about to reach our first scheduled stop," Barbara announced. The tram veered a bit to the right as it passed a large tree, and then the tourists let out a collective "Oooooh!" as they saw what was beyond: a large bubbling pit, about the size of an Olympic swimming pool. It looked like it was filled with molten lava. And things were swimming in it. Lots of them.

It sort of looked the way Christopher imagined the pits of Hell, except that Hell probably didn't have souls in torment leaping out and doing back-flips.

"We have no idea why this pit is there or what those things are that are swimming in it," Barbara admitted. "But it's a fascinating sight, isn't it?"

Not all of the creatures looked like they were

swimming. Some were fighting. In fact, Christopher flinched as it looked like one ripped off the head of another. He was secretly glad when, a few minutes later, the tram pulled away from the pit.

"Spoooooooky, huh?" his mother asked.

As they moved deeper into the forest, the creatures became more and more frequent. They hadn't exaggerated that element at all; the Haunted Forest was *packed* with monsters. Beasts with claws and fangs and tentacles and huge bloodshot eyes and every kind of grotesque appendage he could imagine. Some were recognizable, some were like nightmare versions of familiar creatures, and others bore no resemblance whatsoever to anything Christopher had ever seen.

Despite the knot in his stomach, Christopher knew how this ranked: Best. Halloween. Ever.

The tram stopped.

"Ladies and gentlemen, we are now exactly two miles deep into the forest. And now, for a special Halloween scare, let's look at the forest in its natural glory."

Both the lights inside and outside of the tram shut off, casting them into almost complete darkness.

"We're out here, all alone, with nasty creatures on every side of us," said Barbara. "Can they see in the dark? Who knows? Can they smell us?"

Christopher caught a glimpse of a pair of glowing eyes right outside his window.

"Let's just sit here quietly for a moment, shall we?"

The tourists sat silently in the dark. Christopher was surprised to not even hear nervous giggling. There was dead silence for almost a full minute.

"Okay, let's turn the lights back on," Barbara said.

The lights remained off.

"Lights," she repeated.

Nothing happened.

"Sorry, we're having a bit of technical difficulty. Nothing to worry about."

A set of claws scraped against Christopher's window. He couldn't see what they belonged to.

CHAPTER FOUR

Tommy Walker knew a fake smile when he saw one, even when it was gloomy and kind of hard to see. He liked Barbara, the lady talking to them in the front of the tram, though her voice hurt his ears a little, but he could tell that she was really upset. She walked toward the front of the tram as the things outside slithered and crawled over the exterior.

A few of the people around Tommy looked at the woman with wide, fearful eyes. For his part, he sat perfectly still and chewed on his bottom lip. Mommy and Daddy didn't like it when he made a fuss. They weren't here with him, because they were going through a d-i-v-o-r-c-e, but his Uncle Perry and Aunt Jean were still being pretty calm, so he hoped this meant that the monsters weren't going to get him.

Without saying a word, Uncle Perry, who sat one row ahead, in front of Aunt Jean, reached into his pocket and took out his cell phone. They'd taken away most of the cell phones before the tour began, but Uncle Perry had shown that his didn't have a camera on it.

Aunt Jean reached across the aisle and patted Tommy's knee. "It's okay, Big Tom. They're just trying to add to the scares." Aunt Jean was ten years younger than his mommy, and her hair was red instead of brown, but they looked enough alike that he found the contact comforting.

Tommy was the youngest person on the Haunted Forest Tour, and his eyes were wide as he stared out the window. Something was staring back at him. He couldn't see it all that clearly with the lights off, but he could make out the hard, bony ridges around its burning green eyes and the long segmented body, held up by a series of skeletal arms that ended in hooked claws, as it scrambled over the outside and looked first at him and then at Aunt Jean.

Uncle Perry was punching numbers on his cell phone, mumbling to himself. Maybe Aunt Jean thought they were all adding scares to the tour—which he had to admit was already plenty scary—just for fun, but Uncle Perry was breathing like he'd been running for a long time and couldn't get enough air.

In front of them, a fat man tugged at his tie, pulling it loose and staring out the window as something that looked like it was made of black smoke pressed against the glass and bared wickedly sharp teeth. His wide, flabby fingers grabbed at the edge of Barbara's khakis as she walked past. "Are you *sure* those things can't get inside here? Because I gotta tell ya, that thing looks hungry!"

Barbara looked first at the fat man and then back at Tommy. She was chewing on her bottom lip too, but she suddenly smiled when she looked at the fat man and nodded her head. "Absolutely. It's not possible for anything to get inside one of the tram cars." Her smile still didn't look right. It looked like Mommy's smile whenever she said everything was fine between her and

Daddy. It looked more like a wish than the truth. "Now, just to be on the safe side, I'm going to talk to the driver and we're going to try to get hold of the main office to see if they know what the delay is." Barbara flashed another smile at Tommy and pushed forward.

The snakey-boney-bug thing had slithered off the window and moved on, but there were other things behind it. Something with very thick, powerfully built arms and what looked like three eyes moved past in the trees, but it didn't come any closer. Tommy was glad, because the thing was taller than the tram.

"Son of a whore!" Uncle Perry closed his cell phone and muttered under his breath as several people looked his way.

"What is it?" Aunt Jean gave him a look that said *there's a little kid here, behave yourself*—an expression that Tommy saw a lot whenever his parents were talking in whispers.

"I can't get any reception on this thing."

"Well, we're in a thick forest, honey. I'd be surprised if you could."

"The lady at the store said I should get reception anywhere."

"Perry, it's not a top-of-the-line phone. It doesn't even have a camera."

Behind Tommy, a brown-haired girl around twelve years old let out a piercing shriek as something came lumbering toward the tram car. It had gray skin that fell in thick folds from its neck and shoulders, and if it had a face at all, Tommy couldn't see it. Where the face should have been there was just a warty lump of more gray skin with an upside down Y-shape. As he looked, the slit on the face opened up and revealed row after row of teeth and a purplish tongue that dripped thick, foamy spittle.

The open mouth clamped down on the tram and the window near the girl with a loud rude noise. The girl screamed again and jumped from her seat with both of her hands over her mouth to stop any more screams from getting out. The man across the aisle from her reached over and pulled her into his lap. "Calm down, Carrie. It's fine. We're going to be just fine." He was a big man, beefy with short brown hair. His voice was deep and cheerful as he pulled his daughter closer. Tommy smiled at the sight of him, because he looked large enough to be Superman.

* * *

Neal Whistler looked out the window, and a snake woman looked back. She wasn't really a woman, per se, but she had breasts and she had a nice upper body of a woman, if you looked past the scales. From the navel down her body got scalier and tapered off into a powerfully thick snake body that was coiled below her as she gazed at him.

She had black eyes, just like the garter snake he'd kept as a pet for three weeks before his mom found it and had a fit. That had been messy.

The snake girl leaned in closer and smiled at him with full, sensuous, and slightly green lips. He smiled back, a little nervously. At thirty-four years of age, Neal was still a virgin. He hadn't even tried dating a girl since the one time he'd built up the courage to ask Shaileen Stillers to the prom and she'd laughed in his face in the middle of the cafeteria. He'd been telling himself for years that the problems were glandular, but that was a lie and he'd finally accepted the simple fact that he was fat. Not a little large, not pleasantly plump or big boned, but fat.

It was an ugly truth, but the fifty-four-inch waistline on his pants put an end to his arguments. He'd been forcing himself into pants with a forty-eight-inch waistline for a long time, because the weight around his waist was malleable, but after last week, when he'd blown out the backside of his slacks while trying to sit down at his office cubicle, he'd finally had to accept that some things are inevitable.

Getting new clothes always depressed him but not as much as the idea of dieting. As he was doing both next week, this was his little motivational trip. Today he ate, watched monsters and enjoyed himself. Monday bright and early, it was time to become a better man, even if it killed him.

The snake woman moved closer to the glass, a Mona Lisa smile on her face. She wasn't human, no two ways about that, but she was exotic and he stared, fascinated by her.

Right up until the time she opened her mouth and bared the four-inch fangs that slid out from her upper and lower jaws. The fact that her mouth opened wide enough to swallow his head was a little unsettling, too.

Still, he thought, *she's cute.*

* * *

"Stupid piece of shit."

Perry gave up and shut off his phone. Back in the car, he had a top of the line, state-of-the-art satellite phone, set up to receive a signal anywhere in the world. He'd paid more than most of the people he knew growing up made in a fucking year. But he'd left it behind, because—

oh no!—they didn't dare have *camera phones* in their precious fucking forest. So instead he'd brought this crap phone, that the bitch clerk had promised him would work. The *unemployed* bitch clerk, after he returned home.

He didn't even want to be here. He had things to do, but no, Jean had to watch her little nephew, because her stuck-up sister couldn't keep her husband happy anymore. And who had to pay for it? Perry, of course. He had the money, it wasn't a cost thing, it was a matter of the inconvenience.

Perry didn't want kids, didn't like kids, didn't much care if there were kids anywhere around him. It was just the way he lived. Nothing personal against Tommy—who was a good kid as kids went—but he could have been back at the office or working on the publicity stills for the next movie. He couldn't even enjoy himself on what was supposed to be the coolest tourist attraction ever because he needed to get a few more calls in before he could relax. Instead, they were stuck in the fucking woods.

Tommy looked over his way with wide eyes, and Perry made himself smile. The kid was okay. A pain in the ass, but as long as they had him around now and then, at least Jeanie was shutting up about having kids of their own someday. Having kids would have ruined all the sweet stuff he had going on the side, because you never, ever wanted to risk a family with kids in it. Cheating on Jean was kind of shitty, but cheating on her after they had kids? That was like being a Nazi or something.

Which reminded him, it was time for his monthly check-up. No need to take risks on getting herpes or something worse.

Movement from the corner of his eye caught his attention just in time to let him see a lizard man flick its tongue in his direction. Okay, a nine-foot-tall lizard man, with a dark blue tongue.

Perry opened his phone again and prayed for a signal.

* * *

Up at the front of the tram, Tommy watched Barbara as she spoke to the driver. The driver tried talking into a radio and waited for answers that didn't come. He and Barbara whispered to each other, and neither of them would look back into the car behind them.

In the seat directly behind the driver's, an old man dressed in jeans and a black T-shirt looked out the window and smiled, showing discolored teeth as he watched the things that kept creeping closer in. A baseball cap covered the top of his head. His skin was pasty white and his hands trembled, but he looked like he was happy while almost everyone else was nervous. Tommy kept staring at him, glad to see somebody smiling in the darkness.

Something wet and black oozed across the window near Aunt Jean's head and caught his attention for a moment. Whatever it was, it left a dull red smear on the glass as it slipped past.

* * *

Eddie Turner looked at Barbara and sighed as he set down the radio. "Nothing. There's got to be some major power failure in the tram. I can't even get a signal on the radio. And the handheld is battery operated. I should be able to get through on that if nothing else."

"Jesus, Eddie, what are we going to do if we can't get contact?" She tried not to sound nervous. There had never been an incident of something getting inside the tram on one of her or anybody else's watches, not even the ghosts. Though they'd suffered the occasional technical glitch, nothing like this had ever happened. The Haunted Forest Tour was one hundred percent safe.

Barbara loved her job. The benefits rocked her world and the pay was good enough to cover her college bills, but she had to admit that some of the things she'd seen along the way were disturbing enough to guarantee her nightmares from time to time. The first time she'd seen a giant spider—not an original name, but accurate enough, even if the thing did have ten legs and an unsettlingly human face—she'd almost peed her pants.

The idea of the tram being stuck without power was not at all comforting. "Wait, Eddie, *please* tell me there's some power left on this thing."

"I would, but I try not to lie to people I'm not dating."

"No power at all?" Her heart sped up a bit inside of her chest.

"None."

"So the electromagnet is fried, too?"

"As far as I know. I flipped the switch, so I guess in theory it could be working." Eddie looked a little worried, but he was holding it in pretty well. "The only good thing is I haven't seen anything big enough to be a real threat so far."

"Listen, Eddie, we can't sit out here until night, and if we do, we need to be armed."

"I think it's way too early to worry about that, sweetie." Eddie chuckled and Barbara gritted her teeth.

She hated being called "sweetie" by him. They were friends but sometimes she couldn't decide if the older man was trying to flirt with her or adopt her. Either way, it was a little creepy and a *lot* annoying. Still, she held back from making any comments. "It's gotta be just a freak power failure. We'll be running again any second now."

"Well, to be safe, we should look into opening the weapon chest."

"Are you kidding me? Jeez, you'd think this was your virgin voyage. Relax, sweetie. If it comes down to that, we'll open it, but I don't think that's anywhere close to necessary yet." He looked at the people in the seats behind them. "The last thing we want to do is start these folks panicking, and if they *do* start panicking, the last thing we want is for them to be packing heat."

"Yeah? The last thing I want is to end up as dinner for something with eight mouths." She had to keep herself from yelling. Eddie was a nice enough guy, but sometimes he was condescending as all hell and right now she wasn't much in the mood to be talked down to.

"Don't worry your pretty head, Barbara. If it starts getting ugly, I'll protect you. There's lots of weird stuff out there, but they're harmless. How many workers died clearing out trees and laying out those tracks? Zero. How many got injured? Three. How many of those were injured because of monsters? Zero. I know you're paranoid about getting eaten, but people in this forest don't get et. Just doesn't happen. Go take a bong hit or something to calm yourself down, and let me do my job."

"You don't have a job right now. You can't drive."

"Go away, sweetie."

Before she could tell him off, the tram rocked harshly

and a few of the passengers let out gasps of surprise. Something big had just bumped into them, and big in this case meant hefty enough to rock the four-ton vehicle.

"Okay," said Eddie. "Electromagnet definitely not working."

Eddie let out a gasp as something covered the entire windshield. Whatever it was, it seemed intent on getting inside. Thick claws scraped across the windshield and the tram shook a second time.

The passengers were definitely starting to panic. Barbara looked back to where the people who trusted her to maintain order were all staring out of the windows and either recoiling or pointing.

A *lot* of creatures were moving in for a closer look.

* * *

Everyone around them talked in whispers, the same sort you expected in a church. Brad Landry barely noticed. He was too fascinated by the things outside of the tram. Monsters, demons, and God alone knew what else. Brad had his face inches from the glass and stared out at the things in the woods. Some of the things stared back.

A creature with four arms and warty skin looked right at Tina and licked its chops. Definitely an image she could do without. Still, it was almost worth the nightmares to see Brad so happy.

He worked so hard. Both of them did, but with Brad it was almost an obsession. He wanted them to have the American Dream, and he'd get it for them if it killed him. So it was especially nice to see him having a good time, even if that meant she had to deal with things like the ghost that was shifting and glowing as it moved past the window.

Oh yes, this was going on her long list of places to avoid in the future. Brad was the one that liked horror movies and comic books. He was still a big kid in a lot of ways, but only after he'd finished his duties as The Man Of The House. It wasn't unusual for him to spend ten hours at work, come home and do the monthly bills, and then settle back on the sofa with her to watch one of the *Nightmare on Elm Street* movies. She was okay with those, because even with all the blood, the plots were thin enough to see through.

Brad looked back over his shoulder and pointed at something moving in the distance. She didn't know what it was, but it pushed a tree hard enough to make it sway. Giving it a little thought, Tina decided she was perfectly fine never actually seeing whatever was large enough to knock around a seventy-foot oak tree.

"Did you see that, honey?" Brad's voice quivered with excitement.

"Are we supposed to be waiting this long to move forward? What's taking so long, Brad?"

Brad must have heard the worry in her voice. He smiled and leaned closer, his thickly muscled arm moving around both of her shoulders as he grinned. "Don't worry. I'm betting you they set this up for the extra scares. Remember, this is the Halloween special, right?"

And just like that, some of the tension left her body. Her shoulders relaxed and her chest stopped feeling like it was going to collapse on itself.

"I never even thought about that."

"Trust me." He smiled and nodded knowingly. "If I was the one running this show, that's exactly what I would be doing. Five minutes from now, we're on the way and moving again."

Tina snuggled in closer to her husband of five years and closed her eyes for the moment. Let him have his fun with the weird things lurking outside. She'd had enough. It was better just to think about being back home, where she would be safe and sound.

* * *

He heard the tour guide and the driver talking, of course. He was directly behind them and despite their best efforts to be quiet, Lee Burgundy had made it a point to be in the right place to hear the important conversations that people weren't supposed to hear. He'd had a lot of practice at eavesdropping in his sixty-three years on this planet. It came with the territory and he doubted he could stop if he was suddenly struck deaf.

For the last thirty-five years he'd worked as a debunker, writing under the name Alexis Gander, and his list of fraudulent showmen was almost as large as his bank account. He'd proved hundreds of psychics as grandiose fakes over the years, and if he had a dollar for every "miracle" he'd shown to be nothing more than a clever hoax, he'd have eight hundred and seventy-nine dollars. Fortunately, he had a lot more than a dollar for each one.

For the first time in his life, Lee doubted he'd be able to disprove a claim. Either the Haunted Forest Tour was real, or the special effects being used far exceeded the best he'd seen come out of Hollywood. He'd been on the tour before, of course. First in line when it opened a year ago. It didn't make him a believer. Obviously, the sudden existence of a five-mile forest in the middle of the desert was extremely bizarre, and the creatures didn't *immediately* strike him as fake. But Lee followed a mindset of "total fabricated crap until proven otherwise," and he hadn't been entirely convinced that the Haunted Forest was not a mega-budget Disney-funded undertaking.

He didn't write about it, though. Honestly, the Haunted Forest was a little too big of an endeavor for him at this stage of his life. Too much effort to debunk. He'd gone on the tour, been impressed but not convinced beyond any reasonable doubt of its authenticity, and moved on to more manageable targets.

Hearing the only two employees talking only proved that *they* believed this was all real. The thing with the cat eyes staring through his window was certainly convincing, but again, total fabricated crap until proven otherwise. The beast had a thick mane of fur around its feline face, and when it opened its mouth to yawn he got a chance to count the rows of teeth with decidedly sharp points. It moved closer, and he watched, quietly horrified and fascinated, as the monster's six legs moved forward with unsettling symmetry.

There were more things behind it and the tour guide's words echoed in the back of his head as he tried to comprehend everything he was seeing. *I guarantee that you'll see things you never imagined.*

He had a good imagination, but damn, this was well beyond his wildest hopes.

Despite a long career of revealing the frauds for what they were, he'd longed to see something real. His grandmother had told him fairy tales when he was growing up, and he'd been searching for his entire adult life to find something that could come close to the thrills she'd given him as a child.

A shadowy figure moved closer to the window he was staring out as the six-legged cat-thing jumped onto the roof of the tram. A tattered brown cloak wrapped around the too-thin form and where the feet should have been, he saw what looked like a hundred snake tails writhing in unison to move it forward. A small constellation of glowing lights moved within the hood of the thing's cloak, and after a second he realized the flecks of luminescence were the eyes of the nightmare looking back at him. It moved closer still and its breath cast a pall of frost across the shatterproof surface.

"What the hell kind of thing is that?" He spoke softly, to himself, and almost jumped when he had an answer from the tour guide.

"You know, I don't think I've ever encountered one of those before." Her voice was forced into a cheerful tone that lacked all sincerity. Bless her heart; he could only imagine how she must feel being stuck in her position.

"How'd it get a cloak?" he asked.

"We've actually seen the occasional humanoid creature wearing articles of clothing," said Barbara. "Never anything like a cloak before, but remember, the forest sprouted up on top of an existing town, so we think the creatures sometimes find items that were left behind."

"That makes sense. So I get to name it, right?"

"Well, absolutely!" She smiled brightly, apparently happy to handle something that wasn't part of the crisis. "Did you have a name in mind?"

As Lee watched, a small, humanoid creature with wings got too close to the hooded monster, and the head turned quickly. What looked like at least seven black tongues snapped out of the cowl and wrapped around the delicate-looking fairy. Each tongue latched on firmly and the poor thing was torn to shreds, then pulled back into the depths of the covering.

"Oh my." He swallowed the dust that seemed to have built up in his throat and nodded his head. "Yes, let's call that one a Proof Demon, shall we?"

"A Proof Demon?"

"Yes. I don't believe in the supernatural, but this is as close to proof as I'll ever get."

Barbara chuckled. "Proof Demon it is."

"Do you suppose it's going to be much longer?"

"Before we get the power back? No, I'm sure it will be back any moment now. There's another tram scheduled to show up soon and even if the power failure continues here, they'll be able to radio back for assistance. This is going to be a busy day for the Haunted Forest Tour, and there are contingency plans for situations just like this."

"Really?" He lowered his voice. "Like the weapons cache you have stored onboard?"

"Well, we can't be too careful, can we?" She smiled nervously. "As a matter of fact, in a worst case scenario we'd distribute the weapons, but of course that would be a last resort."

They both flinched as the tram rocked slightly again and something heavy walked across the roof above them. "Sooner might be better at this point," said Lee. "It's been a while, but when I was younger I was quite the marksman."

"Right. I think I'm going to ask a few people as quietly as I can if they'd like to volunteer. If you'd like, I'll introduce you to Eddie up front so he knows who to hand the weapons to. In a worst case scenario. Which of course we don't anticipate."

Lee nodded and slowly stood up. Outside of his window, the Proof Demon let out a wet, croaking noise that rose in octaves and was loud enough to shake the shatterproof glass. Barbara followed him and made the proper introductions.

"Do you think we'll need them?" Lee asked Eddie, who was sweating profusely even though he was apparently trying to project a calm demeanor.

"I doubt it, but I've gotta tell you, I've never seen this many critters around the tram before. I mean, nothing even close. People on the tour don't get ripped off, that's for sure, but the forest things never, ever, ever gather around the tram like this, not at any of the stops. This is insane."

"I have to tell you, I wasn't expecting to see anything like this when I booked the tour."

Eddie nodded solemnly. "Believe me, I completely understand you people being scared shitless."

Lee appreciated the empathy but still wished they were willing to pass out the firearms instead of waiting.

* * *

Christopher was starting to wonder if he'd ever discover what fate awaited him Monday at work. He looked at his mom, who was still peering out the window with fascination. Either she was still having a good time or she was a better actress than anyone ever suspected. The girl a couple of seats behind him had recovered from her perfectly understandable panic attack and was now quietly clinging to her father.

Just past his mother, several sets of eyes stared back, watching every movement that she made; in front of him the little boy and his mom were quiet, both looking at the roof as something heavy paced repeatedly, scraping claws across the top of the tram. The tour guide was leaning over and whispering to a young man two seats ahead of him. Finally, Barbara pointed to the front of the tram and the man nodded his head before getting up and walking past her, shuffling his feet.

Christopher did everything he could to avoid looking out of his own window, because if he kept seeing these nightmarish creatures, even through the protective glass, he was probably going to freak out a little. He hadn't expected to be squeamish, but something about having twelve perfectly round eyes looking at him from above a set of hairy mandibles big enough to eat his face was making him a little twitchy.

Barbara came over, a strained smile on her face, and leaned in close enough that he could smell the perfume she was wearing. It smelled like cotton candy. Nice. When she spoke, it was in a conspiratorial tone. "Hi, listen, we're pretty sure that another tram car is due in a few minutes and that they'll get everything taken care of."

"That's nice. Good to hear. I'm glad."

She continued. "Just as a precaution, we're scouting out a few people who would be willing to carry a firearm if it comes down to that, which it won't, we're certain. We only have a few, plus our driver has something more substantial if it's needed, but I wanted to know if you would consider being 'deputized' until this is over with."

Christopher looked at Barbara for several heartbeats before nodding. "Um, yeah, if you think it becomes necessary. Sure."

"We don't think it will. Have you ever fired a weapon before?"

"A few times." He didn't mention that the biggest thing he'd ever fired was a pellet gun, though he'd almost put out the neighborhood bully's eye with it, so he knew how to do some damage. Besides, he was pretty sure he could figure out how to handle the firearm if the situation came up, and he wanted to be damned sure somebody on board was watching out for his mom.

Barbara smiled again. "Great, thanks. Again, we're certain it won't come down to that, but it's best to be prepared, right?"

"Absolutely." He had a hundred questions he wanted to ask—*Did the weapons come with silver bullets? Was there any proof that some of the things out there were actually susceptible to firearms damage? Were there any cute and cuddly things hiding in the woods, because, damn, the ugly and menacing stuff sure seemed to be in the majority?*—but instead he nodded as Barbara gave him instructions to see the driver and then took her leave, heading towards the drill sergeant-looking man who was holding on to his crying daughter.

Christopher looked over to his window when he heard the scraping noises. The spider-thing was trying to chew through the reinforced window, though, happily, it didn't seem like it was getting anywhere.

Damn bug.

His mom leaned across the aisle and whispered to him. "So you've been deputized. Is that like a guarantee of getting a date with the cute tour guide, or what?"

"I think she's a little distracted right now, Mom." He looked back at Barbara. "Also, a little young."

"Oh, please! Your dad was ten years older than me."

The floor began to vibrate under his feet, and Christopher looked over his shoulder to the back of the vehicle. Through the window he could see a distant pinpoint of light through the murky forest and past the growing numbers of creatures waiting outside.

"I think we might be in luck. I think the next tram is coming."

"Oh, good!" Mindy shifted in her seat and looked back toward the window with him. "This is fun and all, but after a while even staring at all-new monsters makes me edgy."

As they watched, the light came closer and several of the things outside started stepping away as if the oncoming illumination hurt their eyes. That wasn't surprising, since at least three of the things back there had eyes that seemed almost totally made of pupil.

As the things in the world outside of their safety bubble moved away, Christopher caught better glimpses of them in the light and almost wished he hadn't. *What the hell is something with wet tentacles doing on dry land? And why does it have wings?* He wasn't really sure he wanted to know.

The light at the front of the approaching vehicle grew quickly. After sitting in the gloom for a while and watching freakish things move up and over the tram, Christopher's eyes ached as they tried to readjust.

"Say, honey, do you think that thing is coming sort of fast?" His mom frowned as she spoke.

"Maybe a little..." Okay, maybe a *lot*. They hadn't been moving anywhere near the same speed when they'd been touring. It was impossible to see anything past the headlights, but was there something else on top of the tram car? He couldn't tell.

"Seriously, they won't be able to slow down in time."

Christopher nodded and shouted to the other tourists without even thinking about it. "Everyone put on your seatbelts, *now!*" He quickly turned around and began to refasten his. His mom followed suit a second later.

Several other people were looking over their seats now, all of them watching the approaching vehicle. Most listened to his suggestion, but a few of them kept staring, some at the approaching car and others at the beasts around them.

The heavy-sounding beast on the roof suddenly jumped off amid a clatter of scrapes and a loud roar.

Christopher craned his neck around until he could look out the back window again. "You're right, Mom. They're not slowing down." His throat felt hot and dry. His pulse raced at the thought of a four-ton one-car locomotive ramming into them. Oh, this was going to be so very bad...

"Just brace yourself and try to relax, honey. Think solid, immobile thoughts."

Barbara rushed past them, heading for her own safety spot near the front of the tram. "*Everyone please secure your seat belts immediately!*" All pretense of calm was gone from her face.

The heavyset man a few rows in front of them stood up with a stunned expression on his face. Apparently he couldn't believe there was a chance of danger from another group of tourists.

"What's happening?" His voice quavered. "What's wrong?"

Christopher shot him a hard look. "Buckle up and sit the hell down!"

The man got a sour I-just-swallowed-a-thousand-legged-bug expression and opened his mouth to make a comment. Behind him, through the window, Christopher could see the various shapes and nightmares outside the tram backing away. Some of them had faces too alien to read, but a few seemed to be grinning in anticipation.

The light from the car behind them filled the entire cabin of the tram, and the obese man held his hands before his face as if to hide from the light or the full understanding that they were about to get creamed. He let out a bellow of fear and looked away.

There was one loud blast of an air horn.

And then impact.

CHAPTER FIVE

The tram-on-tram collision worked out poorly for all concerned.

The first vehicle, stationary and powerless, moved forward fifteen feet despite the fact that the brakes were down and in a locked position. The rear end of the vehicle rose completely off the ground during the crash. Neal Whistler, who had made countless foolish decisions during the course of his life and whose final decision to stand up instead of strapping himself into his seat continued that trend, was catapulted through the air.

His immense weight meant nothing at all to the kinetic force that smashed him first into the ceiling of the tram and then bounced him across the left side of the car and then down the main aisle.

Neal did not scream as he ricocheted through the interior, but several of the people around him did. Tina Landry let out a particularly hair-raising one as Neal rammed into the back of her husband's seat and cracked the plastic. Brad Landry didn't even see the man coming. He was forced forward as his seat belt tried to hold him in place. The security belt was designed to resist up to 750 pounds of pull before it gave out, and it did the manufacturer proud. Instead of snapping, it held firmly and in the process held Landry's body where it was while his arms flew forward. He nearly blacked out as both shoulders dislocated.

Neal, the airborne human wrecking ball, continued on his trek, slamming into the hard surface of the center aisle and flailing through his path of destruction until he struck the front window. Fortunately, the window was shatterproof. Unfortunately, Neal was not.

The people who were strapped into their seats had a slightly better time of the impact. Those in the back of the tram had the unsettling sensation of being weightless for a moment and then took a blow to their backsides as the car came crashing down. It landed on the front of the tram that hit them, and then pushed forward until it bounced onto the track again. The passengers were all violently shaken as if driving a speeding truck down a mountain of jagged boulders.

Christopher was very grateful for the deep cushioning of the headrests, which he was sure was the main reason a few dozen skulls didn't get cracked wide open and spill their contents onto the tram floor. Aside from Brad's dislocated shoulders and everybody else's countless bruises, most of the people on the tram—save for Neal—were not badly hurt.

The front end of the second tram held up remarkably well to the impact. The windshield spider-webbed but did not explode when the rear of the first tram lifted and then dropped back down on top of it.

For several seconds Christopher sat in a daze, barely able to believe that he and his mother were still alive. The Haunted Forest Tour had sturdy trams, no doubt about it. That would be the one good score on the comment card. He could hear himself asking his mother if she was okay, but it felt like somebody else was speaking through a cell phone with lousy reception.

All around them people were talking at once, with plenty of moans, sobs, screams, and expletives mixed in.

Barbara stood up and shook her head like a heavyweight contender who'd taken three too many shots to the chops. "Is everyone all right?" she asked, turning around to face the passengers. She glanced down at Neal's mangled body and slammed her hand over her mouth.

Brad Landry let out a low, soft groan, causing his wife to immediately begin screaming his name: "Brad? Brad! *Brad!* Are you okay?" Her voice scrolled up through the octaves as she shook him. Brad turned paler and paler until the man in the seat behind Tina grabbed her hand and told her to kindly stop trying to kill him. Whether the man was referring to himself or Brad was unclear.

Christopher unfastened his seatbelt and looked over his shoulder toward the other tram. "Do you think anyone got hurt?"

His mother had already unfastened her belt and joined him. "Honey, I don't see how they could *not* have."

The front end of the other tram looked better than Christopher would have expected—at least in terms of damage to the vehicle. There were huge dents, and the heavy wheels at the bottom of the car had been forced outward at an angle. Some smoke billowed from the bottom. Still, as far as he could see, the passengers were protected inside.

There was no sign of a body where the driver should have been, but a thick spray of crimson had splashed across the windshield.

"Everybody please be quiet!" Barbara shouted. "It's very important for everybody to remain calm!"

Miraculously, the tram went almost silent. Eddie staggered out of the driver's area, a heavy trickle of blood running down the side of his face. "Is everybody okay?" He immediately realized the irony of his question and crouched down next to Neal's body.

"Is he breathing?" Barbara asked. The far-from-natural angle of Neal's neck made the answer perfectly obvious, but she couldn't stop herself from asking.

Eddie pressed his fingers against Neal's flabby wrist and held them there for a few seconds. "No pulse. He's history."

There were several loud gasps from the tourists, even though it was unlikely that any of them had expected Neal to survive the impact.

The little girl who'd been sitting with her father and screaming a while earlier stared out the window. "What happens when the monsters come back?" she asked.

They didn't have long to wait to get the answer. The dark shapes began moving in again, slithering, crawling, or merely charging. They all focused on the second tram.

"They'll be fine...they'll be fine..." Christopher whispered to himself. The tram was badly dented, but the creatures still couldn't get inside. All they had to do was try not to lose their sanity while they waited for help to arrive.

The first true assailant was a humanoid beast that looked almost exactly the way Christopher had always envisioned an ogre. Admittedly, he'd never devoted much time to envisioning ogres, but this thing definitely fit the mental picture. The head was too small for the body, and the arms were as thick around as Neal Whistler's waistline. It pounded on the roof of the second tram with both fists.

It was joined by a ghost, a constantly shifting spectre that was almost as large as the ogre itself. It changed forms almost too quickly to identify them, but Christopher caught flashes of a pirate, a knight, a demon, a shrieking victim, and a seductress.

The ghost passed through the roof of the tram.

Christopher's mother grabbed his arm. Hard.

The tram suddenly seemed to be covered with a thick layer of frost where the ghost passed through. The ogre slammed its fist once more, and this time the roof cracked. It hooked massively thick fingers into the ruptured hull. With a grunt that could be heard from within the undamaged car, it pulled. The scream of tortured metal sent shivers through the onlookers. The monster tore the metal, opening the roof of the tram as if pulling the lid from a particularly stubborn can of sardines, and then reached inside and grabbed two screaming tourists from inside.

Christopher jumped and his mother left out a moan of despair as the ogre turned back to them and stared into the undamaged car. With eyes locked on the interior where they sought shelter, the ogre opened its too-wide mouth and showed them broad, flat teeth that looked like blades on a shovel. A man who appeared to be in his late fifties was the first victim. The man let out a faint scream and struggled violently until the ogre's teeth clamped down and tore his left leg away, chomping and crunching a bloody froth.

The creatures surrounding the ogre—and Lee recognized the Proof Demon as the creature closest to the mountain of flesh—moved forward, surging into the ruined car as the people inside tried their best to hide.

The ogre finished his meal with five additional bites, saving the head for last. Through the entire process, a portly woman that it held in its other hand struggled and screamed. The monster did not eat her. Instead, still looking into the tram with malignant intelligence, the ogre smiled, winked (had it actually *winked*?), and then slammed the woman against a tree. It repeated this several more times, never taking its eyes off the first tram, and then casually discarded her pulped corpse by tossing it over its shoulder.

Beyond the ogre, things were even worse. Numerous creatures of all sorts crawled into the tram. Most of them emerged with live prey.

One man was stuck in a four-way tug-of-war that ended with all of the players feasting on his remains. Most of the victims were devoured—not always quickly—but others were clearly playthings to be mangled.

Christopher was almost willing to rip out his own eyes to spare him the ghastly sight, but he couldn't look away. His mother's grip on his arm was so tight that he thought she might have drawn blood.

It was a toss-up as to who screamed louder, the victims or the witnesses of their demise.

It took Christopher a moment to realize that Eddie was thrusting a rifle at him. "Take this, goddamn it!" Eddie shouted, finally getting Christopher's attention. Christopher heard himself offering up an awkward, "Thank you," and then Eddie pushed past him to distribute more weapons.

Within minutes the worst was over. The screams from outside dwindled and died, replaced by gluttonous roars and the sloppy sounds of feasting.

Barbara stepped over Neal's corpse, then turned around to address the passengers. Eddie stood next to her. "Okay," she said, her voice trembling but coherent, "they don't seem to be paying much attention to us, so we may be able to wait until help arrives. But just in case we aren't so lucky, let's do a quick weapons lesson."

Eddie spoke up. "For those of you with guns, you each have ten rounds, nine within a clip and one in the chamber. The bullets are armor-piercing nine millimeter shells. They should fuck up whatever you shoot with them." He held up his own rifle. "Here's the safety. Do *not* take it off unless it's absolutely necessary. We've got enough shit going down without shooting each other. Everybody understand?"

Those who were able to speak indicated that yes, they understood.

Then they waited.

Five minutes passed as the creatures outside began to take a much greater interest in the tram that still contained live prey. Some of them circled the old wagon like restless Indians. Others seemed to take special pleasure in painting the windows with bloodied tongues and even stranger extremities.

Five minutes for each and every person on the tour to reflect on just how unpleasant their lives had recently become. Three hundred seconds of last minute prayers to various deities and promises to be a better person if He/She/It could just, please, let them get out of this alive.

Christopher quite frankly didn't care if he had a job waiting for him when he returned home. In fact, if he *didn't* get fired, he vowed to march into Mr. Tylerson's office, tender his immediate resignation, and tell Mr.

Tylerson that he could go cheerfully fuck himself.

The lights flickered for a moment.

Everybody stared up at the ceiling. Christopher's mother whispered, *"Please, please, please, please..."* as they waited with communal baited breath.

The lights came back to life, half-blinding every person on the tram and sending several of the things in the forest slinking away. The motor began to whirr.

"Oh, thank God," said Christopher, letting out a deep sigh of relief. Several of the passengers applauded, although it was the numb applause of people who'd just seen forty of their fellow tourists brutally murdered.

Eddie turned back toward the front of the vehicle. "All right, everybody, I'm gonna get us the hell out of here."

And then the pneumatic doors slid open and locked into position.

CHAPTER SIX

Christopher hadn't realized that it was possible for the phrase "*Oh shit!*" to go through his mind so many times in just a few seconds. The sound of the doors locking into place sounded a hell of a lot like the sound of a heavy casket lid dropping closed.

"*Welcome to the Haunted Forest Tour,*" said a perky prerecorded voice. "*Your safety is our primary concern, so please, watch your step as you enter the vehicle.*"

"Close the door!" Tina Landry shrieked.

A creature poked its head inside the tram. The head—which consisted of glistening white skin, slanted eyes, and bloody jaws—was attached to a long neck that uncoiled almost ten feet as it slowly moved towards Tina's face, jaws wide open.

The head exploded in a mess of white slime and flesh pieces as three different people opened fire, though only two hit the mark. Tina screamed as the neck flailed around wildly, scattering chunks all over her and her husband.

"*Welcome to the Haunted Forest Tour,*" the voice repeated. "*Your safety...*"

"Cover the door!" Eddie shouted. "I'll try to get it

closed! Everybody get to the back!"

Sheer panic ensued as three dozen tourists desperately tried to get to the rear of the tram. Several of the armed tourists, including Christopher, tried to push to the front of the crowd. His mother grabbed at his arm but he pulled away from her. They were in ocean-deep shit, but they still only had one opening to protect. A bunch of guys with high-powered rifles should be able to keep the monsters out until Eddie got the door closed again.

A monkey-like creature leaped into the tram, and was immediately shredded by gunfire.

"Don't waste bullets!" Eddie shouted from the driver's seat. "We don't have an unlimited supply!"

As another creature—this one resembling a humanoid lizard—burst into the tram, the tourists ignored Eddie's advice and opened fire repeatedly until the dead creature tumbled out of the open doorway.

"There are lots more monsters coming," said Tommy Walker, peering out the window. The six-year-old was right. All manner of unpleasant creatures were headed for the tram, including the grinning ogre that had ripped open the other vehicle.

Christopher shouted into the driver's area. "Eddie! We'd really, really, *really* appreciate it if you could get that door closed!"

An oversized bat flew into the tram. It bounced against the ceiling and fluttered around, letting out horrible screeching sounds. Christopher took aim, fired, and missed.

A bearded man pointed his own rifle at the bat, then cried out as a shot from one of the other tourists got him in the arm. He dropped his weapon and tried to clutch at the bullet wound, but the bat latched onto the bloody hole before he could get his hand over it.

Another shot rang out, striking the seat next to the bearded man.

"Jesus Christ, be careful!" Barbara shouted. "Don't shoot at him!"

The bearded man screamed as the bat burrowed into his arm. Within seconds its entire head was buried in his flesh. He smashed his arm against the seat, over and over, screaming the entire time. Lee Burgundy dropped his own rifle and grabbed at the bat with both hands. When he couldn't get a hold of the bat, he grabbed the bearded man's arm to make him stop moving it, then dug the fingers of his other hand into the bat's skin. He wrenched the bat out of the man's arm, getting a gout of blood in the face in the process, then threw the creature to the ground and stomped on it as hard as he could. Christopher couldn't see the result, but heard the loud *pop* as its body burst open.

The bearded man clawed at his gushing arm, insane with panic. A white-headed creature exactly like the one that had been shot to pieces in front of Tina extended its head into the tram and clamped its jaws down on the bearded man's shoulder. It yanked him toward the doorway—and right into another bullet. Two more bullets pounded into the man before he was pulled out of the tram. At least eight different creatures pounced upon him and brought him to the ground.

Oh my God, we're going to kill ourselves before the monsters can do it, Christopher thought. Though without the guns, they'd probably be dead already.

So many creatures had now surrounded the tram that there was very little empty window space to see past them. If they all chose to pour into the opening,

Christopher figured they'd last a minute, maybe two if the creatures decided to have a more leisurely meal.

He blinked some sweat out of his eyes.

With a loud whirr, the door slowly began to slide shut. The tram jerked forward, knocking several people off balance, and then began to move forward along the track.

Christopher allowed himself a half-second of mental celebration.

Then the doors stopped.

The ogre climbed into the tram.

All of the rifles seemed to fire at once. The ogre let out a cry of pain that rattled the vehicle, and then it smashed its fists against each side of the doorway, knocking the tram door off its track.

The tourists pumped bullet after bullet into the ogre. Through the red mist, Christopher watched it grab a tourist and bite clean through his arm, swallowing both the arm and the rifle it had been holding. The bleeding ogre grabbed the tourist by the neck and tossed him out of the vehicle. The tourist's single scream ended abruptly.

Christopher fired a shot that, while it was meant for the ogre's neck, hit its right eye instead. The ogre howled and stood up straight, bashing its head against the ceiling of the tram. More and more bullets pounded into its body. It swiped out with its hand, decapitating one tourist and ripping half the face off another.

The tourist with the shredded face fired his rifle several times in a panic. But the ogre's attack had spun him around, and his shots went into the crowd of tourists instead. Christopher's heart jolted as he heard a wail from behind him that sounded like it belonged to his mother.

The ogre's head exploded.

The beast flopped forward onto the first couple of

rows of seats, landing on Neal's obese corpse and revealing Eddie standing behind it. He held a smoking gun with a huge barrel. He quickly glanced over at the doorway and let out a cry of frustration. "He screwed up the door! It's not gonna close again!"

Christopher pushed through the crowd, trying to catch a glimpse of his mother. A young woman in a leather jacket sobbed while the man next to her pressed his hands against her chest where she'd been shot.

After pushing somebody out of the way a little harder than he'd intended, he saw his mother. She looked terrified but uninjured, thank God.

"Can't you make this thing go any faster?" somebody shouted.

"We're lucky it's moving at all!" Eddie replied. He looked through the front windshield. "*Dammit!*"

Christopher turned his attention away from his mother to see what Eddie was talking about. It was hard to see through the throng of people, but he could tell that something was on the track ahead of them.

Something big.

"*Seat belts!*" Barbara screamed. "Everybody sit down, *now!*"

Despite the small thinning of the herd, there weren't that many more seats in the tram than there were tourists, and several of them in the front were covered by a dead ogre. So Barbara's command was met with instant chaos, as the passengers frantically tried to find seats.

Christopher nearly doubled over as the man next to him accidentally smacked him in the gut with the barrel of his rifle. Christopher squeezed his eyes and jaws shut and tried not to vomit.

"C'mon, we have to sit down," said his mother,

tugging on his arm. Christopher forced himself to stand upright again. Now that many of the tourists had found their seats, he could see what was on the track in front of them.

Or at least its head.

Actually, as far as Christopher could tell, it was nothing *but* a head. A giant severed human head that was bigger than the tram. It was lying on its side, allowing them to see the immense bloody stump of its neck. Its black hair was mussed and blood trickled from the corners of its eyes.

"Nobody said anything about giant severed heads!" Christopher shouted. "The commercials promised weird, scary stuff, but there was *nothing* about giant severed heads lying in the middle of the tracks! This is *bullshit!*"

The head smiled, revealing a mouthful of broken teeth.

Christopher sat down across from his mother and fastened his seat belt. They weren't moving very quickly, so the impact wouldn't be anywhere near as bad as the earlier crash, but he still wasn't looking forward to it.

The giant head licked its lips.

The tram smashed into it, jolting all of the passengers forward in their seats. A few people who hadn't been lucky enough to find seats tumbled to the floor. At least a dozen different creatures fell past the windows, obviously having been dislodged from their perches on top of the roof.

"*Guns!*" Eddie shouted.

Creatures began to pour into the tram at a much faster rate than before. Christopher quickly unbuckled his seat belt, stood up, and helped open fire. A scaly red thing with glowing eyes hopped into the tram, bounced over the first few rows of seats, and slashed its claws back and forth across the face of an elderly woman who was still strapped into her seat. It slashed up two more people before a shot to the chest finally took it down.

An oversized brown spider scurried across the ceiling, then leapt down upon a teenaged girl.

Eddie blew away something with a pistol before it could get onboard. "There are too many of them!" he shouted to the passengers. "We'll run out of ammo! We have to ditch the tram!"

"Are you insane?" Lee shouted. "They'll rip us apart out there!"

"They'll rip us apart in here!" Eddie insisted. He paused to shoot a giant millipede. "They know we're in the tram, and they'll just keep pouring in here until we don't have a single bullet left."

"We're still better off in here...at least we have *some* protection!"

"We don't have shit in here once the guns are empty! If we can get out of here, maybe split up, they won't be able to find us as easily. We just have to run like hell for the edge of the forest."

"We won't last three seconds!" said Lee.

"He's right," said Christopher. "There's no way we'd survive out there. Look how many of them there are!"

"I'm making the decision," said Eddie. "And since you only have a few seconds to figure out if you want to join me or die, you'd better think fast."

He held up his other hand, revealing a grenade. He pulled out the ring with his teeth and spat it to the floor.

Oh, this could turn out bad, thought Christopher. *This could turn out real bad.*

Eddie hurled the grenade out of the doorway. "Everybody cover your ears!" he shouted.

Christopher dropped the rifle and slammed his hands over his ears. There was a couple of seconds of silence, and then an explosion that shook the tram and illuminated up the entire forest with a bright white light.

As the roar of the explosion died down, it was replaced by the shrieks of the Haunted Forest creatures as they quickly scurried away from the tram. Christopher couldn't believe how many there were—hundreds of them!

The light began to fade.

"Let's go!" Eddie shouted. "Everybody *run*!"

CHAPTER SEVEN

At least a dozen people were dead, either pulled out of the tram to become meals for the nightmares outside, or mauled inside what was supposed to be a completely safe vehicle, or, unbelievably, shot by their fellow tourists. All in all, Lee could think of better places to be. Like Thunderdome.

Lee looked out the open door and smelled the mixture of blood and cordite wafting through the air. As much as he hated the idea, there weren't a whole lot of options left. Stay inside and die, or go outside and die. He was in good shape for a sixty-three-year-old man, but he wasn't looking forward to having to outrun anything with more than two legs.

He shook his head and shot a withering glare at Eddie, then gingerly stepped through the bloodied remains of several monsters and down the small flight of stairs leading to the outside world.

All my life I've been looking for monsters. I wish I'd been a butterfly enthusiast instead. He held his rifle diagonally in front of his body and waited for the next person to get off the tram.

The woods were hardly deserted, but most of the

things out there seemed like they weren't really in a hurry to get close to anything that bit as hard as the driver's grenade. The ground was littered with pieces of different creatures and a few human remains as well. Most of the pieces were still, but a couple were moving, despite not being attached to their respective bodies any longer.

"You folks better get your butts moving!" Lee announced. "They're not gonna leave us alone forever!" He eyed the woods warily and tried to at least pretend he was brave. He had four, maybe five bullets left, and he didn't want to waste them if he didn't have to.

A teenaged girl and her father came out. The man was sporting another rifle and had a look in his eyes that promised a quick and painful death to anything that came near his little girl. His daughter was wound so tightly around his waist that she could have been a fashion accessory.

A man stumbled on his way out, moving almost like he was drunk as his wife held onto him. His arms both dangled uselessly and his face was so white it almost seemed to glow. His eyes had a glassy glare that made it clear that shock had set in, big time. Right behind them, the poor bastard who'd had his face torn open was stepping away from the vehicle, his shirt caked in blood and a couple of unsightly strips of flesh.

Eddie the tram driver was next. He was sporting a small belt wrapped around one shoulder like a bandolier, but the belt only held two more grenades.

"That's everything," Eddie said as he looked around. "No more weapons and no backup clips of ammunition. We've got to be careful what we fire at." He was trying to sound commanding, but like everyone else, all he managed was to sound scared.

"Maybe next time, you dumb asses will remember a tank or two." That was the man with the little girl. He looked less scared and more pissed off. Of course, judging by the way he carried himself, he'd probably seen a decent amount of time in combat, either as a soldier or a cop. There was an air about him that said he'd managed to handle every ugly situation that had ever come his way.

Several more people poured out of the tram, including a cute little kid whose eyes were currently so wide that Lee feared his eyeballs might roll right out of their sockets. The woman with him kept looking over her shoulder with a deep frown on her face. "Perry? Come on! We have to go!"

Lee turned away from the woman as something moved off to his right. A careful look showed him that something was sliding in closer. He couldn't quite make it out, but it had large eyes that barely even blinked.

"We really have to go now," he emphasized.

Next to him, the man with his daughter in tow took careful aim at the eyes in the distance. "Yeah, bud. I'm with you."

Lee risked a look over his shoulder and saw that a fair-sized crowd had gathered. The redhead with the little boy was looking back at the tram and chewing nervously on her full, lower lip. "Perry? Come on. Seriously. We have to go."

A man poked his head out from inside the tram and shook it vigorously. "No fucking way! Get your ass back in here, Jeanie. We're not going out into the woods!"

"Well, we're not staying here to get eaten!" The boy standing next to Jeanie looked from his mother to his father like an avid fan watching a tennis match.

Eddie grabbed the woman's arm and shook his head.

"Listen. No offense, but we don't have time for this bullshit. If you're coming with us—"

"Perry, *please!*" Her voice cracked as she looked back at the man in the tram's entrance. He was pushed aside as Barbara the tour guide climbed down, now wearing a small backpack. Lee could see that at least a few more people were still inside.

"Don't be an idiot, Jeanie! Get back in here." The man's voice was soft but urgent, a desperate whisper that didn't want to draw too much attention.

Lee looked out into the woods and saw it was far too late for that. The monsters were coming back, surrounding the area, and it was only a matter of time before they came forward again.

His thoughts became fact a moment later, when something landed on top of the damaged tram and let out a warbling roar that was almost loud enough to deafen. Before he could bring his weapon around, the tram driver had opened fire. The first bullet bounced off the top of the tram, but the second struck the creature in the chest and sent it sailing backward.

"That's it. We're outta here." Without another word, Eddie started forward, and the twenty-odd people outside of the tram, Lee included, followed him.

The woman with her child hesitated for a moment, and her face made it clear how desperately she wanted her husband with her, but in the end, she turned and moved into the woods as well.

Not far away, the living severed head, larger than the vehicle that hit it, was bleeding out from the wounds it had suffered—collision, gunfire and shrapnel alike—but it looked like it was trying not to laugh.

They'd only made it a hundred yards from the tram

car, tops, when the people who'd remained behind began to scream. Two of those who'd stayed behind had weapons, and the report from their rifles was dulled by the ululations of the dying.

The sounds were enough to convince even the stragglers to move a bit faster. Unfortunately, running didn't seem to be enough.

The shadows, the trees, even the air seemed to vibrate with menace, and all around him, Lee could hear the sounds of larger things moving through the Haunted Forest.

A high-pitched, cackling laugh cut through the air to his left and was answered from high up in a tree. Despite himself, Lee looked up and saw something moving, leaping from the limbs of an ancient-looking (but of course, only four-year-old) pine and into the branches of a tree Lee couldn't hope to identify.

More of the same insane laughter came from other areas, sending feverish chills running down his spine. He couldn't see what made the sounds, but he had no doubt that they were close and in large quantities.

Just as unsettlingly, the sounds of the other monsters had stopped. The only other noises besides the laughter were the harsh breathing of the other people around him and an occasional curse or whimper.

Lee was feeling every last second of his age, with a bonus decade added on top of it. He paused for a moment and looked over his shoulder, puzzled by the fact that none of the younger folks had passed him yet.

And realized for the first time that there was a good reason for that. Somewhere along the way, he'd stepped away from the others.

He was by himself. In the woods. Surrounded by

laughing things that he still hadn't seen.

The creatures surrounding him laughed again as they slowly moved in closer.

* * *

"I don't wanna die, I don't wanna die, I don't wanna die." A man who was short and pudgy enough to make Christopher feel positively macho was loping along a few feet to his left, speaking the words on everyone's minds as he moved.

He died ten seconds later, as something with the body of an ape and skin like a snake dropped out of a tree and landed on him, pounding his body into the dirt and forest loam.

Christopher thought about trying to save him for half a second and then remembered that he only had a few bullets left and his mother to look after.

The idea had been to run into the woods, but it seemed like some people were taking that to a new extreme. Most of the people around them were at least being semi-cautious, but a few had decided the best way to handle the matter was to try for the hundred-yard dash.

The monsters didn't seem to mind at all. As soon as someone ran away from the main group, they descended, pounced, or flat-out attacked.

A middle-aged man with wide, panicked eyes let out one small gasp of surprise before a shambling mountain of ivy reached out and pulled him into its depths. Only a few seconds later, the man's clothing spat out onto the ground, torn and bloodied.

A woman who looked a little bit like a celebrity

Christopher couldn't remember at the moment (or possibly a porn star from one of the magazines he hoped his mother never found) let out a scream that probably tore her vocal cords when a dark shape crawled over her, literally. One moment the form was merely watching her and the next it fell into what looked like thousands of smaller forms, which began chewing her flesh in an instant. Hundreds of tiny pieces of her body were torn away and devoured as she fell to her hands and knees, unable to take in a second breath and scream again.

Christopher had to sling his rifle over his arm and grab at his mother when she started moving to help the woman on the ground.

"Mom, no!"

"Christopher, I can't stand by and let them eat her alive!" The face he'd grown up knowing so well was made nearly alien by the pain on her features. She fought back, trying to get away from his hands as he grabbed at her shoulders, but after a moment she realized what he already understood: the woman was ruined, not dead but not alive for much longer. A mercy shot to end her pain might use up a bullet needed to save a life.

Tina and Brad moved as quickly as they could. Brad's feet seemed to find good placement more by luck than by any deliberate acts on his part. She looked at her husband and saw the sweat streaming down his face. He was in agony, in shock, and mentally he was nowhere near this haunted little forest. He ran, yes, but only because she told him to.

All around them people ran, and a few of them screamed as the nightmares that lived in the woods became part of their waking world. It was one thing to see the creatures behind a thick layer of special glass with a long scientific name; it was another to see them up close, to smell them, to hear them.

Tina no longer had any chance to lie to herself about what she was seeing. Brad had always been a huge fan of monster movies. If he'd had his way, they would have moved to the edge of the forest two days after the place had grown out of the desert floor. She didn't feel that way at all. She was just fine with the idea of not even knowing that the strange creatures existed. In her perfect world, the closest Tina would ever get to a monster was whatever bad guys existed in the animated movies she'd watched as a child. If it was too tough for Winnie the Pooh, she wanted nothing to do with it.

Up until this trip—paid for by Brad's parents as part of their five-year anniversary gift—-she'd managed to have her way more often than not.

All she'd wanted to do was let Brad have his monsters for a couple of hours...and now? Now all she wanted to do was somehow survive the experience and get Brad to a hospital.

A new rush of screams came from the tram behind them, and Tina looked back as something almost as big as the armored tram car forced its way past the damaged doors. Through the trees, she could just barely see people struggling inside, trying to find a way out of the tram, and she could make out the mouth of the dark shape that lunged forward and shook the entire car. A thick tongue caught hold of one of the people inside and yanked the struggling form into its gaping maw with ease.

She looked away and ran after Brad after she spotted him again, stumbling along in a semi-daze, half-hidden by the trees and the people around them. He'd managed to clear several yards further than she'd expected in only a few moments, and she had to sprint to catch up with him.

"Brad, be careful, honey!"

Brad gave no sign that he'd heard her.

Tina had heard the term *hellhound* before, though she couldn't remember where. That didn't prepare her for seeing one. The black dog that lunged out from behind a black tree trunk bared its teeth and charged for her husband. Flames boiled from where its eyes should have been, and blasted from its mouth and nostrils as it moved. Powerful legs propelled it forward in large bounds, and the turf under its hind claws was torn asunder with each step it made.

Tina had exactly enough time to scream her husband's name before the monster dove at him.

As if suddenly snapping out of his daze for an instant, he ducked. The hellhound's back claws raked against his face, cutting deep. Though the creature could certainly have turned back around and finished off Brad with minimal effort, another man came into view at exactly the wrong time.

Tina wasn't able to identify the man in the split second before the hellhound bit his head in half. She heard the crunch of his bones shattering, saw his head jerk violently to the side, and watched the hellhound chew the remains of the man's face into a bloody pulp surrounded by flames that roasted the meat as the monster swallowed.

She was still staring at the bloodied, blackened teeth of the demonic dog when it turned toward her. The man's body slumped forward and twitched.

Then the hellhound pounced on Brad. He didn't even scream as it finished him off.

CHAPTER EIGHT

No. Absolutely not. It's not true. I won't let it be true.

Tina watched Brad's legs shudder in their death throes, refusing to accept that her husband was dead that quickly. Brad wasn't the most powerful man physically, but he could hold his own. He was smart. He made good money at his job, and he encouraged her to finish her college degree because he knew she wanted to. He was protective but not too jealous. He had such a wonderful, amazing face, and his smile made her weak in the knees after three years of dating and five years of marriage. He was the perfect man for her.

So, really, he couldn't possibly be dead. It was too stupid, too random. He couldn't be dead because they were getting ready to finally have a baby. They'd discussed it for a long time, and at the first of the next year she'd be off the birth control and ready for a new addition to their family. It was time. They'd been patient. They deserved to be happy. So he could not be dead.

All of those thoughts flashed through her head along with a thousand others, even as the hellhound shook its bloody muzzle and started coming for her.

Tina wanted to move. Part of her understood that the

monster was going to rip her apart if she stayed where she was, but the bigger part was still trying to deal with the fact that Brad wasn't just playing possum. He was still in the same spot, and his blood was blackening the already dark earth.

She wanted to move so desperately that she could hear a high keening whine coming from her throat as the monstrous thing walked closer.

Her feet wouldn't lift from the ground. Her arms refused to budge. She couldn't even get her stupid mouth to close.

The hellhound jumped at her.

The bullets that tore holes through its side made it shudder and threw it off course, even as flames blasted from its open wounds. The hellhound fell short of actually hitting Tina, but the flames from its mouth licked across her shins. The flames quickly died, and the hellhound stopped moving.

A man and a girl came toward her. The man reached for Tina's arm. "Move! We have to get out of this area!" The young teenager wrapped around his waist was looking at the dead hound with shocked fascination.

"I—Brad's dead." She tried to explain herself, but the words didn't want to come out right.

"And that sucks, now *go!*" He stepped in closer and slapped her lightly on the face. Not hard enough to knock her down, but enough to make her focus on the here and now instead of what would never be.

The not-quite-dead hellhound reared up and sank its massive teeth into his left thigh and his crotch, biting down almost hard enough to sever his leg.

The little girl with him staggered back and shrieked as her father's blood spilled over her lower body. Tina didn't even think about what she was doing, she merely reached for the girl and pulled her away from the dying man and dying monster.

The man dropped his rifle on the ground and followed it a second later, his eyes bulging and his mouth working uselessly.

She turned to the girl, her thoughts of Brad momentarily pushed aside by the newest horror, and as she turned she saw the hopping thing coming their way.

It almost looked human, with tattered clothing on its emaciated body. The face was skeletal and the body was as thin as that of an anorexic supermodel. Whatever it was, it seemed incapable of standing still. The thick mane of black hair that ran from its head cracked in the air every time it moved, jumping in leaps that would have made a cricket jealous. *Jump*, and it was five feet closer. *Jump*, and it was only seven feet away. *Jump*, and it was next to the body of the man who'd saved her and the beast that killed him. *Jump*, and the little girl was screaming again as the dead-thing caught her in its bony arms and carried her away, still screaming. *Jump*, and it was on a tree above her head, its mouth opening impossibly wide and then sinking into the girl's neck.

The little girl stopped screaming as the thing that had her tore away a thick strand of bloodied meat and swallowed greedily, the skeletal face seeming to grin at Tina even as it sank its teeth into the girl again.

Tina looked around, once again lost in shock, and her eyes found the spot where Brad had fallen. She couldn't see him under the things that were feasting on his remains. Or were they? She only saw the hellhound and its first victim.

What on earth—? Could Brad still be—?

An older woman with tears running down her face caught Tina's left hand and pulled. The man beside her looked her way for only an instant before bringing his rifle up and scouting around them again. When one of the things feeding on the victim who wasn't Brad looked up and hissed through a mouth full of bloodstained teeth, the man shot it in the head.

"Mom, where are we going?" Christopher looked at his mother, who was still holding Tina by the wrist.

Mindy shook her head and spoke in a strained voice. "Anywhere away from the monsters!"

Eddie and Barbara were catching up fast. Christopher looked at the tram's driver and gritted his teeth. He wanted to make a sarcastic comment about their situation not having seen notable improvement after leaving the tram, but it was hardly a good time for that. The creatures were everywhere and they all seemed to think human meat was well worth killing for.

Eddie looked his way and yelled at the top of his lungs: "Hit the dirt!"

And then Eddie pulled another grenade.

* * *

Brad honestly wasn't sure if he was alive or dead. He was concentrating on running, not knowing or caring where he was going. He closed his eyes a few times and then opened them again when he ran into a tree hard enough to rattle his already numbed senses. His arms were screaming obscenities at him and seemed to have no desire to stop any time soon. Tina, whose voice had been his sole beacon for the last few minutes, suddenly wasn't speaking to him anymore.

He hurt in lots of places, but wasn't sure where they were.

When the lack of her cried warnings finally sank in, Brad stopped and looked around. There was nothing to see but trees and more trees.

"Oh brother." He wasn't entirely sure that he'd actually said *Oh brother*, and it certainly didn't seem like the kind of thing he'd say in this situation, but that was his best guess regarding the words he'd panted out. He carefully spun himself in a full circle. "Tina?" He'd definitely said that. He said it again. "Tina?"

Nothing. The closest thing he got to an answer was the sound of laughter up ahead. Brad—*that was his name, right? Brad?*—moved toward the high-pitched cackling, hoping someone up ahead would tell him where he was and what was so gosh-darn funny.

Also, maybe a doctor would be useful.

Instead of directions or instructions, Brad got the sound of something screaming bloody murder. There was the brief *pop* of a weapon going off and then a shriek that cut through his shock. Something fell out of a tree not fifteen feet away from him, yelping in pain all the way down. When it hit the ground he caught a glimpse of a vulpine face distorted by agony. The thing looked like a mix between a man and a wolf with grossly exaggerated features. The blood jetting from its shoulder told him it wasn't long for this world.

Good. It didn't belong in this world.

Before it could even try to stand up, seven more things that looked just like it swarmed out of the woods and attacked it, cackling amongst themselves even as they tore it apart. The laughter and the screams mingled together until only the laughter was left.

An old man looked his way from behind a tree, a horrified expression making him look even older than Brad remembered from when he'd spotted him on the tram.

The old man walked toward him, and when one of the feasting monsters noticed the movement, the old man calmly aimed and fired, blasting a section of the thing's face away. Without hesitation, the other things surrounded the newly wounded one and pounced again.

"Son, we're both lost. Do you remember where you came from?" The old man sounded like he could have used a few hours of rest and maybe a couple of heart pills.

Brad turned his head and nodded over his right shoulder. "That way."

"Then we better get going. It's bad over here."

Brad turned as carefully as he could because his arms were starting to hurt a lot more now that he was coming out of his shock. He followed the old man, focusing on the narrow back and the baggy pants in front of him as if they were a life beacon.

When the old man started jogging faster, Brad did his best to keep up, despite the jarring pains that each step sent through his body. He grunted as his feet moved over a thick root and made him stumble. His arms felt like someone was pumping hot lead through his veins, and the sudden shaking of trying to catch his balance was enough to make the world fade to a dark gray.

The old man looked back toward him, his features pinched with fear. Brad could imagine what was going through his head. Brad was dizzy and barely coherent and close to passing out, true, but he was far from stupid: the man was considering whether it was worth risking his life for a mangled loser with two worthless arms.

He was a better man than Brad, who had to admit that he would've left his own ass behind to die. He turned around and came back. "Come on, son. We don't have time to fall down." The old man put an arm around Brad's waist and started moving again, as quickly as he could with a rifle in one hand and a barely-conscious stranger in his other.

Behind them the sound of laughter faded. Ahead of them, the screams of other people grew louder.

* * *

The explosion shook the trees and stunned most of the people around them for a few heartbeats. No one was prepared for the impact of the grenade going off, even with the warning that Eddie called out. The tree closest to the impact spot had a small crater blown through the coarse bark and bled a thick red sap.

Christopher's ears were ringing and he'd caught enough of the flare from the detonation to leave him blinking spots out of his eyes. Still, it had worked. There were much fewer of the monsters around them now; most had bolted as soon as the grenade was airborne and the few that hadn't had a chance to get away were now bloodied confetti on the ground.

Barbara pointed and yelled. He could almost make out the words through the ringing in his ears, but he got the obvious gist of it: they had to go the way she pointed. His mom nodded her head and started running, pulling along the woman she'd already grabbed.

Something moved. Christopher didn't know what it was and he didn't care anymore. His nerves were shot.

He swung the rifle around and aimed even as he pulled the trigger.

The rifle made a clicking noise that he barely even heard. "Aw, crap." Just to make sure he was as screwed as he thought he was, Christopher pulled the trigger seven more times, with the exact same result each time.

"Oh, that's...that's not fair!" He looked at his mother, who was running hard, to see if she agreed. As she was currently dragging another woman behind her and, well, running like an intelligent person would in this situation, she had no words for him.

The big thing that came out of the woods made Christopher really wish that he had not just run out of bullets. It charged in his direction on two reptilian legs, snorting heavily as it ran his way, all four of its eyes looking directly at him.

Christopher stared long and hard as the monstrosity flapped vestigial wings and lowered its head coming for him, the long neck that held the head in place weaving slightly like a snake's.

He pulled the trigger a few more times, just in case he'd been mistaken about having no ammunition left. He hadn't.

As the thing moved closer still, picking up speed along the way, Christopher tossed the rifle into the air and called on old instincts to save his ass. The barrel of the weapon shifted by one hundred and fifty degrees, until it was almost pointing at him. His hands caught it in a death grip, leaving the heavier stock pointing at his impending doom. It had been a long time since he'd played Little League baseball, but some lessons were hard to forget. Christopher had always sucked at catching a baseball, and his pitching skills left a lot to be desired, but when it came to hitting, he was pretty damned good.

He cocked the rifle over his shoulder as he crouched. The monster opened its slobbering jaws wide and lunged forward, the neck first coiling and then releasing at high velocity.

Christopher got a home run for the first time in over two decades. The hardwood stock of the rifle cracked with a loud snapping noise, as did the skull of the thing that was trying to eat him. That did not stop the six-hundred-pound creature from slamming into him at high speed and knocking him completely off his feet. Christopher let out a loud yelp as the lizard-thing landed on top of him, its body shuddering and spasming. The beast's skin was hot and dry, like having sun-baked stones set on him to pin him in place.

He pushed against the flesh and felt his palms stinging from the heat, his muscles quivering with exertion. The damn thing weighed too much! He couldn't get out from under it.

Christopher grunted as the weight slowly increased, pushing him lower and lower, back into the thick loam of the forest floor. He tried to catch enough of a breath to call out for help, but the pressure kept increasing across his body and the thing was still suffering death throes.

More and more, it looked like he was going to meet his doom crushed under the thing that had been ready to eat him only a few seconds earlier.

CHAPTER NINE

Tommy felt like his heart was going to explode inside his chest. His sides ached, and it was almost impossible to catch a breath.

He'd lost his Aunt Jean, and then he'd lost everyone else around him. They were all gone and he was alone in the woods, with monsters moving between the trees and sniffing around for more people to eat.

He wanted his mommy.

He knew the other people were nearby, but he was too scared to scream. What if the monsters heard him first? There were a lot more monsters than there were people.

Tommy stopped running, trying to keep the sounds of his ragged breaths as soft as he could. His legs shook and his hands trembled. Just to make sure he didn't fall over, he leaned against the rough bark of a black tree that had enough leaves to make everything under it seem as dark as bedtime.

For the first time in a very long while, the world around him was quiet, save for the pulse of his own beating heart. The air was sticky and just warm enough to keep him sweating.

Something moved on the other side of the tree. He

didn't hear it, but he felt it: a delicate tapping that vibrated through the heavy wood and made his back tingle where it touched the bark.

Tommy took a deep breath and let it out in a trembling gust. He didn't know what was causing that vibration, but he knew it would be bad. Everything around him was bad.

"Aunt Jean?" His voice refused to go over a whisper, and maybe that was a good thing.

"Little boy? What are you doing all by yourself?" He looked over to the voice that came from his right and saw six people he'd spotted on the tram car earlier. They were all looking as frightened as he felt, but the one closest to him was a tall woman who was as big as his Uncle Perry, with dark red hair pulled into little pigtails on the sides of her head like puppy ears. She stared at him for a second while he tried to remember how to make his voice work, and then she came toward him, taking mincing steps, as if the ground beneath her feet might be thin ice over a very cold river.

"Come over to me, okay? My name is Becca and I won't hurt you, but you need to get away from that tree."

The people behind her—two more women and three men, most of them already injured and bloodied in the attacks from the bad things—took a step back. Tommy knew that if he turned around and looked at what was behind him, he'd start screaming and never stop. The looks on the faces in front of him said that whatever was there had to be worse than the Boogey Man himself.

Becca came a step closer, her skin as white as a glass of milk.

"Come on, hon. You come over to Becca, okay?" Her voice shook as she spoke and her hand rattled in the air.

Tommy's heart beat faster than ever before, and he resisted the urge to look at the monster he knew was behind him. His daddy always said you should face your fears, but he thought Daddy was wrong this time. You only faced them when they couldn't hurt you in real life and this, whatever it was, it could do more than hurt him.

Though the forest was gloomy and filled with shadows, the large shadow behind him blocked out all of the others, spreading over him like a black pool as the thing moved closer.

Tommy ran, pumping his short legs for all they were worth, and Becca crouched to pick him up. One of the men standing behind Becca aimed his rifle and pulled the trigger. One bullet left the weapon and whizzed past Tommy's head. He never saw if the bullet hit its target. He closed his eyes instead, as Becca turned and the thing that had been behind the tree came into view for one split second as the wood and bark he'd leaned against splintered and broke with a sound like thunder.

The massive tree toppled, falling in what seemed like slow motion before bouncing off another trunk and rolling to the side, instead of crushing them all into the ground.

Before Tommy could worry about how close he came to dying—the tree had missed him by less than three feet—the thing that had knocked the tree aside seared itself into his mind.

Every nightmare he had ever had was moving behind that tree. The shape was massive, so big that his mind wouldn't allow him to see it completely. The skin of the thing was mottled in shades of gray and black, with pale splotches that wanted to draw his eyes, because they moved and there appeared to be screaming faces within them. There was too much skin on the nightmare monster, it moved in ways that made no sense, and parts of it stretched toward him, hungering and shrieking in high, piping voices. Did he see eyes? Yes, oh yes, far too many. Did he see mouths? Yes, more than he could count, each filled with teeth that wanted to tear his flesh away from his bones and chew him into tiny pieces. Were there limbs? He thought so, but none of them looked like anything he'd seen before.

He squeezed his eyes shut.

Becca ran, her breaths blowing past him, her legs lifting and falling without any rhythm or comforting pattern. She screamed each time she exhaled and her hands, clutched at his back, hooked into claws as if she were afraid she would drop him if she didn't sink her nails into his tender skin. He felt her nails cutting but didn't dare protest. She might drop him if he did, and then he would be dead.

His face was pointed at the nightmare, but his eyes remained closed. He heard the wet, meaty sound of the others dying but did not see it. Tommy knew deep in his heart that if he dared look, he would never, ever be able to forget what he saw.

Becca let out a scream. Not the high, whiny sounds she'd made before, but a yowl of pain, and Tommy couldn't help but open his eyes again.

Some part of that hideous, mottled thing had reached Becca and touched her. Where it touched, her skin was distorted, pushed out of place as more of the gray thing pushed forward and deeper into her skin. Her eyes rolled almost blindly, and her face twisted into the ugliest mask he had ever seen, purple and red and filling with blood like the blister he got once when he pinched his skin in a door hinge.

Still, Becca saved him. She bent forward and lowered him almost to the ground, even as he tried to catch her hands in his because he knew what was going to happen.

Becca straightened up and threw Tommy as hard as she could. Tommy's fingers lost their grip, and the nails in his back let loose of him, sending him arcing away from her.

Tommy saw Becca's body torn apart. Whatever was within her sloughed away her skin and drew in the muscles and blood and bone that had been inside of her. Even as he saw her die, his body rolled over the top of the sprawled tree that had been his shelter only a few minutes before. He hit the heavy bark and rolled across the top of it, scraping his legs and hands and face in the process, and then he was over the side and falling, trying to grab with his hands, trying not to fall too fast.

The ground punched him hard, stole his breath away, and bloodied his lips.

Tommy gasped on the floor of the Haunted Forest, his mouth tasting of blood and dirt and dead leaves, and then he started to cry.

On the other side of the fallen tree, something screamed with a thousand voices. At least one of those voices sounded like Becca's.

CHAPTER TEN

"So, Lee moved quietly and slowly, fully aware of the man staggering along beside him. He didn't know his name and didn't want to take the time to ask it in case there might be something listening for human voices.

Not far away, he heard the deep groan of a tree falling. The impact was enough to shake the ground under his feet.

He should have been petrified, and certainly he was very scared, but he was also remarkably calm, all things considered. Despite the death and violence, he still felt exhilarated. Every few minutes he would pause to reassess where they were, and every time he did so the thrill came back into him. A lifetime of skepticism had been dispelled in a minute, and the wonders around him, deadly as they obviously were, still made him punch drunk.

Or, maybe he'd just gone mad.

The man behind him groaned again and stumbled. Lee caught him by the chest and eased him to the ground as best he could.

"Can you keep walking?" he whispered, hoping that

the other sounds around him would keep anything from actually hearing him.

Brad nodded his head. "Brad. My name is Brad. Yeah, I think so, just give me a minute."

"Well, Brad, I'm Lee." He looked Brad over and shook his head. "Listen, your arms are dislocated, and I think I can get them back where they belong. I might need to, because if we have to climb over any obstacles, I'm just not strong enough to carry you. Do you understand?"

Brad's eyes rolled in his head for a moment and then closed. Lee thought the man might have passed out, but finally he nodded his head and opened his eyes again.

"Yeah. I understand."

"Okay, now for the tough part. This is going to hurt, probably a lot. And I need you to be quiet and suck it up. Can you do that?"

Brad worried his bottom lip and shrugged. "Is there something I can bite down on?"

Lee thought about it for a few seconds and then pulled his wallet from his right rear pocket. "It's leather," he explained. "Soft enough that you won't break your teeth."

He helped Brad wedge the old, battered billfold in between his teeth, and then considered the best way to proceed. After a moment's debate with himself, he moved over to Brad's right side and gently worked his fingers around the gap between the man's heavy arm and his shoulder. He moved Brad's arm and heard the man groan.

There had been a time, when he was much younger, that Lee had managed to do similar damage to his left arm. A medic in Vietnam had placed his shoulder back into its socket by pulling on the arm and wiggling it around until the joint reconnected itself. Lee had let out several loud screams before the pain made him pass out. He couldn't afford screams right now.

Not far off, something let out a wail that would have shamed an air raid siren, and Lee took advantage of the noise, roughly pulling Brad's arm with as much strength as he could manage and twisting the limb at the same time. Brad bit down hard enough on the wallet that his teeth suddenly seemed to vanish within the leather, and howled in agony. His body thrashed as he tried to get away from the pain. The sound was muted but still loud. Fortunately, the thing in the distance was much louder.

A moment later, Brad's fits calmed down and left the poor bastard whimpering around the spittle-drenched wallet in his mouth.

Lee ran his hands delicately around the swollen joint and felt the lack of a gap between the bones. It was the best he could do for Brad, and it was definitely better than nothing.

Before the man could recover enough to protest, Lee went to work on his other shoulder, once again wrenching the arm around until it finally slipped back into its socket with a meaty popping noise. Brad let out one high-pitched grunt and then slumped back loosely, unconscious.

"Damn!" Lee looked around and shook his head. The last thing he could afford to do right now was watch over an unconscious man. The best thing he could do to keep his sorry ass alive would be to leave the man where he was and head on his way.

He sighed and settled down next to Brad, because he didn't have it in him to leave the stranger defenseless in a forest filled with monsters.

Shit.

* * *

Mindy looked around for her son and failed to see him. That put an immediate end to the idea of following everyone else. The woman with her, Tina, had no intention of going anywhere without her, so they both doubled back to see if they could find Christopher.

Having nobody else to turn to now that her husband was dead, Tina had apparently decided that Mindy was her life support. Mindy thought she could've made a much better choice of a protector, since Mindy's only weapon was her patented "Stern Mom Look." That only worked on Christopher, and one man who'd been trying to slide closer to her on one of the rare occasions she went to a movie by herself. Stern Mom Looks, scary as they might be, were nothing compared to the faces of a few of the things she'd already seen in the last hour.

There were several monsters lurking nearby, which was an obvious source of concern. The good news seemed to be that most of them were already engaged in eating their latest meals. If she didn't dwell on what they were eating, it was possible she'd get through the search for her son without breaking into hysterical laughter and awaiting the arrival of a tour tram with padded walls.

She heard Christopher before she saw him. He was currently pinned under what looked for all the world like a four-eyed, scaly chicken of epic proportions.

"Honey, are you okay?"

"Mom, I can't really breathe here."

Tina reached down and grabbed one of the thick, muscular legs on the chicken-thing and pulled with all of her might. Mindy joined in and a few seconds later they'd managed to move the thing enough for Christopher to climb out from under it.

Mindy looked him over from head to toe the same way she had whenever he'd come home from school when he was younger. Everything that was supposed to be attached to him was there and mostly intact. His eyes were wide and a little wild, but that was perfectly understandable under the current circumstances.

"Thanks for coming back for me." He managed a quick smile and gave his mother a one-armed hug.

Tina looked at them both blankly for a moment and then said, "Maybe we should go now? Before we lose everyone else?"

"Yeah, or before anything else comes along to eat our faces." Mindy looked down at the remains of the chicken-thing and shook her head.

"It looked a lot scarier when it was alive." Christopher sounded embarrassed, as if being pinned under a monster that he'd killed instead of being swallowed by the same thing was somehow a reason to feel ashamed.

"Honey, believe me, it's plenty scary right now, too."

"It looks like a scaly chicken now. It looked more like a Chinese Dragon when it was coming for me."

"Either way, it's a giant scaly chicken and more than scary enough. I've seen some mean chickens in my time."

Tina started walking again but called over her shoulders, "Geese are worse. And swans. They may be cute, but they're mean as all hell."

Mindy and Christopher—now once again carrying his empty rifle, because any weapon was better than none—followed her. Tina plodded along, her eyes mostly focused on her feet. Her new friends watched for the things in the woods, several of which had almost finished their meals.

After almost five minutes of walking through the dark woods, Mindy heard the sound of a boy crying. Not a man, but a boy. It was a sound she and countless other mothers knew very well, and she stopped the other two in their tracks and told them to wait a moment.

She looked around the area carefully. There was a tree down, and she could tell just by looking at the path of destruction from where it dropped that it was newly felled. In front of it the ground was blackened and the air smelled of blood and worse. Behind it, she could hear the sounds of the child crying.

"Wait right here and keep a look out," said Mindy. It wasn't a request. Where the safety of children was involved, there were no requests.

There was just that one little obstacle, the tree. She had to climb it if she wanted to get to the other side, or she had to go around it. She thought briefly of going under it, but she'd have to dig to find a spot big enough and didn't really like the idea of being trapped under the tree if something came along to devour her. Climbing would probably be safer. Anything could be hiding on the other side.

Mindy climbed carefully. It wasn't the biggest tree she'd ever seen, or even large in comparison to some of its neighbors, but scaling the thing wasn't easy with all of the tall, thick branches in the way. It was nice that the branches gave her plenty to hold on to, but pushing through them was nearly impossible, so she was doing more climbing than walking. Once at the highest point, she saw a lot more than she expected to. First, she saw the little boy, maybe five years old, maybe a little older.

She also spotted Lee and Brad a short distance away.

Lee spotted her, too. He waved carefully, looking around first to make sure he didn't get any unwanted attention.

She waved back just as carefully and then held up a finger, telling him silently to give her one minute. He nodded and maneuvered around again, his rifle held close to his body.

Off in the distance, Mindy saw a shape that didn't belong in a forest. She couldn't make it out clearly, but it looked like a building. Real walls, and solid if they had lasted the last few years.

She started the task of climbing down the other side of the tree. After only a couple of missteps, she was next to the tyke who was curled up into a fetal position and crying to himself.

"Hey, come on, let's get you out of here, okay?"

The boy looked at her with frightened, tear-stained eyes and nodded silently. He didn't protest when she picked him up, and his arms instinctively wrapped around her neck. She started moving almost immediately, climbing over the branches and marveling at how little the boy seemed to weigh. She'd seen him with the group earlier, firmly attached to a redhead who was nowhere to be seen.

He didn't weigh much, but having him wrapped around her neck and waist made the already-difficult climb a lot harder. When she finally reached the highest point a second time, she waved Christopher and Tina over. They were both looking everywhere around them, and it took a few seconds to get their attention.

"Where did you find him?" Christopher started climbing and stopped halfway up the tree.

"Well, my other son is starting to get too old for spoiling properly..."

"Ha ha." He smiled.

Mindy's expression turned serious. "There are two more people on the other side of the tree. One of them looked unconscious. Why don't we get together with them and see if we can find our way out of here?"

"What about all of the other survivors."

"Christopher, I don't know if there are any other survivors."

He looked at her and nodded, his brow drawing in like a gathering storm. "Okay, good point. Lead on, Mom."

Christopher helped Tina after he was done climbing over the branches of the felled tree, and all four of them maneuvered around carefully. They looked first at the stone structure Mindy had discovered, and then let out a few startled screams as the demon-spider dropped down from above them.

It wasn't really a spider. Mindy could have probably handled one of those; she'd squashed quite a few of them in her time. No, this had more legs and a longer body. Also, it had twelve glossy green eyes in a perfect circle, just above the mandibles that tried to cut the kid wrapped around her body in half. Tommy was now wide awake and let out a few screams worthy of a rhesus monkey as he started scrambling over Mindy's head in an effort to get away from the thing.

Mindy lost her footing and fell backward. Christopher caught her and let out a few monkey screams of his own as the mandibles chopped through the air where she had been standing a second before. The spider let out a low growl that sounded like a few thousand pissed-off bees, and as Mindy finally cleared the kid out of her view, it let out another scream.

It lunged forward, the thick claws on its feet grabbing at Mindy's legs and slicing into her socks with ease.

It would have been less painful if she had actually been wearing socks. Mindy cried and, without even thinking about it, threw the scrambling kid toward Christopher, who caught him. If she was going down, she wasn't taking the kid with her. That was all there was to it.

Mindy kicked hard with her left leg, taking a few layers of skin away as she wrestled free of the claw. She cocked her right leg back to land another kick, and then the spider-thing's face exploded.

Rather than continuing to attack her, the spider shuddered and twitched and drooled a lot of purplish goo out of the stump where its head had been.

Christopher let out a muffled curse as the kid his mother had thrown him started climbing over his head. Tina caught the kid before he could fall and hurt himself, and just to make sure he didn't go anywhere else, she wrapped her arms around his trembling body.

Down on the ground, she saw the old man from the tram, Lee, slowly lowering his rifle.

"Weren't we going to go down to save him?" Christopher wondered aloud.

Lee took two steps forward, and Tina dropped the kid she'd been holding as she got truly lively for the first time since they'd met her.

"Brad!" Her shout was loud enough to guarantee that every monster hiding in the trees around them would hear, but she was too busy scrambling down the fallen tree to even notice. Somehow she managed to keep her footing. She ran right past Lee and charged over to the man on the ground, stopping only when she could see him clearly and then hug his unconscious form.

Lee looked back at Tina with a combination of surprise and severe annoyance on his face, while Mindy scooped up the kid who was once again curling in on himself. He latched on to her and she climbed down without any incidents.

Christopher made it almost all the way down before he tripped, but he managed to land on his feet.

"You folks all right?" Lee came over to them, moving with the particular stride that seemed to be reserved for old men.

"Yes we are," said Mindy. "Thank you!"

"Well, it was the last bullet, I think, but that thing was looking uglier than most."

"Damn." Christopher looked at the top of the tree. "I dropped my rifle."

"Honey, the rifle is broken."

"Yeah, Mom, but it's a rifle."

"Let's just get Tina and her not-so-dead Brad and find that building, okay? Maybe there's something there that can help us."

Christopher looked less than thrilled about the idea. "Maybe there's something there that can eat us."

"If it's got walls, it's a start." Lee smiled as he spoke. "Except for the ghosts, not too much around here that seems to come through the walls. That means we can at least get a little protection."

"Brilliant plan," said Eddie, suddenly stepping into view. Barbara the tour guide was with him. Eddie waved his rifle at Tina. "You. What's your name?"

"Tina."

"Pleased to meet you, Tina. Don't ever scream like that again, okay?"

HAUNTED FOREST TOUR

"I—I won't."

"Good. Let's get moving."

CHAPTER ELEVEN

The few survivors of the Haunted Forest Tour walked quietly but briskly through the woods. Eddie took the lead and blew away the occasional ghastly creature, while Barbara walked just a step behind him, pointing out the occasional approaching ghastly creature that he might have missed. Mindy, holding Tommy's hand, was next in line, speaking softly to the young boy to keep him calm.

Christopher and Lee followed behind them, carrying Brad's semi-conscious form. Aside from the occasional loss of footing, they kept up a solid pace. Tina walked with them, stroking her husband's hair and quietly crying.

"Hey, you—Betty, is it?" Lee asked. "Tour guide lady."

Barbara glanced back at him over her shoulder. "Barbara."

"Right. Sorry. Aren't you supposed to be telling us about this place? I paid good money for this tour, and I'm hardly learning anything."

Barbara smiled. "What would you like to know?"

"What kind of tree is that?"

"Which one?"

"I can't point while I'm holding this guy. Any one."

"Well…that tree to our left is tall and brown. Its scientific name is the tall, brown tree. Its primary function in the ecosystem of the forest is to stand there and be tall and brown."

"What about the green parts?" asked Lee.

"The green parts are actually an optical illusion. If you look at them in direct sunlight, they're actually brown."

"Fascinating."

"Thanks for the improv," said Eddie. "Now that we've shared this lighthearted moment, I'm not scared a bit. Remember when that one lady got ripped apart and eaten? Man, that was fuckin' hilarious, don't you think?"

"Shut up, Eddie."

"What about all the corpses we left back in the tram? I get giggly just thinking about it. The funniest part was all the gushing blood."

"*Enough*," said Barbara.

"Just relax, Grenade Guy," said Lee. "We're trying to make things seem like they aren't completely hopeless. Sorry if that offended you."

Eddie kept walking without further comment.

Brad's body was starting to get really heavy, but Christopher didn't want to request a break. If Lee wasn't complaining, Christopher certainly wasn't going to. Even under extremely stressful circumstances, he had his sense of pride.

Brad coughed, spraying a bit of blood on Christopher's shirt. The poor guy looked absolutely terrible. In fact, though Christopher didn't say this out loud, unless they happened to stumble upon a completely equipped medical team, he didn't think Brad had much time left.

One more death to add to the dozens.

They walked silently for a while, interrupted only by Tina's occasional sniffle, Brad's occasional groan, and Eddie's occasional gunfire blast. And then, hidden by trees so thick that they were practically right on it before they even saw it, they reached the concrete structure.

"What do you think this is?" Lee asked.

"I'm pretty sure it's the water reclamation plant," said Barbara. "Most of the structures in Cromay were completely destroyed when the forest appeared, but a couple of the larger ones did survive, if the foundation was strong enough."

"So where does that put us in the forest, location-wise?"

"I'm not sure exactly. Still a couple of miles from the edge, I think."

"Isn't that about where we were when things became unpleasant?"

Barbara nodded. "But we can defend ourselves better with concrete walls."

"No argument there."

They walked around the edge of the round building, trying to find the entrance. Though Christopher couldn't honestly say that he was disappointed by what appeared to be a lack of bloodthirsty creatures in the area, he had to admit that the silence was more than a little eerie. Anyway, just because they weren't attacking didn't mean that the creatures weren't watching.

Barbara took off her backpack and unzipped the top. "I've only got three flashlights," she said, "but we'll probably need them inside."

"Anything else useful in there?" Lee asked.

Barbara shook her head. "Bug spray."

"*Big*-bug spray?"

"No. Mosquito repellent. I think it was a joke. But at least we have flashlights."

"Here we go," said Eddie, taking one of the flashlights as they came upon a small staircase. Christopher watched as he cautiously disappeared up the stairs, then called out, "We're cool!" a moment later.

The survivors walked up the flight of stairs (getting Brad up them was a real bitch) and followed Eddie into a small room. It had a desk, some computer equipment that was covered with a thick layer of dust, and a couple of chairs. Somebody's office.

As Barbara shut the office door and waved her flashlight around, Christopher and Lee carefully lay Brad on the floor. Tina cradled his head in her lap.

"This seems reasonably safe," Eddie noted. "Everybody take five and then we'll figure out what to do."

"What are the chances of a rescue party finding us here?" asked Christopher.

"Unless we can find a way to contact headquarters, I'd say it's pretty much non-existent. The only way they'd find us is if we stayed near the tracks. But, of course, if we stayed near the tracks, we'd all get eaten."

"So what do we do?"

"Me, I'm going to rest up here for a while, then I'm heading back."

Christopher gaped at him. "Are you serious?"

Eddie nodded. "Hell yeah."

"Why would you come all the way over here, and then go all the way back?"

"We had a feeding frenzy going on. Think of it like sharks. You can float around in the ocean for quite a while without getting bothered by them, but if you're swimming with somebody who cuts their finger and those bastards smell blood, you're screwed. There are monsters chowing down on whatever's left of the tourists right now, but once they finish their meal, they'll wander off. I'm not saying it's gonna be *safe*, but it shouldn't be anywhere near as bad as it was before. Anyway, it'll just be me."

"Let's not split up just yet," said Lee. "Maybe we can contact somebody. I'd much rather hang out here than in the forest." He flipped on the power switch to the computer. Nothing happened.

"You didn't really think that was going to work, did you?" asked Eddie.

"No, but we would've felt pretty stupid if we waited here for two weeks and then found out we had a live high-speed Internet connection available."

"Touché."

"Do we really want to just wait for help?" asked Mindy. "It seems to me like we'd be better off doing what we've been doing, and see if we can just walk out of here."

"Well, see, that's another possible plan," said Eddie. "Our opportunities are limitless. The whole world is in front of us, if we just hitch our wagon to a star."

"You're a very obnoxious young man."

"An obnoxious young man who saved all of your asses."

"An obnoxious young man who put our asses in danger to begin with."

"I beg your pardon? Are you trying to blame this on *me*?" Eddie stepped forward, looking way too pissed for Christopher's comfort.

"Hey, whoa, everybody settle down," said Christopher,

stepping between Eddie and his mother. "We're supposed to be taking a break. Let's just catch our breath, gather our thoughts, and figure out how we're going to get out of this mess."

"Here's what we're going to do," said Lee. "We're going to go around the room, and everybody is going to share one unusual thing about themselves. We'll start with our driver."

"Screw you."

"One unusual thing. Let's hear it."

"I'm not in the mood for games, old man."

"It's a team-building exercise. C'mon, now, you can't tell me that somebody who carries around grenades doesn't have anything unusual to share about himself."

Eddie gave him the finger.

"We'll come back to you." Lee turned his attention to Tina. "What about you? One unusual thing."

"I don't want to play."

"Sure you do."

"I...I can touch my nose with my tongue."

"Let's see it."

Tina extended her tongue and briefly touched it to the end of her nose.

"That is absolutely astonishing," said Lee. "I salute you. What about you, young man?" he asked, ruffling Tommy's hair. "What's weird about you?"

"Lots of stuff."

"For example?"

"I dunno."

"Just name one."

"I can burp longer than anybody in my class."

"No, you can't. A little guy like you? I don't believe it."

"I can."

"Prove it."

Tommy took a few gulps of air, closed his eyes, then let out a belch that lasted for a full ten seconds.

"I stand corrected!" said Lee. "You are truly a talented young man. Someday you'll be president of the United States. Keep up the good work." He looked at Christopher. "And you?"

"Well, I don't know if I'll have a job when I get back on Monday."

"And that's unusual?"

Christopher chuckled. "Maybe not. I do have to say that the experience of facing my boss doesn't seem so bad anymore."

"Perhaps Eddie will let you borrow one of his grenades."

"Now there's an idea."

"Okay, I'll let you get away with the job answer," said Lee. "What about you, Barbara?"

"Before I got this job as a tour guide, I used to work at a meat packing plant, and I'm a vegetarian."

"You were a vegetarian before you got the job?"

"Yes."

"And it didn't make you want to become a carnivore?"

"Nope. It solidified my decision."

"Okay. Good answer. And you, Mindy?"

Mindy smiled. "I like Rob Schneider movies."

"No, you're supposed to share a *true* thing about yourself."

"It's true. I have them all on DVD."

"She's telling the truth," Christopher admitted. "Oh, God, how I wish she weren't."

"Okay, well, let's move on. Brad, what about you? Brad?"

Brad lay silently on the floor.

Oh, shit, thought Christopher, staring at the man's unmoving body. But, no, he was still breathing, if only faintly.

"We'll excuse him," said Lee. "Back to you, Eddie."

"Screw you still."

"Why do you find it necessary to be so rude?"

"I guess I'm just an unpleasant human being."

"You realize that there'll be book and movie deals galore once we get out of this. Do you really want to be known as the prick?"

"Fine. I have a tattoo of a cougar on my ass. How about that?"

"That's sufficient. No evidence is necessary."

"So what about you?" Christopher asked Lee.

"Oh, there's nothing unusual about me. I'm just your standard-issue debunker."

"What's a debunker?" Tommy asked.

"Somebody who proves that monsters don't exist. Otherwise known as a complete idiot. So let's discuss our plan of action."

"Okay, here's what I think," said Christopher. "We need to figure out exactly where we are. The best way to do that is just climb a tree as high as we can. For all we know, we're five hundred feet from the edge of the forest."

"You volunteering?" asked Eddie.

"Sure."

Mindy looked as if she wanted to protest, but then lowered her eyes and said nothing.

"You can't go by yourself," said Lee. "Who knows what kind of things are lurking in those trees? And no, I'm not volunteering. I'm in pretty good shape for my age, but I'm well past my tree-climbing days."

"I'll go," said Tina.

Christopher looked at her in surprise.

"I don't climb trees in my spare time, but I used to be a gymnast. I'll go with you."

"Okay, that sounds good to me."

"I'll search the building," said Barbara. "There might be a more secure place for us to hide out. Eddie, do you want to help me?"

Eddie shook his head. "I should head back to the tracks. If they've got things working again and send another tram, I want to be there."

"Are you sure that's a good idea?" Christopher asked.

"No, I'll probably get eaten."

"You should at least wait until Tina and I scope out our location. Like I said, we could be close to the edge."

Eddie shrugged. "Fine. You two let me know if it's a merry little stroll to safety, then I'll head off to the tracks. Anybody want to come with me for bait?"

"I'd go, but I think I'd slow you down," said Lee.

"Yeah, I think you would, too. Maybe I'll bring Brad along."

"That's not funny," said Tina.

Eddie glared at her, then softened a bit. "Yeah, you're right. Sorry. Okay, so, you and momma's boy are going to climb a tree. Barbara's going to look for a better hideout..."

"I'll help her," said Lee.

"...with Lee as her chaperone."

"Mom, do you want to stay here and make sure nothing happens to Tommy and Brad?"

"I can do that, sure."

"Good. So let's go."

CHAPTER TWELVE

"You know, this may be a terrible idea," said Christopher, gazing up into the tall pine tree. Not much light streamed through the branches. Lots of places for nasty things to hide. And, even if the tree was monster-free, he could always have a nice long fall and break his neck.

"Yep, definitely a terrible idea," Eddie agreed. "I sure as hell wouldn't go up there. Have fun."

"We're trusting you, Eddie,," said Christopher. "If anything scurries toward us, shoot it."

Eddie nodded. "No problem. What percentage of your body do you want to be eaten away before I deliver the mercy shot?"

"You're a very grim man."

"It's a very grim forest."

Christopher turned to Tina. "You ready?"

"Sure." She sounded like this was a big fat lie, but Christopher wasn't about to call her on it. "If we watch each other's backs, we'll be fine, right?"

"Absolutely. Which side do you want?"

"The one with the fewest monsters."

"Fair enough. What do you think: slow and easy, so we

don't wake anything up, or as fast as we can?"

"Slow and easy."

"Hey, if you want me to spot you, you'd better go with the 'as fast as you can' idea," said Eddie. "I'm not hanging around here much longer."

"Well, that answers that," said Christopher, reaching up and grabbing the lowest branch. "Let's get a move on."

Tina walked around to the other side of the tree. Christopher pulled himself up and stood on the lowest branch. It seemed to be perfectly sturdy. He could only see Tina's arm as she pulled herself up to the lowest branch as well.

They began to climb.

The branches were thick and difficult to maneuver around, but there didn't seem to be anything living in them. Nor did any of the branches spring to life and try to impale Christopher or toss him into the air, which was nice. He asked Tina how she was doing every minute or so, even though she was outpacing him by a full body-length.

"Oh, gross," said Tina from the other side.

"What?"

"Sap. But it's green. Kind of looks like snot."

"Maybe the tree has a cold."

"That would be our luck. It'll probably sneeze."

"Stop talking about sneezing trees and climb, dammit!" Eddie called out.

They continued to climb. The first sign of life crawled over Christopher's arm when they were about fifty feet high.

It looked like a ladybug, although it was one hell of a ladybug, approximately the size of a computer mouse. It left Christopher's arm before he could even flinch and moved around to the other side of the tree.

"Watch out for the bug," he said.

He heard Tina gasp. Seconds later, the ladybug flew past him and fluttered away.

"See, not every creature in the forest wants to devour us," Christopher remarked. "Some of them are rather...oh, crap..."

Hundreds of oversized ladybugs streamed down the tree towards him. They washed over him like a ladybug shower, as Christopher squeezed his eyes shut and tried not to panic. *It's okay...it's okay...they're probably not carnivorous...*

Tina screamed on the other side.

Then, as quickly as it had begun, the flood of ladybugs ended. Christopher watched as the red tide moved down to the bottom of the tree. Eddie stomped a few times as they moved past him.

"You okay?" Christopher asked Tina.

"Delightful."

They resumed climbing, picking up the pace. The trees were all very similar heights, so it looked like they were going to have to go all the way to the top—two hundred feet or so—to get a good vantage point.

"You okay?" Christopher asked.

"Quit asking me that."

"Sorry."

Christopher froze and stared up into the darkness. Had something moved above him, or was that just a rustling in the wind? He didn't see any glowing eyes or gleaming fangs. Probably just a rustling in the wind. Definitely just a rustling in the wind. Best to be optimistic.

He looked down and was suddenly much less optimistic.

The panther—at least it *looked* like a panther—struck Eddie from behind before Christopher could even start to call out a warning. Eddie hit the ground hard, but quickly rolled over on his back as the panther lashed out at him with its front paw.

Christopher let go of the branch with his left arm and waved it in the air. "Hey! Hey, you! Up here!"

"What the hell are you doing?" Tina asked.

"Drawing it away from him!"

"Well, *don't!*"

Eddie squeezed off a shot. The panther yelped as a streak of red appeared on its side. The beast leapt off of Eddie and onto the tree that Christopher and Tina currently occupied. It started to climb at a much more rapid pace than Christopher had been able to achieve.

"Shit!" he shouted, because it seemed appropriate, as he frantically grabbed for the next higher branch. "Eddie, shoot it! Shoot it! Shoot it! Shoot the damn thing!"

Christopher heard the shot as Eddie fired. The bullet sliced across his upper arm. It took a moment for the realization to sink in (*"That son of a bitch shot me!"*) and another moment for the pain to kick in.

He'd just been grazed, but damn, it stung.

The panther was climbing fast.

Another shot. The panther yelped and stopped climbing...but only for a second. Then it let out a loud, unnerving snarl and resumed its upward movement. Christopher tried to grab the next higher branch, but his arm wasn't working right and he missed. He tried again and managed to get hold of it, and a bolt of pain shot through his arm as he pulled himself up, enough to make him feel dizzy. He was going to have to do this with one arm.

Tina was now two full body-lengths above him. He thought about the old joke with the two friends and the bear: "I don't have to outrun the bear; I just have to outrun *you*."

"Crap!" he heard Eddie say. Christopher was pretty sure this meant "Crap, I'm out of ammunition."

At least it's going to be a macho death, he thought. *How many people get killed by panthers, after all?* There was no shame in going that way.

The panther snarled once more, and then opened its mouth wide. Its tongue shot out, frog-style, and wrapped around Christopher's foot. He hadn't expected that. He smashed his other foot against the tongue, and it quickly withdrew back into the panther's mouth.

Now the panther seemed to be just as angry as it was hungry. As it crawled up the tree after him, Christopher realized that there was simply no way he was going to outrun it. He also probably wasn't going to defeat it in one-on-one combat. His only option was to hope that Eddie was able to quickly reload his rifle and then shoot with improved aim.

Or...kick.

He kicked the panther in the face so hard that he thought something in his foot might have snapped. The beast seemed unphased. His second kick got it right in its open mouth, knocking out some teeth. The panther slashed with its front paw, creating a two-foot-long gash in Christopher's pants, as well as his leg. A third kick connected directly with its skull, and the panther fell out of the tree and landed on its side on the ground below.

It immediately got up, shook itself off, and climbed

back up the tree. This was a very resilient panther.

"Jump to the next tree!" Tina shouted.

The closest tree was about four feet away. Not that much of a jump, unless your leg had recently been savaged by a panther's claws.

The panther was moving fast. Christopher decided that Tina's advice was sound and leapt toward the next tree. Several branches scraped him all over, and the pain in his leg exploded as he made the leap, a sensation that was only slightly less intense than the pain when he landed on the other tree.

His foot struck the intersection between two branches, and he lost his balance. Though he kept from plummeting to the ground below, thanks to lots of very sharp branches that blocked his fall, he found himself lying on his side, frantically struggling to get back to a standing position.

Tina leaped onto the tree, landing above him with a hell of a lot more grace than he'd managed. Some pine needles rained onto his face as she hit.

The panther climbed up to Christopher's level and looked over at him, as if trying to decide whether to make the jump. Christopher was pretty sure it was going to. He pulled on some branches to lift himself up, but his foot was tightly wedged.

Oh no. No way. I can not be stuck in this frickin' tree. My life can not be a comedy of errors like this.

He yanked as hard as he could, confirming that his foot was indeed stuck. Tina hurriedly climbed down toward him. "What's wrong?"

"My foot's stuck!"

"Are you fucking kidding me?"

The panther leaped onto their tree, landing right

beneath Christopher.

"Go!" he shouted at Tina. "Get out of here!" No sense both of them getting ripped to shreds just because he was an incompetent klutz.

Tina ignored him. She dropped down onto the large branch that was supporting most of his weight and snapped off one of the smaller branches.

The panther lunged upward.

Tina slammed the branch into its eye.

The panther let out a howl of such extreme agony that Christopher couldn't help but feel a little bit sorry for it. Not too sorry, though. It dropped off the tree and struck the ground a second time, landing on the branch and driving it into its skull. This time, the panther didn't get back up.

Eddie shot it.

"Oh, that was *real* helpful!" Christopher shouted at him.

"Screw you."

"You shot me, you penis!"

"Your arm got in my way!"

"You were supposed to be protecting us!"

"Screw you."

"Um, how about we focus on your foot before another one of those things shows up?" asked Tina.

Christopher nodded. Tina grabbed onto one of the intersecting branches with both hands and pulled. Christopher popped his foot free.

"Thanks."

"No problem. Do you want to head back down?"

"No, no, we still need to figure out where we are."

"I can do it."

"Nah, we should still watch each other's back." That

was only part of the reason. Christopher didn't relish the idea of returning to the others with a report about how he'd nearly gotten killed, forced Tina to risk her life, and then failed to accomplish anything worthwhile. He was completely willing to admit to himself that he suffered from macho pride, and going back in disgrace would hurt much more than his leg and arm would as he climbed to the top.

That said, the actual climb threatened to prove him wrong. Every step was like a rusty fishhook jabbing into his body. Fortunately, though, there were no other wild animal attacks, and even the ladybugs stayed away.

They reached the very top of the tree, which swayed in a rather unnerving manner, and gazed out at the thick forest. There were a few clearings and a narrow winding path, but it was impossible to see what lurked beneath the trees.

"That path is where the tram goes, right?" Tina asked.

"Yeah, I think so."

She sighed. "Then we ran in the wrong direction after the accident. We went deeper into the forest."

"Yeah, but still, if we just go *that* way," Christopher said, pointing to the nearest edge of the forest, "we can be home free in just...what, two miles?"

"Two long miles."

"At least we have a direction now. That's a start."

Swish swish swish...

Christopher spun around. "Did you hear that?"

"Yeah. What *is* that?"

Swish swish swish...

"Let's climb back down before we find out," Christopher suggested.

"Good idea."

An instant later, a bird flew above the trees, less than twenty feet from them. A *huge* bird, at least the size of a car, with black feathers and red eyes.

It flew at them, claws outstretched.

Christopher had just enough time to say "Shi—!" as the bird snatched him out of the tree and flew away, its talons digging deep into his chest.

CHAPTER THIRTEEN

Mark Harper had gone nearly an hour without flirting with Hannah, and it was starting to bug him. He hoped to get in several more clever bits of subtle and not-so-subtle innuendo before the day ended a few hours from now. Then he could head home and take his three kids out trick-or-treating. Later he could have sex with Chloe, since of course his wife was the only woman he would have sex with.

And of course, Hannah was not the only reason he lived for working on the Haunted Forest Tour. It wasn't often that a cryptozoologist got such a high-profile, well-paying position. He thoroughly enjoyed cataloguing the new life forms they discovered inside the forest, and Hannah's presence was a mere bonus.

God, he wanted to do her. It could be in a tender romantic manner or a rough animalistic manner, quietly or noisily, but he wanted to do her.

But as she stepped into their shared office, all thoughts of bending her over his desk and pounding away vanished. She looked more stressed out than he'd ever seen her.

"What's wrong?" he asked, standing up.

"The shit has hit a million different fans. Main control room. Now."

He followed her out of the office. "Seriously, what happened?"

"Two of the cars haven't returned. One lost power completely and the other one went out of control."

"Are you kidding me?"

She turned around and glared at him. "Do I *look* like I'm kidding?"

"Whoa, calm down. I didn't mean anything by that."

"We have eighty-four people unaccounted for. All we know is that the trams collided. After that, we lost contact with the second vehicle as well."

"How is that possible?" Mark demanded. "Those things don't just lose power. They've got backup generators, redundant communication systems, fail-safes out the ass...unless a nuclear missile plowed into one of them, there should be no way to completely lose track of them. There are military tanks that are less secure than our tram cars."

"You're preaching to the choir."

"Is Booth flipping out?"

"Nobody knows where he is."

"*What?*"

Hannah nodded. "Nobody can reach him."

Mark was so dumbfounded that for a long moment he couldn't even speak. How the hell did the head honcho of H. F. Enterprises go AWOL at a time like this? Unless...

"You think it's sabotage? Maybe somebody kidnapped him?"

"I'm not even going to pretend to speculate." She

resumed walking down the hallway toward the main control room.

"So what's Steve doing?"

Steve Bradford was second-in-command at H.F. Enterprises, and the guy who presided over most of the day-to-day operations of the company. Mark liked him a lot. He was basically the rich kid who liked to share his playground with his employees, and as corporate superiors went, Mark had never had a better one.

"He's called in the Security Detail."

Mark nodded his head. The Security Detail was a troop of heavily-armed soldiers with the best body armor around and enough firepower to take over a small nation, at least according to Steve. They were all familiar with the Haunted Forest and had done duty inside of it. They were the guys who kept the construction crews safe when it came time to put down more tracks. Screw the National Guard. He'd bank on the Security Detail every time. The guy who was in charge of them, Hal Ordover, was as scary as half the monsters Mark had seen. Only half of them, true, but still an intimidating man.

Mark and Hannah walked into the main control center. Steve sat there, his thinning hair soaked with sweat. The other H.F. Enterprises employees in the room spoke in hushed, panicked whispers, and several of them frantically typed on keyboards. At least half of the monitors were blank.

Moments later, Ordover came into the room dressed in his heavy armor and carrying what looked like a howitzer on his shoulder. Steve moved in his direction quickly, not even acknowledging that Mark had joined them. Mark might have been offended under some other wildly different circumstances, but not these.

"We're ready to go in." Hal's voice was as gravelly as ever, as if he'd been gargling with hot sand. Every time the man spoke, Mark wanted to offer him a cough drop, but it was just his natural voice, which seemed to feel the need to be as harsh as the rest of him.

Steve nodded his head and shrugged his shoulders simultaneously in a gesture that looked uncomfortable as hell. "We've got to get those people out of there. Let's do this. Be safe, Hal."

Ordover nodded and turned away, already speaking into the com-link he wore on his head. As he walked, he slipped his helmet in place. The uniforms were red, white, and blue, not your standard-issue military olive. Made them stand out better while they stood guard over the workers in the forest, giving the often-reluctant but well-paid employees a better sense of security.

Mark watched the security team's progress on one of the working monitors as they left the western side of the building and marched toward the three trucks meant to take them to the tram line.

The oversized trucks were gone from sight within four minutes.

"Do you think they'll be okay?" Hannah's voice was very small.

Mark looked at the entrance into the Haunted Forest and shook his head. He had his doubts. "Christ, I really hope so.""

CHAPTER FOURTEEN

Barbara and Lee paced around the building for a few moments, and while they did, Mindy did all she could to make Brad comfortable. He was looking anything *but* comfortable. In fact, he looked like a man who was half a foot away from death's door and about to step onto an oil slick. His skin was so pale that it almost looked translucent, except for the deep gashes on his face, which emphasized the sickly tone of the rest of his flesh.

Lee came back into the room and stared at Mindy for a moment before turning his attention to the little boy who was currently drawing on the dusty desktop with his fingers. He sighed sadly and looked back at Mindy. "Listen, if you get too bored waiting for everyone, you can keep trying the computer and the light switches. A lot of these municipal buildings have backup generators or even bomb shelters. We're going to see about finding one of those while we're looking. Who knows, maybe we'll get lucky and find both."

"Okay, Lee, I can see the generator, but why a bomb shelter?"

The older man smiled. He must have been a knockout in his earlier days, because that smile brought back a ghost of his youth. "It's a stretch, but you never know. If there is a shelter, they might have bottled water or even some food. I don't know about you, but I could use a drink of water and some canned green beans right about now."

Part of Mindy didn't think she'd ever be hungry again, but the idea of a glass of water was mighty appealing. "Well, good luck, and be careful, Lee."

"Don't have to tell me twice." He looked away from her and focused on the boy. "Tommy, you take care of Brad and Mindy, okay? I'm counting on you."

Tommy nodded his head a little listlessly but managed a weak smile.

A moment later Lee was gone and she was alone with the boy and the man lying nearby, sweating and whimpering in his restless sleep. Mindy didn't like to think about it, but Brad's chances were not good. Not at all. Aside from the whole monsters-are-trying-to-eat-us issue, he was suffering from God alone knew what sort of internal injuries. Even if they were sitting in a top-notch medical facility instead of an abandoned building, she didn't think he'd make it through the night.

Lee and Barbara were gone, and Tommy, bless his little heart, was staring into space and writing on the dust that covered the workspace as if his life depended on it. She didn't want to think about what scars his young psyche was already experiencing, and she definitely didn't want to be the one to pay the bills. Near as she could tell, that particular privilege was going to whatever state he was from, or to his next of kin. His dad hadn't gotten off the tram in time, and she hadn't seen his mother in a while.

God, what if he'd seen his mother get eaten? The

thought made her shiver.

Mindy looked around the office space and tried to take in any details that could keep her occupied. There was mold in all of the corners, which wasn't very surprising for a water reclamation plant; the humidity almost guaranteed the growth of some sort of fungus. Water stains covered the lower edges of the walls, and if she dwelled on it, she could smell the musty odor of the black spots that were pushing through the paint. Four years of going unattended hadn't hurt the place too much, but there was no escaping mold and the like. They were almost as inevitable as death, taxes, and tedious celebrity scandals.

Brad coughed violently, his face getting actual color for the first time in a while. He sat up long enough to heave a few drops of dark red spittle across the front of his shirt.

He opened his eyes for a moment and called Tina's name. When he didn't get an answer, he settled back down and started whimpering again.

Baby sitting. That's what I'm doing. I don't mind really, but what if Christopher needs me? She pushed the thought away angrily. Her son was a grown man, and there was a little boy right over at the desk who needed watching. She turned to look at Tommy, who had already gone through so much in just a few hours.

Tommy was gone.

"Tommy?" Her voice was soft and scared. Mindy stood up quickly and almost lost her balance. Her heart was jack-hammering away merrily in her chest as she scanned the room and tried to see where he might have gone.

She looked under the desk and saw nothing. Next she

looked behind the two chairs. They were actually too small for him to hide behind, but it had been a while since she'd dealt with a five-year-old and anything was possible.

She was turning toward the door when she spotted Tommy, his hands up against the wall, staring directly ahead as if the paint might reveal some deep, hidden secret.

"Tommy? Honey, are you okay?" He didn't respond to her at all, and Mindy moved closer, wondering if he'd gone into shock. He'd already seen so much death...

Mindy moved closer and put her hands on his narrow shoulders. He barely even noticed her, but his entire body was shaking.

The wall under his hands was covered with the same black mold that ran along the floorboards and her heart stuttered beneath her ribs. God! What if that stuff was just another monster in this madhouse? What if it was eating the poor boy's hands even as she touched him?

Mindy pulled him roughly away from the wall and spun him to face her, looking at his hands to see if there were any signs that the flesh had been marred. All she saw was that the mold was crusting over his fingers and palms, little more than dirt and sludge.

Tommy sucked in a massive lungful of air and shivered, his eyes moving wildly in his head. And then he let out a loud, braying scream, not of pain, but of sorrow so deep it seemed to almost rip him in half.

"Oh, baby boy..." Mindy's heart broke for him. None of them deserved this, but Tommy? He was a child, still with his baby teeth for Christ's sake. Mindy squatted until she was almost his height and he wrapped his arms around her neck, still crying out his anguish. He buried his face against her shoulder, his hot breaths washing over her as the sobs continued to spill from him.

And what else could she do? She held him and made comforting lies come from her mouth, the sort that mothers always told children after a nightmare. The ones that promised everything was all right and would stay all right, even when the parent knew otherwise.

He tried to speak, but the words came out as more muffled cries and gasps. She just nodded her head and said, "I know, baby, I know."

* * *

Behind her, on his back, Brad opened his eyes and stared at the ceiling. His skin felt wrong, tight and restrictive, and his arms, oh Lord, his arms were on fire, burning and throbbing with every pulse of his heart.

Almost everything that had happened was a blur, from the time the obese, screaming missile had slammed into his seat to this very moment. He remembered Lee fixing his arms—that sort of pain, he suspected, was something he wouldn't forget anytime soon. He remembered Tina calling his name and holding him close when she saw that he was alive. He remembered her hot tears spilling down his face and chest as she praised God that he was alive, even though he was pretty sure he was in fact dead. But all of it was muted. The colors were washed away, and even the sounds of the things in the woods and his fellow humans perishing were bleached-out echoes.

A black shadow slid across the ceiling above him, a shadow made of mold spores and rancid water. As he watched, the shadow took form, blistering the acoustic tiles and staining their lacquered finish until a lopsided face looked down at him. Funny how the mind could play tricks, wasn't it? Here he was, aching throughout every cell in his body and his mind wanted to make pictures out of the clouds. Of course, he was inside, so the water stains would have to do in a pinch. The notion brought a weak smile to his face. It was the best he could manage under the circumstances.

Not far away, he heard a little kid crying, and the whispers of a woman offering comfort. *Tommy, I think. And maybe the older lady is Mindy. Yeah, Mindy.*

He slid his eyes away from the stain above him and saw Mindy's hair, pinned as it was by the arms wrapped around her neck. Tommy's face seemed to almost sprout from her shoulder, and that was kind of weird-looking, but also kind of nice. He understood how the kid felt. Brad felt a little like crying himself, and he might have, if he could have found the strength.

A drop of water fell down and hit his cheek. Brad looked back at the ceiling. The stain was bigger now, almost as big as a man, and shaped like one, too, if he let his imagination stretch a bit.

It would have been funny if the man hadn't looked so sinister, with that wide, ugly smile and those splotchy patterns that almost looked like eye sockets above the grin.

The tile split right where that mouth was, and a stream of water fell down, splashing into his mouth before he could turn his head away. The water was cold, colder than he would have expected, but it wasn't refreshing at all. It tasted like sewage, with a side of moldy bread.

Brad tried to spit it out, but the stuff clung to the inside of his mouth with the tenacity of industrial adhesive. When he tried a second time, he must have moved his muscles the wrong way, because the foul-tasting piss-water slid into his throat and trickled down into him. He wanted to gag, but nothing happened. The smell and taste of the stuff was overwhelming, strong enough to make his eyes water. Still, he couldn't get up the energy to cough it out of his mouth and throat.

Five feet away from him, Mindy held Tommy as he cried, and Brad lifted the hand closest to them, praying one of them would notice that something was wrong.

Instead, Tommy cried harder and Mindy rocked him gently, with the practiced moves of a mom used to comforting a frightened child.

Above him the water stain's smile grew even wider as the stream of nasty fluids poured down into his mouth and filled it completely. He couldn't cough, couldn't move at all, no matter how much he wanted to. He was completely powerless.

Though he didn't swallow, Brad felt the cold water slip down into his throat, chilling his body as it descended.

What a stupid way to die.

The chills got worse, until he felt like his whole body had been filled with ice.

Up above him the waterworks stopped.

The water stain did the impossible—there was a lot of that going on as far as Brad was concerned—and grew smaller.

A few moments later it was completely gone and even the mold that had started out as a shadow receded, sliding down the wall as silently as night falls.

Brad stared at the ceiling, unable to move, and felt the new pains start in his body, pushing their way through the bitter cold and cutting like lightning strokes through every nerve in his body.

I think I figured it out, he mused, still trying desperately to get his body to move, goddamn it, and give him a chance to fight back. *Yeah, I did. I'm already dead. This is just Hell. One of those fucking things got me and ate me and now Satan himself is gonna come pay me a visit and tell me how it only gets worse from here.*

If he could have cried, he would have.

Instead he looked back at Tommy, who was finally calming down a little. He'd left a trail of tears and mucus on Mindy's neck and shoulder.

Tommy could still cry.

The lucky little shit.

Brad felt his chest rise and fall, heard his own heart beat, and struggled to do anything but just stare at the ceiling while wave after wave of pain chewed away his insides.

I'm in Hell. I fucked it up good today and I'm in Hell.

His pain got even worse, while not far away, Mindy laid Tommy on the musty carpet to sleep. She turned Brad's way and looked at him for a moment, her face showing nothing but concern for his condition.

He'd have laughed if he could. He'd have cried. Deep inside, he did both. If Mindy noticed, she never gave a clue."

CHAPTER FIFTEEN

As he walked through the forest, Eddie felt bad about leaving the others, but not *too* bad. They'd be better off hanging out at the water reclamation plant, and he definitely didn't need them slowing him down or doing anything stupid that would get him killed.

Tina had scrambled down the tree, screaming that Christopher had been carried off by a giant bird. That sucked. It really sucked. But it didn't suck any more than what happened to the dozens of other tourists, so Eddie found it hard to get all choked up over this new development. Tina had been wailing, "*We have to go after him! We have to go after him!*" but that was ridiculous. What the hell were they going to do, sprout wings and fly after him? Swing from tree to tree like Tarzan? Jump really high? Jesus. If Christopher got out of that mess, great, Eddie would give him a high-five. If he was dead, well, it wasn't like their situation was all that much worse.

Now, if Christopher had been carrying the last grenade when he got carried off, *that* would have been cause for panic.

He'd wasted a couple of valuable minutes trying to calm Tina down, and then sent her back to the office where the old chick, the kid, and the half-dead guy were hanging out. Then he set off on his own. H.F. Enterprises would send help, and that help was coming on the tracks. So he'd return to the tracks and follow them until either the cavalry showed up or he wandered out of the forest on his own.

As long as the others stayed put, he'd send the frickin' Justice League of America in to get them out of there. If they were dumb-asses, well, they deserved whatever they got. Shouldn't have gone on the stupid tour anyway.

The forest was quiet. Almost peaceful. If Eddie had his iPod, this could've been a nice, pleasant walk.

Okay, okay, he had to admit that he did feel bad about accidentally shooting Christopher. That wasn't very cool. But when you're up there climbing trees like an idiot, you can't expect completely proficient gun coverage, right? The guy was lucky he didn't get shot in the head.

Eddie stopped walking for a moment. Had he heard something?

He listened carefully.

Nothing.

He resumed walking. He was moving at a fast pace but resisted the temptation to run. Running would make it difficult to remain totally aware of his surroundings, and the last thing he needed was for something with lots of teeth to jump out at him when he wasn't paying attention.

Okay, okay, he *would* feel bad if something happened to Barbara. She was a nice girl. He'd definitely do her, if the opportunity presented itself. In theory, the opportunity could present itself back at the water plant, if he tried the old "Gosh, we could die at any time, I wonder what we could do to make our last hours on

Earth more enjoyable?" trick, but that would greatly increase the chances of something with lots of teeth getting him while he was distracted.

She probably didn't put out on the first date anyway, regardless of impending doom.

A monster stepped out from behind a tree, maybe a hundred feet away. It kind of looked like the traditional descriptions of aliens, the "grays" or whatever the hell they were called, except that it was sort of a sickly yellow color. But it did have that weirdly-shaped head with the big eyes.

Eddie stopped and pointed his rifle at it. He wouldn't waste the bullet if he didn't have to, but he'd sure blow that yellow alien away if it took a step toward him.

The alien-thing looked at him and tilted its head, as if trying to figure out what sort of creature Eddie was. It regarded him for a few moments, then turned and walked away.

Good. That's what he wanted the forest creatures to do. Walk away. If he could keep that tradition going for the rest of his little stroll, they'd all get along just fine.

He wondered if Barbara was okay.

Sure she was. She had that old guy to protect her. Larry or something. Lee? Yeah, Lee. Cool guy.

Something moved to his right. Another yellow alien-thing stepped out from behind a tree, about the same distance away as the other one had been. That probably wasn't good. Eddie pointed his rifle at that one as well, ready to put a bullet right between its oversized eyes if it tried anything.

It stared at him for a long moment.

Better move your yellow ass if you want to live long and prosper, Eddie thought. His finger tightened on the trigger.

The alien-thing turned and walked away.

Eddie resumed his brisk pace, feeling extremely uncomfortable. What if there was a whole bunch more of these things, setting up an ambush?

Well, then they'd be very unhappy to see his grenade.

He wiped some sweat off his forehead. What a horrible way this would be to die. Alone out in the woods. His body probably never to be found. Nobody to mourn him at home.

Eddie's parents had died when he was ten, in car accidents. Separate car accidents, within a week of each other. On a Thursday, Eddie was pulled out of class so that the school nurse could tearfully tell him that his mother had been struck by a drunk driver. The son of a bitch was on the road drunk at ten in the goddamn morning. His mother died instantly. The drunk guy lived out his last few years as a vegetable.

Eddie's father had cried a lot (he'd *never* before seen his father shed a single tear) and promised Eddie that they'd be okay, that they'd get through this. He barely even remembered the funeral, except that a whole bunch of people had told him how *brave* he was being, as if he were just the most precious little thing for not bawling his eyes out.

The following Thursday, his father died. Not a suicide drive, where he decided that he just couldn't live without his wife and did eighty in the wrong direction on the freeway. Nope, he was on his way to the grocery store, three blocks away, to pick up some charcoal so they could grill some burgers to distract themselves from their loss. Stopped at a red light. Guy in a truck behind him lost his brakes. Slammed into the back of Eddie's father's car. Smashed him against the steering wheel. Severe internal bleeding. He'd died three hours later.

Cruel goddamn joke.

He went to live with his grandparents. They weren't mean people, but they'd already raised their children and they had no interest in starting the process over again. Eddie got a roof over his head and food in his belly, but that was about it. They didn't care about his grades, so neither did he. He finally flunked out his sophomore year in high school, moved into his own apartment, and got a crap job washing dishes. Eventually he worked his way up to a crap job waiting tables.

He had some beer-drinking buddies and a few short-term girlfriends, but that was about it. On his thirtieth birthday, he did a rough estimate of all of the tables he'd waited on in his life, cursed several times, and then quit his job the next day, giving the finger to every person he walked past on his way out of the restaurant.

He spent a couple of years moving from one crap job to another, hating them all. Then he got a job washing tour buses. This job sucked. A few weeks later, he was driving the bus with a license that wasn't necessarily 100% legal. This job sucked substantially less. He didn't much care for listening to the exact same spiel from the tour guide every single day, but he did enjoy driving the bus.

This led to a job driving a bus with a much better company, and an actual legal license.

Which led to him meeting Cindy, who was extremely impressed with Eddie's bedroom skills, and who was in charge of hiring drivers for this top-secret project.

And so, after weeks of intense training, Eddie found himself driving a tram on the Haunted Forest Tour. Cindy took another job and moved out of the country shortly after that, but Eddie didn't mind. He was finally sort of content. It was easy work (there wasn't actual "driving" involved, since of course the tram just moved along the track) with lots of cool, new stuff to see every day. The training was only in case everything went to shit.

He wondered what he was going to do for a job after this.

Assuming he didn't die out here.

Alone.

Something moved behind him. Way too close. He spun around, expecting to see another one of those yellow alien-things.

He did.

Then there was movement on all sides of him.

Several more alien-things stepped out from behind trees. At least six or seven of them...no, make that eleven or twelve. Not good. Not good at all. And he particularly didn't like that they were smart enough to hide themselves. Eddie much preferred the "dumb animal" variety of creature opponent, thank you very much.

One of the aliens spoke in what sort of sounded like a series of clicks. Other aliens responded with more clicks.

Eddie didn't have enough bullets to take them all out. He could use his last grenade to clear a nice path, but he wanted to save that for an absolute I'm-totally-screwed situation, and he wasn't *quite* there yet. The alien-things were kind of skinny. Maybe he could beat them in a fistfight.

The first alien who'd clicked began to click again, much louder. It raised its arms in the air. This had the potential to be very, very uncool.

The aliens—and now there had to be at least twenty—all ran toward him at once. Their mouths were open wide, and all of them were clicking.

Eddie fired twice in front of him. Two aliens took chest hits and fell. He sprinted in that direction as fast as he could, leaping over their bodies, which were still very much alive, and—

—immediately collided with another alien as it stepped into view.

The alien dropped to the ground as Eddie bounced off it and slammed into a tree. His entire right arm went numb as his shoulder hit, and the rifle fell out of his hand.

The clicking was becoming almost maddening.

Eddie reached down for the rifle with his other hand, grabbing it by the barrel. Another alien-thing collided with him and slammed its mouth against his lower arm.

The pain was incredible, as if his flesh were being twisted to the breaking point, like the mother of all hickeys. He punched the alien in the face, hard enough that it felt like the bones in his hand had been shattered into splinters. It let go of his arm, leaving a ghastly red and purple welt.

Eddie spun around in a quick circle. He was completely surrounded by aliens.

He adjusted his grip on the rifle and opened fire. One alien's face exploded at close range, spraying yellow gook all over the weapon. He fired again, right through that alien's destroyed head, and got the one behind it.

He pulled the trigger again. He couldn't hear it over the other clicks, but the rifle had made a clicking sound of its own.

Another alien latched its mouth onto his arm, getting him in almost the same spot. The pain was even worse this time, and as Eddie screamed he dropped the rifle once again.

He kicked an alien out of the way. Two more took its place. Where the hell had all of them come from? The bastards were everywhere now.

He frantically kicked, threw punches, and even tried a head-butt, but it was only seconds before the aliens pulled him to the ground.

One of them latched its mouth onto his ankle. As Eddie screamed, he pulled out the grenade. This was definitely an I'm-totally-screwed situation.

If he had to die, he was going to take out a shitload of these aliens with him.

But he really, really didn't want to die.

An alien reached for the grenade. Eddie yanked it out of the way just as another alien pressed its open mouth against Eddie's cheek.

Another alien grabbed the grenade and tugged on it.

The pin popped out.

The sudden pain in Eddie's face was so incredible that it provided a split-second distraction from the fact that he was now holding a live grenade with nowhere to throw it.

He really should've offered to help Tina follow the giant bird.

CHAPTER SIXTEEN

Christopher sailed about five feet above the treetops, the bird's talons digging painfully into his shoulders, which already hurt from being shot by that prick Eddie. This was definitely a "lose-lose" situation for him, or even what his mother would call (in one of her rare bad moods) a "You are in *infinite* trouble!" situation. He was pretty sure that the giant bird was not carrying him off to a sunny beach populated by nubile nymphomaniacs; more likely, it was going to drop him into a nest of giant baby birds that would peck him to death. Of course, lots of birds ate their prey and then regurgitated the remains into the mouths of their young, so he might even have that to look forward to.

That was the "lose" part.

Unfortunately, though his destination was unlikely to be pleasurable, he also couldn't try to free himself from this bird, because otherwise he was going to enjoy a nice plummet to the forest floor and go splat. Sure, *maybe* he could grab a branch and save himself, but more likely he'd find himself impaled from rectum to cranium. Not good.

So, basically, he had to let the bird finish up its flight

pattern and hope that wherever his travels took him, it wasn't immediately fatal.

You know, you did pay for this vacation, he thought. *It's a beautiful view, and despite the agony of the whole business with the bird talons puncturing your skin, maybe you should just try to enjoy the moment. Let out an excited whoop or something. After all, how many people have ever been flown around by a giant bird? If you're lucky, maybe somebody will snap a picture.*

Christopher did not let out an excited whoop, since he knew quite well that his line of thinking was strictly intended to keep him from going completely insane. It didn't feel like it was working.

At least I'm not airsick.

As if reading his thoughts (hell, maybe it *had*) the bird swooped down so that Christopher's feet scraped the tops of several trees, then swooped up high again, making his stomach lurch.

So much for that positive element.

Just up ahead was a small clearing in the forest. Though he wasn't high enough to get a true sense of exactly where they were, he was pretty sure that this clearing was somewhere in the middle.

A couple of minutes after the flight-o-terror began, the bird swooped down into the clearing. Instead of the dirt floor Christopher was expecting, he saw...ice.

The bird set him down, much more gently than anticipated, and then flew away.

Christopher stood there for a moment, trying to process the fact that he was now standing on a makeshift ice rink in the middle of the forest. Then he slipped and fell on his ass.

The ice floor was circular and just a little smaller than a hockey rink. The edges sloped up about eight feet into the air, effectively putting him inside a giant ice bowl. The ice had a blue tint, like the Alaskan glaciers he'd seen on television.

He placed his palm on the ice to push himself up, then quickly winced and pulled away. It was *cold*, much colder than standard-issue ice.

He managed to get himself back up to a standing position. In theory, the ice bowl should not have weirded him out this much. After all, an entire freakin' forest had sprouted in the middle of a desert, and was filled with dozens (Hundreds? Thousands? Millions?) of bizarre creatures, many of whom had killed his fellow tourists. In the grand scheme of things, the ice was a minor oddity, barely worth a raised eyebrow and the word "Hmmmm." But for some reason the ice creeped him out. It was just...*unnerving* somehow.

He took a step forward and ended up on his ass again. As a child, he could just barely ice-skate successfully when he was wearing regulation skates and his mother was holding his hand, and there was no reason to believe that his skills had improved.

Instead of getting up again, he scooted along the ice on his knees. His jeans didn't do much to keep the cold out and his knees immediately went numb, but that was better than breaking his neck after falling another sixty-seven times. It wasn't like there was anybody around to see him.

He reached the edge of the ice and stood up. Though the top of the ice bowl was low enough that he could reach it, he definitely couldn't do it with bare hands, unless he wanted his fingers to instantly freeze and snap off, which he didn't. He wished he'd worn long sleeves, so he could just tug down his sleeves to cover his hands, but he hadn't expected cool weather in the New Mexico desert.

Christopher let out a small cry as he pulled off his shirt. Though his shoulders weren't bleeding much, nor was his admittedly superficial bullet grazing, they hurt like hell. If merely removing his shirt was a painful process, pulling himself up over the edge of the ice bowl was going to really, really suck. But it was either that or stand here and freeze and/or starve to death.

He folded his shirt in half, then draped it over the top of the bowl. He reached up, letting out another cry, grabbed the edge of the ice, and tried to pull himself up.

Two seconds later, he was back on his butt.

He cursed and stood up again. After all he'd been through, he was most assuredly *not* going to die trapped in a giant ice bowl. Just not gonna happen. No matter how much his shoulder hurt, he was going to pull himself over the top.

He reached up and got as solid of a grip on the top of the ice as possible. He took a deep, cleansing breath, and focused all of his energy on the task at hand. *Ignore the pain and pull yourself up. Don't die here just because you have an ouchie on your shoulder. That would be stupid.*

Christopher closed his eyes, exhaled, and then used every ounce of his strength to pull himself up.

So much pain ripped through his shoulders that he thought the skin might split open.

His feet slipped uselessly against the ice wall.

He pulled himself up so that he could almost see over the wall...and then he fell again, this time taking his shirt with him. Instead of landing on his ass, he landed on his back, which hurt a lot more.

He lay there for a while, thinking that dying here might

not be so bad. It might even be relaxing. He could just close his eyes, start snoring, and wake up on the other side, greeted by his father and thirty-seven virgins.

Or not.

He wondered why the bird had dropped him off here. Why pluck him off the top of a tree and drop him in an ice bowl? There certainly weren't any baby birds around. Was this a nest of some sort? Was the bird coming back, possibly with a whole flock of buddies?

Or was he trapped here awaiting something else?

Something much worse.

Christopher thought about that. Considering the way things were going in his life, "something much worse" was the most credible answer.

He got back up.

"I'm not gonna die here," he said out loud, as if it were more convincing spoken than thought. "I'm gonna give it one more try, and even if my goddamn arms rip right out of their sockets, I'm going to get over that wall."

He looked at the wall more carefully. Though it was a different type of skating, he'd seen kids on skateboards ride something similar to this. They'd skate along the floor, go right up the side, and then come back down. Perhaps if he got a good running start, he could slide up the wall and leap to the other side...?

Um, no. Not even if he had a skateboard.

Christopher cursed again.

Then his feet crossed beneath him and he fell yet again.

Now death was *definitely* starting to look like the more appealing option. Even if he went below instead of above, how bad could Hell really be? If nothing else, it would certainly be warmer.

He turned his head to the side and sighed.

Then he frowned.

"What the hell...?"

He got onto his knees and peered closely at the ice floor. It looked like there was something etched into it. He couldn't quite make it out, but it looked like a face. A screaming face.

He rubbed his shirt on the ice as if polishing the surface, then looked again. Definitely a face, with a hand on each side, palms-up, as if somebody were trying to push through the ice.

Creepy.

Christopher looked at the ice to his right. If he got down close enough...yes, another screaming face. And another. He scooted around, looking carefully, and it appeared that the ice was *filled* with images of screaming faces.

At least he hoped they were just images.

He reached into his pocket and took out his car keys. It suddenly occurred to him that he could probably use the keys to chip a foothold into the ice wall, which would get him over the side. Excellent. He was saved. But first he had to see what the story was with those faces.

He gathered the keys into one unit, then struck the ice. Though he'd somehow thought it might be magic ice that was impervious to key-related damage, the ice chipped away with no more difficulty than breaking through typical frozen water.

Within a few minutes, he'd broken away a couple of inches' worth of ice over the left eye of one of the faces.

He really hoped it was just an image of a face.

He looked into the hole. There was only a paper-thin layer of ice remaining over the eye, or the image of the not be so bad. It might even be relaxing. He could just close his eyes, start snoring, and wake up on the other side, greeted by his father and thirty-seven virgins.

Or not.

He wondered why the bird had dropped him off here. Why pluck him off the top of a tree and drop him in an ice bowl? There certainly weren't any baby birds around. Was this a nest of some sort? Was the bird coming back, possibly with a whole flock of buddies?

Or was he trapped here awaiting something else?

Something much worse.

Christopher thought about that. Considering the way things were going in his life, "something much worse" was the most credible answer.

He got back up.

"I'm not gonna die here," he said out loud, as if it were more convincing spoken than thought. "I'm gonna give it one more try, and even if my goddamn arms rip right out of their sockets, I'm going to get over that wall."

He looked at the wall more carefully. Though it was a different type of skating, he'd seen kids on skateboards ride something similar to this. They'd skate along the floor, go right up the side, and then come back down. Perhaps if he got a good running start, he could slide up the wall and leap to the other side...?

Um, no. Not even if he had a skateboard.

Christopher cursed again.

Then his feet crossed beneath him and he fell yet again.

Now death was *definitely* starting to look like the more appealing option. Even if he went below instead of above, how bad could Hell really be? If nothing else, it would certainly be warmer.

He turned his head to the side and sighed.

Then he frowned.

"What the hell...?"

He got onto his knees and peered closely at the ice floor. It looked like there was something etched into it. He couldn't quite make it out, but it looked like a face. A screaming face.

He rubbed his shirt on the ice as if polishing the surface, then looked again. Definitely a face, with a hand on each side, palms-up, as if somebody were trying to push through the ice.

Creepy.

Christopher looked at the ice to his right. If he got down close enough...yes, another screaming face. And another. He scooted around, looking carefully, and it appeared that the ice was *filled* with images of screaming faces.

At least he hoped they were just images.

He reached into his pocket and took out his car keys. It suddenly occurred to him that he could probably use the keys to chip a foothold into the ice wall, which would get him over the side. Excellent. He was saved. But first he had to see what the story was with those faces.

He gathered the keys into one unit, then struck the ice. Though he'd somehow thought it might be magic ice that was impervious to key-related damage, the ice chipped away with no more difficulty than breaking through typical frozen water.

Within a few minutes, he'd broken away a couple of inches' worth of ice over the left eye of one of the faces.

He really hoped it was just an image of a face.

He looked into the hole. There was only a paper-thin layer of ice remaining over the eye, or the image of the eye. He gently blew on his index finger to warm it up, then stuck his finger into the hole and pushed down on the eye.

His finger cracked through the ice layer and sunk to the first knuckle in warm, wet ooze.

You have got to be kidding me.

There were real people beneath the ice.

So it was no longer a case of merely needing to get out of the ice bowl to avoid freezing to death. Now he needed to get out before these frozen people came to life, broke through the surface, and lumbered after him zombie-style, moaning and shambling and devouring flesh.

Or something like that.

He quickly wiped his finger off on his pants, leaving a white streak. He got up and started chipping away at the ice wall. Get himself a nice foothold and he'd be able to leap right over. Then everything would be fine. No more creepy faces and potential zombie intruders.

A gust of wind blew past his ear.

That was okay. He could handle spooky wind.

He continued chipping.

Something moved behind him.

Christopher spun around. Nothing there.

"Go away," he told the nothing that was there.

He chipped some more, hoping that the ice wall would be considerate enough to simply collapse, allowing him to step over it and move on with his life.

Something else—or the same thing—moved behind him.

Still nothing there. But this was *not* a trick of his imagination, unless he'd gone insane. He was headed in that direction to be sure, but Christopher wasn't quite ready for the padded walls and comfy straitjackets yet, and there was no doubt in his mind that something had moved behind him, even if the ice bowl remained empty.

He went back to work.

The goddamn thing moved again.

Christopher spun back around. This time he did not see nothing. He saw a humanoid figure, at least seven feet tall. Its flesh was dark blue, much bluer than the ice, and it was covered with scales that sparkled with frost. It had the build of a weight lifter and wore a pair of silver shorts.

The creature's hand shot out, grabbing Christopher by the throat. Its skin was as cold as the ice.

It grinned, revealing enormous fangs that were clear, like pieces of ice in its mouth.

"Hi, Christopher."

CHAPTER SEVENTEEN

"It's quiet. Almost...*too* quiet."

Lee chuckled at Barbara's words, which was good, because that was exactly what she was hoping to achieve. A few jokes now and then, even really lame ones, helped ease the pressure.

And it was stupid, but she almost felt better when the monsters were in front of her. At least then she knew they were there. This? Shining flashlights around a musty old building and waiting to see if something was going to pop up and go *booga-booga*? This was suspense, and suspense always screwed her up.

They were ten minutes along, moving through dark hallways and stepping over the rubble from where at least one tree had taken out part of the building. Not her idea of a jolly good time.

"So, do you think we'll find a generator? Or even a few decent supplies somewhere in this place?" Lee looked at her as he spoke. His eyes were almost buried in the shadows, and the effect was unsettling. He was just the right age to turn into a Creepy Old Guy when the lights were off. He'd been nothing but polite and friendly, but the way the darkness gathered on his face gave him a sinister aura.

She shook the thought away and then sighed. "I don't know. I hope so. Anything positive would make me feel a lot better now, I have to tell you. Even if we just found a cookie crumb."

"I would be disappointed if all we found was a cookie crumb," Lee admitted. "I'd much prefer a full cookie, accompanied by a fresh plate of Buffalo wings with bleu cheese dressing and celery."

"Are you trying to torture me?" Barbara asked with a grin.

"Are you a Buffalo wings person?"

"Vegetarian, remember? But I do like bleu cheese dressing and celery. And cookies." She forced a chuckle, and then her grin slowly faded.

Lee looked at her for a long moment, his eyes on hers and his face almost expressionless. "You know it's not your fault, right?"

"What's not?"

"Any of this. You didn't do it."

Barbara felt the heat run through her face and knew she was probably blushing. She didn't think there was any way that anyone could know what she was feeling and then Lee nailed it in one.

"It's kind of hard not to feel at fault. I mean, there was no way I could help what happened with the tram, or the crash, but maybe if we'd handled things better when things started getting out of control—"

"You didn't do anything wrong. Neither did Eddie. He may be a bit of an ass—okay, several bits of an ass—but you've both done everything possible to keep things sane. So when this is all over, and we walk out of the woods and go home to our regular lives, don't blame yourself."

"My regular life is being a Haunted Forest tour guide."

"You know what I mean. It's not your fault."

Barbara had no idea what to say to that, so she simply nodded her thanks.

Lee reached out and touched another of the doors. This one was different from the cheap wooden ones they'd already encountered. It was metal and painted white. The knob turned easily enough, but the door itself seemed almost fused in place. Lee slammed his shoulder against it three times before shaking his head.

"Stuck."

"But of course." Barbara pointed to the base of the door. "Looks like it's blocked." A thick black substance oozed from under the doorjamb. "I think something's growing on the other side."

Lee's face pulled into a wrinkled look of disgust. He was handsome in a grandfatherly way, and the expression added ten years to his apparent age. She was tempted to tell him to stop pouting, but she resisted.

"I think we can get it open, but how about we try a few more doors first and come back here if we have to, okay?"

It took her a second to realize the words were aimed in her direction. Barbara wasn't really used to the idea of people asking her opinion, especially people who were a good deal older.

"Um, okay." What else could she say? There were still plenty of doors they hadn't looked through yet.

Lee smiled again, and the added decade slipped away from his face. "I have a quarter that says we'll have to check it anyway, but now I can let my shoulder have a rest before I try again." He winked. "Never does me any good to have a pretty girl knowing I'm as old as I am, you know." He slumped his shoulders and pushed his belly out in an impressive imitation of a man twenty years his senior. "The body goes to hell after fifty."

While Barbara was still chuckling, he opened the door to one of the rooms. There was no natural light at all. There were no windows, apparently. Given the circumstances, that was a plus and a minus. No windows probably meant no monsters, but then again, no light meant anything could be hiding inside.

Lee shone his flashlight into the room, which was actually a small storage closet. Nothing interesting. A couple of folding tables propped up on their sides and a stack of plastic chairs. He moved forward and sniffed the closet. After a few seconds he shook his head and stepped back.

"What's wrong?"

"Nothing, but the room smells funny."

"Funny how?"

"Chemical funny. Like cleaning supplies."

"After five years?" Barbara frowned. Even if someone had left a bottle of bleach out with the lid off, the smell would have faded eventually, wouldn't it?

"That's why I don't like it. Especially since I don't see any cleaning supplies in here."

"Good point." She eyed the door dubiously.

Lee walked down the hallway and tried the next door. It was locked. Barbara was beginning to feel like she was stuck in one of her younger brother's *Dungeons & Dragons* games.

The door opened easily, and Lee backed away from the foul odor that escaped it. Light spilled in from above due to a collapsed ceiling. More of the same black substance they'd run across at the metal door covered the floor.

Lee gagged.

A large pile of bones rested in the corner of the room. Several human skulls were clearly visible.

Lee hurriedly pulled the door shut. "I think we know what happened to all the people working here."

"Big surprise."

"It shouldn't still smell like that, though. Those skeletons are long-decayed. I think I'm gonna—" Lee slapped a hand over his mouth and turned away.

Barbara watched him for a long moment.

Lee turned back around and removed his hand. "Okay, I avoided puking in front of the young lady. That's one point of dignity in my favor."

They moved on, checking door after door. If they were locked, they were ignored. Most of the doors were locked, or maybe just wedged shut by years of unrelenting humidity.

"So what do you know about the town that used to be here, Barbara?"

"Not much, really. There were some survivors, but near as anyone can tell, the entire town was destroyed inside of an hour."

"The trees grew that fast?"

"According to one of the people who made it out, the trees came out of the ground so fast they seemed to be fully grown."

"And the monsters came with them?"

"Nobody knows if they were waiting inside of the trees or if they came afterward."

Lee scratched at his chin for a moment. "I can't imagine they were hiding in the trees."

"Well, there are a huge number of things we can't

explain about the forest. Why don't the creatures ever leave the perimeter? How come so many of them seem designed for other than forest climates? And, starting today, how come they all turned bloodthirsty when previously they only *looked* scary?"

Lee nodded his head. "True enough." He smiled. "I remember when the forest first popped up, all the news on the television and all the theories that came out of it. I think my favorite was the one about a writer who claimed to have written a book just like that, and wanted to sue the town and the state for stealing his ideas."

Barbara laughed at that one. "I remember that! You know what? He couldn't even find the manuscript he'd allegedly written when the time came for a court case. He said it had been stolen by goblins or some such and tried to prove that the Haunted Forest was all the evidence he needed."

"Please tell me he lost the case."

Barbara nodded emphatically. "Oh, yes. He lost. Then he came down to the actual forest and spent two months carrying a sign around that claimed the monsters inside were plagiarists."

"Seriously?"

"Hand to God." She crossed herself and lifted her right hand in a salute to heaven.

"Whatever happened to him?"

Barbara shook her head and smiled despite her desire to be serious. "I think he got an actual book deal based on the publicity."

"Bastard."

"Yep."

"Well, at least he was dedicated in his dementia." Lee was about to say something else when they heard the sound of something moving its way down the darkened hallway. He held up one hand, made a shushing gesture, and shut off his flashlight. Barbara did the same.

Whatever was heading in their direction had a breathing problem. The sounds it made were phlegmy and strained. Barbara's cousin Amelia had asthma, and the worst attack she'd ever witnessed sounded mild in comparison to the noises coming from down the hallway.

Lee urged her back against the wall and she followed his lead, moving out of the hallway to give whatever it was coming their way plenty of space. Of course, she also made sure that her pistol was in the right position and that the safety was off, just in case whatever came along was hungry.

Lee leaned against the wall next to her, and the fact that he was trembling was oddly comforting. If he'd been steady and calm, it would have meant she was either the only one of them that was weak and cowardly, or the only one that was human. Either way, having him with her and just as nervous made her feel a little stronger.

Whatever was coming their way was also dripping fluids. The sound of the liquid splashing along the tiled floor was very distinctive. It was also loud enough to tell her that the thing was very, very wet.

It stopped moving. The noisy breathing calmed down and the constant trickle of water came no closer.

Barbara had the sudden need to sneeze. Her nose tingled and her sinuses felt clogged. Her eyes started watering and she resisted the urge to sniff as best she could while her whole face seemed determined to build into the sort of sneeze that would blow down walls.

Lee twitched next to her and sniffled faintly. It seemed he was having the exact same problem.

The stalled trickles started moving forward again. She looked past Lee and saw nothing at all. Not so much as a shadow moved, but she still heard whatever it was in that area.

Lee's hand moved slowly over to hers and tapped lightly at her wrist. Because she knew he was there, she managed not to scream. She looked away from the empty hallway and over toward him. When she finally saw Lee in the darkness and moved her hand to let him know, he took his fingers from her wrist and pointed upward.

Barbara looked and saw the thing slithering across the ceiling. All she could really make out was the uneven shape in the darkness and the oversized eyes that glowed very dimly.

Neither of them moved, and though the stuck sneeze kept threatening a rebellion, Barbara eventually won out. Lee watched the ceiling right along with her until the big-eyed monster was out of sight. It slithered along the tiles until it came to a hallway, and then turned left, into the area they hadn't yet explored.

Barbara no longer wanted to explore it.

Lee must have been reading her mind. He leaned in close and whispered, "Screw this. Whatever else we can say about that first office, it's safer than anything we're going to find down here."

"Yeah," she agreed. "And at least we know the way out of the building if we need to run."

Slowly, reluctantly, they headed back the way they'd come, checking every door and the ceiling above them to make sure nothing was waiting to pounce.

CHAPTER EIGHTEEN

Mark shook his head as he watched the four Security Detail trucks drive single file into the Haunted Forest. He wanted to see what was about to happen. Part of him wanted to know that the good guys were winning the battle. Another part of him—a part that did not make him proud—wanted desperately to see some of the Haunted Forest's denizens in action. Seeing a creature, marking its height, probable weight, and body structure and listing large conjectures on what it might be capable of doing, that was all good and well, but to actually have visual documentation of the damned things in action...*that* he wanted to see.

Not that he'd get to. Along with the complete communication failure, none of the cameras in the Haunted Forest were working. It was as if the equipment, trams, and people inside had simply ceased to exist.

The trucks would have to stay near the tram track, since that was the only area cleared out enough for a vehicle to drive through. Hopefully the tourists were just sitting patiently in their trams, awaiting assistance.

"Absolutely bizarre, isn't it?" asked Steve, who Mark hadn't even realized was standing behind him. "How the hell did something take out power to the entire line of cameras?"

"Should've been impossible," said Mark, turning around to face the man who, until Booth returned, was responsible for the whole operation and did not look happy about it. "They're on different feed lines."

Steve nodded. "Yeah, near as we can figure, either we had a catastrophic computer failure, which we didn't, or something out there destroyed a lot of cameras all at once."

"There's over a hundred camera feeds out there. There's no way one thing could have done that."

Steve looked him in the eyes and nodded again. "I know. That means it was a lot of things working together."

Working together? In all of the time since Mark had taken the job and started observing and making notes on the different creatures in the Haunted Forest, he'd never run across a case where any of the different creatures out in the woods worked in unison. Well, okay, there were packs of gigglers working together, because that was how they hunted, but none of the creatures he'd ever seen in the woods worked with other life forms to do anything.

"That's crazy," said Hannah. She'd been standing there the whole time, and not once had Mark thought about her breasts. This was a bad, bad situation.

Steve shook his head. "No, that's scary."

Several of the people at the windows let out a unified gasp, and Mark, Hannah, and Steve all turned as one and moved over to see what was happening.

The entrance to the Haunted Forest was monitored constantly by the now-defunct cameras, but it was also easily seen from the control center. The heavy armored bay windows—the entire facility was built to withstand unexpected visits, even though nothing had ever visited—showed a clear view of the forest and both the entrance for the tram cars and the exit a hundred yards away. Aside from the rails that ran into the woods and the carousels where the trams were stored and turned to be sent back into the forest, there was nothing to see on most days but the almost impenetrable wall of trees that stood taller than should have been possible.

Fifty feet into the thick woods, the tracks vanished into shadows. Beyond that, they'd always depended on the cameras.

Something was different this time. There were flickers of light coming from the depths of the forest. They couldn't hear anything, because the heavy windows were virtually soundproof, but they could see the flashes of activity that made it quite obvious that the security team in their armored vehicles had encountered something already.

Mark pressed himself up against the window and blocked out the lights behind him with his hands, the better to make out the details of what might be going on down there. Hannah did the same thing next to him, her body pressing against his as the crush of people increased.

Something enormous came into view a moment later.

Mark couldn't see the creature clearly, but it was, what, fifteen feet tall? It looked like it weighed as much as one of the trams. It was the biggest thing Mark had ever seen inside the Haunted Forest...and it looked like it was coming *out*.

Nothing anywhere close to this big had ever been seen this close to the edge of the forest. Even the smaller creatures never actually came out of the forest. Not ever.

More flashes of light and the creature backed up, its impossibly large mouth open in a wide scream of rage. Then it stepped forward and lashed out at the source of the light. Bright, tacky outfits or no, the security guard was barely visible in the heavy darkness. Only the flash from his weapon's muzzle gave him away.

A half-mile worth of open dirt and sand separated the forest from the offices; a tempered piece of nearly indestructible translucent acrylic almost a full foot thick was an added barrier. Mark would have sworn on a stack of Bibles that he heard the soldier scream when the creature tore him limb from limb. But consciously, he knew that the only thing he heard as the soldier's blood painted the monster was the sound of people around him squealing in panic. Not that he could exactly blame them, as he was seriously considering a good solid shriekfest of his own.

The creature walked closer, and Mark finally got a good look. He recognized it immediately: an ogre. But an ogre that was a hell of a lot bigger than the one he'd sliced up on his autopsy table.

This was bad.

It got worse when the second ogre came into view. And then the third. And the fourth.

The security detail had armor and weapons. The ogres had their own bodies and their teeth. Mark hoped it would be an unfair fight, advantage going to technology over nature, but there was so much pure *rage* on the hideous faces of the ogres that they looked like they might take a direct missile hit and keep coming just out of malice.

The security team was good. And they should have

been well prepared. But it seemed like for every bullet that landed, another soldier got pounded into the ground. One ogre fell. The other three—that he could see—remained standing and angry.

Several people staring out the window moved away to be sick. For every person that left, someone else was more than willing to come over to get a better view of the carnage. Mark didn't move. Part of him wanted to, but the professional cryptozoologist in him refused to budge. Hannah was the same way. His inner chauvinist felt the need to protect the pretty girl from the horrors they were watching, but he managed to control the impulses to gently usher her away.

At least fifteen soldiers came running out of the forest, hauling ass with all of their energy, and Mark followed them with his eyes until he saw why they were moving so fast. Two additional ogres hurled one of their trucks after them. The truck was on fire, and barely recognizable as an American-made automobile.

The flaming truck bounced awkwardly and then rolled after the soldiers, who scattered before it could finally land. Not that it did them much good, because the gas tank exploded on impact and sent a fireball and debris sailing everywhere. Mark couldn't tell who was merely stunned by the impact and who actually took shrapnel.

And then the ogres emerged from the forest in hot pursuit.

Mark's stomach felt like it had become one giant ulcer. Was it just these particular creatures that were defying four years of "no creatures leave the forest" tradition, or were the camera and communication problems related to some sort of horrifying free-for-all?

More people moved away from the window as the

ogres got serious about their carnage. Mark kept watching, wondering how many of the tourists had suffered the same fate. He had no doubt that he would be looking for a new job in the very near future, because all the insurance in the world wouldn't save the company when the lawsuits started coming in.

He made a mental note to start copying all of his files and smuggling them home. Somebody should have all of the information that the courts would probably demand be locked away or handed over to national security for the purpose of wiping out the forest. Also, he'd been meaning to write a few articles for a while now, and if the company couldn't defend itself from the lawsuits, he'd need all the money he could get. *The Weekly World News* would pay a fortune, he was sure.

"Jesus, those bastards from CNN are recording all of this." Steve's voice was asthmatically weak.

"Oh yeah, we're boned." Hannah had suddenly developed a tendency for stating the obvious.

Mark looked out the window.

"Why the hell are some of those reporters still out on the field? Get them out of there!" He couldn't believe how stupid some people were.

Steve laughed bitterly. "Yeah, yeah, I'll get right on that."

"No, seriously, Steve. How much more added litigation can we handle?"

"Shit." Their acting-boss jumped toward the closest phone, but it was already too late. A cameraman below was actually walking toward a pair of the ogres. The results were exactly what Mark expected, and when they were done wishboning the bravest little moron on the planet, two of the ogres charged the remaining news people.

Fortunately, not all of the security team had headed into the forest. There were still a few posted discretely in bunkers around the perimeter. Mark had to give H.F. Enterprises credit. They'd understood just how bad it could get if anything from the woods ever came out to investigate. The cement and steel bunkers were never without at least a few heavily armed guards. The combination of firepower from the bunker guards and the remaining security team members on the field felled the two ogres before they could reach the news crews, though it was close enough that the second ogre nearly fell on top of them.

The reporters were apparently not suicidal. They ran like hell for the safety of the building. They made it. One more ogre died in a hailstorm of literally hundreds of bullets, but the rest proved that they had some survival instincts and took off for the forest.

Down below, he could see the reporters enter the building, or at least reach the overhang that stopped him from seeing the front doors. For all he knew they were locked out and the people inside were making faces from the other side of the glass.

Hannah tapped Mark on the arm and leaned in close, so that no one else could hear her. "So," her voice was as soft as a lover's first tentative caress, "when are we going to duplicate all of the files? And where are we going to hide them?"

Mark gave her a grim smile. "I think there might be time right now, actually." Neither of them planned on doing anything with the files as long as H.F. Enterprises was in business, but if it went under, that was a different story. There's a difference between loyalty and stupidity.

Besides, someone needed to know what they'd been doing, needed to understand the wealth of information they'd accrued. Also, it was about the best hope either of them had for getting another job that paid as well.

Mark and Hannah looked at each other and headed for their offices. They'd made it out of the control room before the first tremors shook the building. The vibrations weren't epic, but they could be felt. The ground beneath their feet shivered slightly and every window in the building rattled. Being much stronger than the average panes of glass, none of the windows broke, but the rattling noise was enough to catch everyone's attention.

Hannah looked his way with wide eyes and shook her head. "What now?"

"I'm not sure I want to know." It took a hell of a lot more than a gentle breeze to rattle this building. The foundation was made with four feet of solid concrete and extra layers of rebar, just in case any new trees ever tried to sprout.

The miniature earthquake stopped for the moment and both of them moved faster, heading for their shared office. They had to get this done as quickly as they could. If something was coming that could damage the building they needed to have all of the data and be on their way to whatever safety they could find.

Neither of them said what was on their minds, which was that anything down there big enough to cause a tremor in this very well-fortified building was larger than anything they'd ever encountered.

There was no time to lose if they wanted to get their research to safety, because even the backed-up information was kept in the facility. No data ever left

H.F. Enterprises. And if the threat was as serious as they suspected, there would be no second chances to get what they needed and get the hell out of Dodge.

CHAPTER NINETEEN

Mindy looked at Tina, and any pretense of cheer slowly fell from her face as she mulled over what the younger woman had said.

Just to make sure she'd heard correctly, she repeated Tina's statement in the form of a question. "A big bird swooped down and snatched Christopher from the tree?"

She realized that she must have been staring bloody murder at Tina just then, because Tina flinched and nodded silently.

"Yes, ma'am."

"I want to make one hundred percent sure I heard you right, Tina." Mindy was trying to discuss things in a logical and sane manner, but her ears were ringing and she was feeling a bit dizzy and she wasn't really sure if she was doing a good job being logical or sane. "A big black bird zoomed down out of the sky and snatched my baby boy like an owl grabbing a mouse. All this after Eddie accidentally shot him. Is that right?"

Tina nodded her head and did her best to hide behind something while standing perfectly still. Mindy closed her eyes and tried to imagine her son being stolen away by a gigantic bird with blazing red eyes. Despite everything that had happened, it wasn't as easy to do as she would have expected. Not because she had any trouble dealing with the idea of a giant black bird, but because it was impossible to imagine her world without Christopher in it.

He was more than just her son; he was her best friend and the one person she could always depend on. When her husband Thomas died, it was Christopher who took care of the funeral arrangements and stood by her side and gave her strength. She could remember seeing him in his suit, looking like a little boy playing dress-up for all the sorrow that he was drowning in, but he still managed to handle all of the details and arrange for the viewing and the wake. Christopher was stronger than he knew and, damn it, the idea of a world without him for moral support was a bleak one.

In a much smaller voice, Mindy asked the question she dreaded the most: "Is he dead?" She kept her eyes closed, because if she opened them the tears would start. She didn't want to cry in front of these people. They were strangers, really. The man on the ground, the boy now once again sitting in front of the computer and drawing on the desk, and the woman who'd just witnessed her son being ripped away from her life, her world.

Tina shook her head. "I don't know." Her voice came in hitches, and Mindy opened her eyes to see the woman cover her face to hide the tears.

Mindy nodded her head and rose from where she'd been sitting near Tina's husband. Brad seemed to have recovered a bit from his earlier troubles, and though he wasn't speaking, at least he didn't seem to be suffering quite as much. Good for him. Good for Tina. Peachy, really. But at this moment Mindy couldn't stand the idea of being around either of them. Call it sour grapes, call it whatever the hell they wanted, but she needed to get some space.

Mindy brushed past Tina and walked as calmly as she could out of the office and toward the entrance to the reclamation building. She needed fresh air in the worst possible way, and the scent of mold and mildew was so thick that she couldn't even remember what fresh air smelled like.

The door was closed, but she had no trouble opening it. The forest greeted her with heavy shadows and not nearly enough actual light to help warm her from the chill she'd developed. Somewhere out there, Christopher was probably dying or—more likely—already dead. She'd seen enough people torn apart since the day started to know that his chances were almost nonexistent.

Still, she didn't want to think about her son being dead. There was an old saying of her grandmother's that stuck deep inside of her and echoed up to her conscious thoughts: "No parent should survive their children."

Truer words were never spoken.

Of course, Gramma was still very much alive, and after today might very well have survived her children, grandchildren, *and* great-grandchildren.

Mindy sat on the highest stair and stared out into the gloom, fully aware that there might be any number of creatures staring back at her. Then she cried. Soft, quiet tears of desperation, and she prayed as hard as she could to whatever gods might listen, begging for her son's safety.

* * *

Lee walked along the corridor as carefully as he could, and told himself that the tightness in his chest was just simple anxiety, nothing more. If he could convince himself that his ticker was just fine, it might do him a little good. On the other hand, in a worst-case scenario, he could always go for the nitro tablets in his pants pocket.

He thought about his next book. This one was going to be very different. A cautionary tale. *Don't Go on Tours into Haunted Forests, Dammit.* Solid advice for the new generation.

Thinking about his next written endeavor was a great distraction to keep him from screaming like a little girl or putting one of his remaining bullets in his own head. Two bullets were left in the rifle, and Barbara had told him she only had one shell left for her pistol. If he thought about the sheer volume of nasty things lurking inside and outside of their shelter, he wasn't completely sure he could keep moving. His childish glee from before was officially history. So instead he thought about what he could write when the nightmare was over. How exactly would he describe that giant head on the tracks?

His musings helped, but not a lot.

Barbara looked his way again and tried to smile. It wasn't very effective. She was a pretty little thing, but the stress she was under stretched her smile into an entirely different, somewhat ghoulish expression.

"Are we ready for this?" He tried on a smile of his own as he asked the question, but it felt wrong so he got rid of it.

Barbara looked at the door to the room where they'd left the others and chewed on her lower lip. It might have been a fetching gesture under different circumstances.

"Yeah, let's do it."

Lee opened the door carefully as Barbara held her pistol at the ready. They were prepared for trouble, but they didn't get any. Instead, they saw Tommy writing on the dust that covered the desk and Tina sitting Indian-style on the floor next to Brad, her hand stroking his forehead as she looked in their direction.

"Did you find anything?" Tina's tone held a slight warble of desperation, as if they might have somehow run across a fully functioning emergency ward and a staff of doctors to help her husband.

Lee shook his head solemnly. "No, I'm afraid not. There's not much beyond this room that I'd feel comfortable calling safe."

Tina took the news poorly. He couldn't really blame her, but when she started crying, it made him feel like the worst kind of heel.

Barbara saved him from the awkward situation, moving past where he stood and looking down at the husband and wife. "How did it go? Did you see which direction we need to head?" Her voice was almost as desperate as Tina's had been and Lee knew the answer before the young woman spoke.

"We're in deeper than we thought. It's at least two miles."

"Is Christopher out scouting a path?"

"No." Tina looked down at the musty carpet beneath her feet. "He got carried away by a giant bird."

Barbara looked at her for a few seconds before answering. "Oh."

Lee coughed into his hand. "Where's Mindy?"

Tina managed to look even more wretched when she answered. "She went outside. I think she needed to get away from me."

Lee nodded slowly and double-checked his rifle, hoping that a few more bullets had magically appeared. They had not.

"She shouldn't be out there by herself," he said. "I'll go check on her."

Barbara looked his way, worried. "Be careful."

"My dear, I am far too old to behave any way *but* careful." With that, Lee headed for the main entrance a level below and tried to talk his knees out of violently knocking together. He wasn't much into dying, and the notion of getting anywhere near the front door seemed like a pretty good way to get himself killed. On the other hand, he certainly wasn't into the idea of watching someone else die, especially when it could be avoided.

He found Mindy sitting on the stoop, her elbows on her knees and her hands holding up her tear-streaked face as she looked out into the forest. Lee stood silently and watched her for several moments, alternating between trying to find the right words to say and making sure that nothing was waiting out in the darkness.

Mindy spoke before he could find the right words. "I'm fine, Lee." She looked over her shoulder at him, her lower lip trembling a bit. "I just need to think for a while."

"Might be safer in the stairwell, Mindy." He thought about it for a second. "Maybe not a *lot* safer, but still..."

"I don't think Christopher is dead." Her voice was small, smaller than at any point he'd heard her speaking before.

"Well, I didn't get all of the details." What else could he say? The chances that Christopher was still alive were about as good as the chances that Lee would suddenly grow a poodle tail and win a dog show. This didn't seem like a wise point of view to share at the moment.

"Tina said he got snatched by a giant bird. She didn't say anything about him being dead."

Lee nodded his head. "It's always possible. I mean, really, for all we know there's something more to what's going on than just a bad case of hungry creatures." *Even so...*

Mindy shook her head. "I dunno. Maybe. Or maybe the damned thing wanted to feed my boy to its young. Who knows?"

Something shuffled through the woods, low to the ground by the way it sounded, and Lee could see a few leaves shivering in the gloom not too far away.

Mindy noticed it too. Her head turned in that direction and her entire body tensed up. Lee lifted his rifle and sighted into the woods, aiming where the bushes and undergrowth rattled the most.

"I think you're right, going inside sounds good. How many bullets do you have left?"

"Just two."

"Yeah. Inside then. Let's go." Mindy stood up.

The bushes trembled and something burst forth from them, moving fast and panting.

Lee added pressure to the trigger and reminded himself to breathe in nice, shallow breaths. He almost pulled the trigger completely before he recognized that the shape was human.

"Stop right there. I've got a loaded rifle aimed at you."

"Don't shoot! Oh God! Don't shoot!" He recognized her as she stepped closer. A cute redhead with a body that spoke of many, many hours in a gym, and clothes that cost far too much for her to be running around in the forest.

"You're Tommy's mother, aren't you?"

"Oh God, is he here?"

"Yes, he's inside."

"Oh thank God! His mom would kill me."

"You're not his mom?" He frowned. Tommy and the woman even looked a little alike, give or take the gender and age differences.

"No, I'm his aunt." She moved closer, heading toward them at high speed. "I need to see him, make sure he's okay."

Mindy stood up to let her get past, and Lee lowered the rifle again. Who would have thought anyone could survive out there without a weapon? That thought got him frowning.

"Wait a second. How are you still okay? I mean, there are things out there eating people left and right, and you're fine?" He blocked the door as he spoke, and Mindy frowned for a second before understanding came to her eyes.

Jean looked at him as if he'd lost his mind. "I've been trying to follow you guys. I saw the direction you went. Thanks for coming back when I called for you, assholes."

"We never heard you." Lee looked her over from head to toe, and she took his eyes on her as a personal affront, judging by the way she put her hands on her hips.

Her clothes were filthy, and she was drenched with perspiration. No blood, though. But it wasn't like monsters were popping up every ten seconds. Maybe somebody could quietly sneak through the woods by themselves without any weapons.

"Okay, let's all go inside."

"If you're done ogling me—"

Lee shook his head. "I'm trying to make sure that you're exactly who you say you are."

"What do you mean?"

"I mean we're in a forest filled with monsters, and for all I know you could be a shape-changing thingy."

"Oh, give me a break! I've been alone in the woods all this time and my husband is probably dead, but you don't see me accusing people of being shape-changing thingies. Are you some kind of fucking idiot?"

"Just being careful," Lee said, admitting to himself that it did sound kind of silly and paranoid. Her tone was annoying him, but Lee did his best to ignore it. The tensions were high enough without his adding to them. He knew better, that was the saddest part. He knew not to piss people off in stressful situations. Another survivor was a good thing. A miracle.

"Who died and made you the general around here anyway, mister?"

Mindy stepped between them. "Let's just all calm down and see what we can do about getting you back together with your son, okay?"

"He's not my son."

"Good for him." Mindy turned and headed inside. Jean followed her a second later, and Lee headed for the entrance himself when he saw movement at the edge of the forest.

His hands twitched, and he almost dropped the rifle but managed to recapture it before it could fall.

The shape coming toward him was familiar enough. He'd studied it earlier when it looked him eye to eye outside of the tram car.

The Proof Demon moved closer as the door closed next to Lee. It moved quickly, and he wasn't sure he could aim the rifle before it was upon him.

CHAPTER TWENTY

Eddie wrenched his head away from the alien's open mouth. It let out a shrill cry that ripped through his ears. As the alien thrust its head toward him for a second bite, Eddie slammed the grenade into its mouth, shattering several of its teeth.

Eddie wanted to quickly roll over, but the other aliens had him pinned down. He settled for holding up his hand as a semi-shield.

The alien's head exploded, spraying yellow chunks and slime all over the place, though mostly on Eddie. It wouldn't be biting anybody else's face any time soon. The alien was motionless for a moment, as if coming to terms with its lack of a cranium, and then it collapsed.

One down, a shitload more to go.

The head of another alien exploded. Eddie hadn't anticipated this one and thus hadn't protected his face or mouth. Then another one burst, followed immediately by a third. One after the other, the aliens' heads exploded in a voluminous shower of yellow goo, completely drenching Eddie.

About thirty seconds later, Eddie lay in a small pond of alien remains. The smell was not pleasant.

He sat up. His ears were filled with gook, but he had nothing slime-free available to use to wipe off his fingers so he could get it out. Instead he got to his feet and trudged through the yellow pond until he reached a tree. He wiped his fingers on the trunk and then went to work trying to get the slime out of his ears.

So what was up with the mass explosion? All of those aliens *had* pretty much come out of nowhere. Maybe they were all part of one creature that split itself into multiple parts that all shared the same consciousness and receptiveness to head-exploding or some science fiction bullshit like that.

Then why hadn't they all died when he shot a couple of them in the head?

Maybe it was some sort of psychic connection between them all, and the mental stress of having its head completely explode impacted the others as well, thus causing their own heads to explode.

Fuck it. They were dead. He'd ask somebody about it when he got back.

He stepped forward. Something wrapped around his ankle and yanked him upside down. Eddie found himself dangling from a tree branch, his head swaying three feet above the ground.

Great.

Who the hell had set up a booby trap out here?

He swayed back and forth a bit, slime dripping off his body onto the ground.

Hopefully this was a trap set by humans to catch a monster, and not a trap set by monsters to catch a human. The situation was messed up enough without these things being able to use tools and set traps.

He tried to pull himself up, but he had no energy left.

He'd just have to dangle here for a while and get his strength back.

Some slime oozed down into his nostril. He frantically pinched his nose to squeeze it out.

Shit.

Double shit.

Triple shit to the twelfth power.

The rope around his ankle tightened.

He looked at it more closely and realized that it was not, technically, a rope, in the sense that the standard definition of "rope" did not include eyes, teeth, or any degree of writhing. The thing that held his foot wasn't exactly a serpent, but it was close enough.

Eddie yelped and kicked at the snake-thing with his free foot. Its grip on his ankle tightened.

"Let me go, bitch!" he shouted at it, now grinding his foot against its head. It tightened around his ankle even more, so that it was starting to hurt. He kicked and kicked at it, but the serpent wasn't letting go. So Eddie switched tactics and tried to grind his shoe against its neck as hard as he could, hoping its head would explode just like one of those aliens.

Its grip loosened.

Eddie's foot popped free and he fell to the ground. Though he cushioned his landing with his outstretched arms, it was still quite a jolt, and he lay there, dazed.

The snake-thing dropped onto his face.

He yelped again and grabbed at the serpent as it slithered underneath his neck. He got a good grip on it and tried to pull it away, but the damn thing was too strong, and before he even realized what was happening it was double-coiled around his neck.

"Oh, no, you are *not* going all boa constrictor on me!"

he told it, although his current lack of breathing ability made the words sound much more similar to an incoherent groan. As it squeezed his neck, he squeezed its body, trying to dig his fingers into its skin and rip it apart.

Its tail slapped against his cheek, as if trying to add insult to injury.

Eddie sat up. Now he truly couldn't breathe, and he was pretty sure that passing out was in the near future for him. He got to his feet and stumbled against the tree, waiting for the inevitable crack of his neck as the serpent's grip continued to tighten.

He noticed something on the ground.

An alien's jaw.

He reached down and picked it up. He slammed its teeth against the snake-thing and moved the jaw back and forth in a rapid sawing motion.

He couldn't see what was coming out, but his fingers were getting wet.

The serpent tightened and tightened as he sawed and sawed.

Then, all of a sudden, it released its grip and dropped to the ground.

It tried to slither away, the front half of its body dragging the partially detached bottom half. Eddie slammed his foot down on it, missing the head but crushing the tail.

The snake's head slipped underneath the right leg of his pants. Eddie hurriedly lifted his foot to try and shake it out, which he immediately realized was a very big mistake because it freed the creature and allowed it to slip completely into his pants.

"Shitshitshit!" he screamed, frantically punching at the

creature as it made its way up his leg. His blows didn't seem to be doing any damage, and the snake slid past his waist into his shirt, giving his testicles a swat with its tail as it passed.

Eddie desperately tried to get a grip on the snake as it darted up toward his neck, but it slipped effortlessly through his hands as he grabbed at it through the fabric.

It popped its head out of his collar, and suddenly the snake was around Eddie's neck again. It tightened around him, and Eddie's breath stopped in mid-gasp.

He clawed helplessly at the creature, then bent down and scrambled to find the alien jaw again.

The snake bit his chin.

Eddie cried out and tried to pry its fangs loose. The snake's head wouldn't budge. He poked at its eye and missed.

It hurt so badly that he couldn't even say "shit" again.

Eddie slid his fingers along the portion of the serpent that was wrapped around his neck, stopping when he reached the half-severed portion. He crushed it in his fist.

The snake dug its fangs deeper into his chin.

Eddie squeezed harder. Something spurted.

Then he ripped the snake away from his neck. Its fangs took a generous piece of his chin with them as they pulled free.

Eddie whacked the snake against the tree.

It continued to writhe in his hand.

He whacked it again and again.

It didn't stop moving.

Eddie whacked it against the tree trunk repeatedly, counting each blow. Ten...eleven...twelve...

The snake was almost in two pieces, but it was still alive and struggling.

Eighteen...nineteen...twenty...

The damn thing just wouldn't die!

Twenty-six...twenty-seven...

Now pieces of snake were flying into the air with each hit,

Thirty-three...thirty-four...

It wasn't struggling quite so much anymore.

Forty...forty-one...

It had stopped moving.

Forty-seven...forty-eight...

By the fiftieth hit, Eddie was certain that the snake was dead. He kept whacking it against the tree until he'd counted to seventy-five.

He let the pulpy mass drop to the ground, then he stomped on it ten times.

Then—fuck it, nobody was around to see—he sat down against the tree and cried.

* * *

Eddie's chin hurt like hell, but there was nothing to indicate that he'd been injected with venom. Not that Haunted Forest snake venom would necessarily follow the standard poison rules, but as far as he could tell, the only damage came from the deep twin holes.

He walked through the forest, still dripping yellow alien slime. He wondered if the others were faring any better. Christopher in particular had seemed like a pretty decent guy, and Eddie hoped that he'd somehow survived his encounter with the giant bird.

He doubted it, but, hey, nothing wrong with hoping.

Eddie walked as quickly as he could while still paying close attention to where he stepped. He didn't think he could handle another encounter with one of those snakes. Actually, the way he felt at the moment, an ambitious hamster might be too much for him to handle.

And then, finally, he saw the tram up ahead. Not the one he'd been driving, but the one that had been ripped open.

He'd hoped to see an additional tram with a rescue team waiting inside, smiling and waving and bearing Starbucks, so he was disappointed by the lack of reinforcements. At the same time, he'd feared that he might see a couple of extra wrecked trams littered with corpses, so it could've been worse.

He reached the tracks. The tram was silent.

Okay, best-case scenario, a rescue tram was on the way at this very moment. Somewhat less than best-case scenario, the rescue tram had been ambushed before it reached this point, preventing anybody else from getting through on the tracks.

He had to assume that waiting around for help wasn't going to get him saved, and just make his way along the tracks by foot. If reinforcements showed up, fantastic, if not, he'd just have to get out of the forest without their help.

He walked over to the wrecked tram. He didn't expect to find any survivors, and quite frankly didn't need anybody slowing him down, but there might be some useful stuff in there.

He stood outside the tram for a moment and listened. Nothing seemed to be stirring.

He stepped inside.

A man, seated in the second seat back, pointed a rifle at him.

Eddie put his hands in the air. "Whoa, hold on, I'm

here to help."

The man looked at him closely. The stress of the situation made everybody look older than they were, but Eddie pegged him to be in his forties or so. He had short hair, which was sticking up in the back, and a neatly trimmed mustache and goatee. He was wearing a black jacket, and though Eddie's fashion knowledge didn't extend past Levi's, it looked damn expensive.

"You're the other driver, aren't you?" the man asked.

"Yeah."

"We crashed into you."

"I know."

"You shouldn't have stopped."

"Yeah, well, they weren't perfect driving conditions." Eddie lowered his hands.

"Get them back up!" the man said.

"Are you kidding me?"

"I'll shoot you. I swear I will."

Eddie sighed and raised his hands in the air again. "I'm not here to hurt you. I don't want anything from you. Okay, that's not true, I'd kind of like the gun, but I'm just here to find something to defend myself with while I try to get out of the forest."

"You can't have any of this."

"You're just going to let me die out here?"

The man shrugged. "What's one more?"

"What's your name?"

"None of your business."

"I'm Eddie. Pleased to meet you."

"Don't try to make friends with me," the man said. "I'm serious. Turn around and leave this tram, or I'll kill you."

"Listen," said Eddie. "I understand that none of us are

having a very good day. I'm not here to cramp your style or steal your seat. I'd just like a weapon."

"Get one from someplace else."

"Your best chance of survival is if I get out of here. If another tram was coming, it would be here by now. So help ain't on the way, buddy. If I can get out of the forest, I can tell the cops, military, coast guard, and everybody else exactly where to find you and the other survivors."

"There are other survivors?"

"Yeah. Not many, but a few."

"Where are they?"

"At a water reclamation plant. And one guy got carried off by a giant bird, but he's probably dead."

"Interesting."

"Yeah, yeah, it's fascinating. So why not be a pal and let me borrow a gun? It doesn't have to be the one you've got pointed at me."

The man shook his head. "Get out."

"You know you're committing suicide, right?"

"Get out!"

"Whatever." Eddie turned and stepped out of the tram. Great. Just when things could work out in his favor, he had to meet some whacko with a—

Lots of creatures were staring at him.

Dozens of them, no two of the same species. Things with fangs, things with claws, things with spikes, things with horns, and even a fuckin' thing with a giant mouth on its stomach.

Where the hell had they all come from so quickly? Even when the trams first collided, all of the creatures hadn't arrived this fast.

There was something very, very wrong here.

JAMES A. MOORE & JEFF STRAND

Moving as one, the creatures rushed forward.

CHAPTER TWENTY-ONE

"How do you know my name?" Christopher asked.

The scaly blue creature smiled. "It's written on your underwear."

"What?"

"I'm kidding."

"What?"

"Let me introduce myself before you get too confused to speak properly." The creature let go of Christopher's neck and shook his hand. "My true name is very long, difficult to pronounce, and rhymes with one of my native language synonyms for 'penis,' so I prefer not to use it. Instead, you can call me Pestilence. That's a suitably disturbing name, isn't it?"

Christopher just stared at the creature.

"If you continue to look at me that way, I shall be forced to pluck out your eyeballs and encourage you to eat them," said Pestilence. "I won't cook them or disguise the flavor with any spices or sauces to make it more palatable. It will be two raw eyeballs, straight up, and you won't enjoy it. Do you understand?"

Christopher nodded.

"Please do more than nod."

"Yes, I understand."

"Good. So, we've now established that you're Christopher and I'm Pestilence. We should also establish that you're a weak, puny human, and I am an extremely powerful demon. Do I look powerful to you?"

"Yes."

"You're too kind. Flattery will get you everywhere." Pestilence winked at him. "It may have crossed your mind to wonder why you're standing on a patch of ice in the middle of a hot forest. Then again, it may not have. It's sometimes difficult for me to understand the human mind, despite its simplicity. So, were you wondering about the ice?"

"Uh, yeah."

"You're not just saying that so I think you're more inquisitive than you really are, are you?"

"Are you going to kill me?" asked Christopher.

"At some point, I suspect that your death is a strong possibility," said Pestilence with a shrug. "In the meantime, I'm just in the mood for some scintillating conversation. So be scintillating. If you're not scintillating, I'll kill you sooner rather than later, and then you'll be dead and nobody will converse with you ever again."

Christopher had no idea what to make of this demon. His best theory was that the last time he slipped on the ice, he'd cracked his head and was now seeing a very realistic, very demented hallucination. One realistic enough that his neck still felt frostbitten from where the demon had clutched it.

"So...what's with the ice?" he forced himself to ask.

"I despise hot weather," said Pestilence. "These scales really soak up the sun, and once it hits seventy, eighty degrees, I'm dying. You can tell by my blue color that I was built for colder climates. And, hey, I may not be all-powerful, but I'm powerful enough to bring along some ice, so there you go. I hope it's not too cold for you. Is it too cold for you? I could procure a sweater."

"No, I'm, uh, fine."

"Good. We're both comfy, then. So how has your tour been so far? Worth the money? See anything interesting?"

"Yeah, I..." Christopher trailed off. "Sorry, this is very weird for me."

"Talking to a demon? Why's that weird?"

"I've never done it before."

"Well, you've probably never stapled a carrot to your nose before, and *that* wouldn't be weird. Okay, it might be a little weird, but weirder things have been done in your universe, I assume?"

"Yes."

"I thought so. So, Christopher, how was the flight over? Sufficient leg room? No mechanical delays, I hope."

"You mean the bird?"

"Yeah, I mean the bird. Don't be such a dumb-ass. How about you answer me this question: Why do you think you were brought here?"

"I have no idea."

"I know you have no idea. But you've got to have a guess, right? Even if it's something like 'I was brought here because I'm a snazzy dresser.' If you truly have *no* idea, then your mind must be blank, and even though you're limiting yourself to short, uninteresting sentences I'd be very surprised if your mind was completely blank. Why were you brought here? Go on, guess."

"To...negotiate?"

"Ooooh, good one. You were brought here to negotiate for the lives of your fellow survivors. I like that. It's wrong, but I like it. Actually, the truth lies more along the lines of you being, y'know, a sacrifice."

Christopher nearly lost his footing, but somehow managed to keep himself upright. Pestilence chuckled.

"Yep, a good old-fashioned sacrifice. Also, here's another trivia fact that you might find interesting. You know my charming personality? It's really just to lull you into a false sense of security."

Pestilence punched Christopher in the side of the head, hard enough to make his ears ring. This time Christopher did fall. As he struck the ice, Pestilence kicked him in the side of the leg. Christopher slid across the ice, his teeth clacking together on his tongue as he bashed into the far wall.

An instant later, Pestilence hovered over him again. "Did that hurt? I hope it hurt. I do so enjoy causing pain and suffering." The demon grabbed Christopher's foot and flung him across the ice again. He slammed into the wall, almost certain that he'd broken a few bones this time.

This time Pestilence walked toward him in a casual stroll. "Yep, Chris, things aren't going to work out well for you, I'm afraid. Being a sacrifice for a demon? Not fun. Too bad you're not my human host. That's a fun gig. But you'll be dead before I get to that part."

Christopher sat up against the wall, the cold biting into his shirtless back. "Why me?" he asked.

"No good reason. I sent my birdie to grab somebody and you were the closest. I know, I know, it's a disappointment, isn't it? You were all excited thinking that you were the Chosen One or something like that. For what it's worth, of all the people who've died on this lovely Halloween, your death will be the messiest, and that's saying something."

Christopher spat out some blood.

"Now, now, don't waste it. Waste not, want not, that's what I always say. Well, not really, but I should start. There's wisdom in those words, don't you think?"

Christopher spat out some more blood. "Fuck you."

The demon stopped. "Oooooh, now we're getting feisty, huh? I didn't expect to hear the F-word pass through your lips. I like your spark, young man. How about this? Look at me really sternly and tell me that you're gonna kill me. Go on, do it. As stern as you can."

Christopher used the back of his hand to wipe some blood off his mouth, but said nothing.

"Oh, c'mon, be a sport! Give me a mean ol' look and tell me that you're gonna kill me! Do something that'll send a chill down my spine and make me think 'Oooooh, this guy is a bad-ass, I'd better be concerned for my personal safety!' Scare me. Go on. Make me tremble."

"I'm not playing your games," said Christopher, with approximately twenty-five times more courage than he actually felt.

"I wouldn't call this a game," said Pestilence, resuming his stroll. "Games are supposed to be fun for both players. This is more like amusing torture. You're not gonna try to intimidate me, huh?"

Christopher didn't respond.

"That's fine, that's fine. We'll just get right down to business." The demon gracefully slid across the last ten feet of ice, and grinned at Christopher. "What part of your body would you miss the least if I sliced it off?"

"Fuck you."

Pestilence frowned. "Now you're just being redundant. I hate redundancy. It's a waste. And now that I think of it, the human body has a lot of redundancy. Two eyes. Two ears. Two arms. Two legs. Hell, you've even got two kidneys. What's up with that?"

Pestilence crouched down next to Christopher. He held up his clawed hand and waved it in front of Christopher's face. "I could slice your nose off before you could even sneeze. You're aware of that, right? Of course, your nose isn't redundant, but the twin nostrils are. I guess I could slice your nose in half. What do you think of that?"

Christopher was absolutely petrified, and he was pretty sure that at any moment he might vomit, lose control of his bladder, cry, or all three. Instead, he forced himself to stare directly into Pestilence's cold blue eyes. "Touch me and I'll kill you," he said.

Pestilence threw back his head and laughed. "Now *that's* the kind of spark that entertains me! Yeah! Your personality isn't a complete void after all." Pestilence quickly swiped his claw across Christopher's cheek, slashing him from ear to chin. "Did that hurt? I hope it hurt, because that was my intent."

"I swear I'll kill you."

"Oh, now you *swear* you'll kill me! Even better! Here, have another painful slash." The demon sliced Christopher's other cheek.

"I don't want to build up your ego too much," Pestilence said, "but you look really cool with those slashes on your cheeks. Like some macho warrior or something. Believe me, if I weren't the powerful demon ruler of this forest, I'd be intimidated as hell."

Pestilence clapped his hand over his mouth. "Oops! Did I let that out? You were just supposed to think I was some common hooligan, not the big bad guy. But, hey, it's out there. I'm the leader. The boss. The video game villain at the end of the level. The guy you love to hate and hate to love. Hard to believe that there was a time when you thought that the bird was your biggest problem, huh?"

"You're lying," said Christopher.

"I beg your pardon?"

"Do I need to repeat it?"

"So you're getting into the tough-guy act. Cool. I encourage that. You think I'm full of shit, huh?"

"Yeah."

"Well then, let's discuss that interesting point of view. Is it okay if I slice and dice you while we're conversing? Good."

Pestilence slashed a line across Christopher's chest. "Tell me, Chris—oh, hey, is it okay if I call you Chris?"

"Nobody calls me Chris."

"Fair enough. How about I call you Prey? Or Plaything? Or Poor Bastard Who Is Going To Die A Horrible Gruesome Blood-Spurting Death?"

"Whatever."

"Okay, Poor Bastard Who Is Going To Die a Horrible Gruesome Blood-Spurting Death, what do you know about inter-dimensional travel?"

"Not much."

"I didn't think so. Let me explain it in a way that won't hurt your brain too much. Look around you. Go on, look around you."

Playing along, Christopher glanced to his right and to his left.

"Everything that you see is part of your dimension. A dimension is very vast. It goes way past the stars and all that stuff. With me so far?"

"Yeah."

"Good. I think your chest would look good with a checkmark." Pestilence slashed a checkmark-shaped line on Christopher's chest. This one cut deeper than the others and he grimaced.

"What the overwhelming majority of you humans don't realize is that all of the vastness around you is just part of one dimension. Let's call it Dimension #1. Meanwhile, in another plane of existence, there's Dimension #2. This dimension isn't quite as nice as yours. Most of the denizens aren't very polite at all. It's also much smaller than your dimension and a lot more crowded. Still with me?"

Christopher nodded.

"Good. How about a smiley face next?" Pestilence slashed a large smiley face into Christopher's chest.

Christopher spat blood into his face.

"Okay, now you're taking the macho thing too far," said Pestilence. The demon grabbed Christopher's leg and flung him across the ice, much harder this time. Christopher struck the opposite wall with such force that his vision went black.

"Stay with me...stay with me..." said Pestilence, shaking him. "You fall asleep, the skin-flaying begins. You won't like the skin-flaying."

Christopher looked up at the demon and said something, but he wasn't sure what.

"Anyway, I'm a powerful guy, but the kind of project I wanted to accomplish required a lot of resources. And by resources, I mean sacrifices. Those sacrifices just piled up, believe me. Body parts everywhere. But it was worth it, because I then was able to push Dimension #2, mine, into Dimension #1, yours. That's where the forest came from. Never knew that, did you?"

Christopher forced his mind and vision to focus. "So you did all this just to give tours?"

Pestilence laughed. "No, no, no. I found a human and he struck a deal with the devil. Or a deal with a demon. Whatever. The people running your little vacation may think that they're just in the business of giving tours, but their real boss has much more nefarious intentions. It took a while to set the whole thing up, but hey, I'm a patient demon. But believe you me, Chris, it won't be long before your whole precious dimension turns into our own personal tourist buffet."

Pestilence licked his lips. "In fact, why don't we get started with that little sacrifice I mentioned earlier, huh?"

CHAPTER TWENTY-TWO

"Did you ever lose anyone close to you, Lee?" Mindy's voice was laced with sorrow, but as much as he longed to comfort her, he didn't move forward. It would be inappropriate, all things considered.

"Oh yes." He looked past her for a moment and stared out at the well-kept lawn a story below and the bright stars that shone down from above them. He felt almost suave in his tuxedo, a rental, and she looked stunning in the strapless black affair she was wearing. Thirty other people milled around in small groups on the marble balcony, moving with the casual pace of folks just having a good time. Not far away from her, Barbara was looking his way, almost begging for his attention.

"I lost my wife, Angela, to cancer almost fifteen years ago. I lost my son, Jeff, to Operation Desert Storm." He sighed and looked back at Mindy. She shook her head in sympathy, the loss of her own son still fresh in her eyes, even six months after everything that had happened on that damned forest tour.

"How did you ever cope?" Her voice faltered and almost broke, but she held herself together.

"It wasn't easy, of course. I'd been with Angela for

close to thirty years. I woke up with her every day and went to bed with her every night." He felt the sting of tears start at his eyes, but did nothing to stop them. "I spent every minute I could with her, because she made my world a brighter place. Even when she was dying, when the chemotherapy failed to stop the cancer and I knew she was in agony, she made my world better."

Barbara nodded from off to the side and moved closer. Tina wasn't far behind her. Tina's losses were just as fresh as Mindy's and both of them looked at him as if he could somehow offer them the wisdom to survive losing a loved one. There was no wisdom to offer, of course. Condolences, yes, but he'd learned nothing of how to grieve painlessly. He still suffered from the losses every day.

"You're a very brave man, Lee. You've been through so much." The redhead, Jean, Tommy's aunt, was the one who spoke now, moving in on the other side of Mindy. Four beautiful women, dressed to the nines, and all of them with him at the remembrance of the fateful events that occurred half a year earlier. It was also the debut of his account of the affair. The publishers had pushed hard to get the book ready as quickly as possible, and Lee had delivered. He knew how to write a fast book, and in this case the story was easy to research. He'd lived it, after all.

"What will you do now, Lee?" It was Mindy who spoke again. Or at least he thought it was. It could have been Barbara, or even Jean. They all sounded a lot alike, really.

He frowned at that. No, they didn't sound that much alike. Not when you got down to it. Jean had a California non-accent, and Barbara sounded like she was from

Arizona. And Mindy? Mindy was pure southeast, one of the areas where other accents had merged and diluted the gentrified southern accent, but definitely from that area. They didn't sound much alike at all, at least they hadn't before tonight.

Mindy put a hand on his arm and smiled up at him. She was a beautiful woman, no two ways about it. She opened her mouth to say something...and then screamed instead. Part of her face exploded away from her skull, leaving a cavernous hole where her left eye had been.

The women in front of him shimmered and the world around the balcony where he stood celebrating his literary victory grew blurry.

Lee shook his head again and looked at Mindy. She was gone. He could still feel her hand on his arm, but she was gone. He looked at his arm and saw the wriggling mass of serpentine fingers that gripped his shirt and sank into his flesh. The pain hit a second later.

"Ow! Damnation!" His voice was a dry croak, and his ears were ringing.

"Get away from him!" Mindy was back, only this time she was covered in sweat and dirt and her clothes were disheveled. She'd never looked lovelier.

Without a legitimate weapon to use for attack, she'd resorted to swinging a metal hole punch she'd found somewhere inside the office up one flight of stairs. Not far away from her, Barbara was aiming her now-empty pistol at the ruptured cowl of the Proof Demon, which still held onto his arm with its wicked talons.

Lee yanked his arm back and lost a generous portion of skin along with his shirtsleeve. The sting from where the sharpened nails had dug in was like a slap in the face and helped knock the cobwebs out of his head.

Mindy swung with her makeshift weapon and struck the mostly undamaged side of the cowl covering the demon's face. What passed for blood spilled out of the ruin on the opposite side of the monster's head and it stepped back, hissing. Several shapes moved under the hood, and the entire form under the draped cloth shivered violently.

Mindy moved in to swing again but the creature was too fast, slipping away from where it had been a second before and rearing up in front of Lee with all the speed and grace of a cobra.

"*We...will...meet...again...Lee...*"

Lee didn't need that. The Proof Demon's voice was creepy enough without adding "Lee" to the end of the sentence. He really didn't need that.

The brown cloth and everything under it fell backward and dropped over the side of the small stairwell, landing in the darkness below.

Lee grabbed for his rifle and tried to aim, but by the time he was ready to draw a sight, the monster was gone.

* * *

"We can't just sit here."

Barbara looked at Tina and tried not to sigh with exasperation. Tina was right, of course. No one would find them anytime soon if they stayed in the water reclamation plant, and it wasn't like they had any supplies to keep them alive during a long wait for the search party. They didn't even have an aspirin to help Brad, whose face was far beyond simply being "pasty." Barbara didn't say anything, of course, but the man looked absolutely terrible.

"We have to, at least for now." Barbara leaned in and spoke as calmly as she could. "Eddie is out there trying to get help for us, and there's just no way we could get out of here with Brad. When Eddie does bring help, he's going to bring it here, not to some other random location in the forest, so we need to stay put. And it's going to start to get dark soon. It's dangerous enough when we *can* see. The flashlights aren't going to keep us from getting ambushed."

"Well, we can't stay here forever," said Jean.

"I'm not suggesting that we stay here forever. We'll wait until tomorrow morning, sunrise, and then we'll go. Maybe we won't have to wait all that long. Maybe Eddie will come back with reinforcements before then. For now, we have shelter, and it's best not to leave it."

Jean slid her arm around Tommy, who was staring at the wall again, fascinated by whatever he was seeing. There was nothing on the wall, of course. Tommy's only reaction to his aunt's touch was to blink and look back at Brad where he rested on the ground.

"I realize it's still very early, but I think we all could at least use a nap." Lee spoke softly, his face haunted. The encounter with the Proof Demon, as he called it, had obviously rattled him badly. He wouldn't even look at anyone else. "When assistance does arrive, it may not be an armored tank. We may still need to be awake and alert, so now is a good time to get some rest. I propose a watch."

Mindy nodded. "I'm for that. We'll take it in shifts. Maybe two people at a time, just to be safe."

The others agreed immediately, except for Jean, who said nothing.

"We can barricade the doors," said Barbara. "That's a

good starting point."

They all grew silent for a few moments. Lee's haunted expression faded, and he got an ornery smile on his face. "So who knows a few good ghost stories?"

Jean practically exploded. "*You think this is fucking funny?*" She stood up, knocking Tommy aside without even seeming to notice it. Barbara looked at the woman and ground her teeth together. Jean was not finished with her rant. "I lost my husband earlier today! We're stuck in the middle of this goddamned dump, which is in the middle of this fucking forest full of fucking monsters and you want to crack jokes? Fuck you!"

Lee glanced at Jean for a moment and shook his head. His lips pressed together firmly.

Barbara looked from one to the other, wondering what she could say to defuse the situation.

Mindy stared only at her hands as she spoke. "You should have shot her, Lee."

Jean's head snapped around fast enough to cause whiplash. "What the fuck did you say?"

"I said he should have shot you. It would have been a mercy killing."

Jean sputtered in return, her mouth gaping open and snapping closed a dozen times.

"You think you're the only one, is that it? You lost your husband? I lost my son. So don't you dare whine about how shitty your life is. We all get it."

Jean didn't answer. Instead she settled back against the desk and leaned her head back. She closed her eyes and acted as if none of them were there.

Lee coughed softly. "Everyone get some rest. Who wants to join me on watch?"

Barbara settled in as best she could, while Mindy and

Lee took the first watch. She did not sleep. Exhausted as she was, she had trouble believing she'd ever sleep again.

* * *

But they slept, most of them, as well as was possible in the cramped, spooky quarters. Tommy tried to join them, but after a while he sat up because he could feel the nightmares coming. They were trying to sneak into his head when nobody was looking, and he didn't trust them to stay away.

Nightmares were always trying to do things to him. Like what they were doing to his parents. Mom and Dad would go to bed at night and sometimes he'd hear them when the nightmares got to them. He could hear them crying out, or arguing because of the bad dreams.

Mr. Lee was talking in his sleep. Aunt Jean was crying, but he couldn't tell if she was awake or not. She'd been crying a lot. He wished he could help her, but he was afraid to move. The Gray Man might get him if he moved. Everybody else called him Brad, but to Tommy, he was the Gray Man. Mostly because his skin had lost all of its tan and gone a sickly shade of gray. Miss Tina was worried about him and kept checking on him and saying she loved him, but Tommy wasn't worried about him.

He was worried about the thing inside of him. Tommy couldn't see it, but he could smell it. So could everyone else when they got close to the Gray Man, but they kept looking around like the smell was coming from somewhere else. Tommy knew better. He'd walked around the room a few times earlier, and he knew the stinky mold scent came from the Gray Man as surely as he knew that his uncle was dead and the nice lady, Becca, was dead too.

Tommy closed his eyes for a second and then opened them again, wishing that he was back in his bed. Even if Mommy and Daddy were fighting, it would be better than this place.

Something moved off to his left, where the Gray Man had been resting. He heard a dripping noise, like water trickling from a busted pipe—Daddy had fixed one of those last year and he still remembered the sounds—and then the smell from the Gray Man came along, stronger than before.

Tommy tried to make a noise, but no sound came from his mouth. His voice was frozen.

The Gray Man moved again, letting off more wet noises. It sounded like his clothes were soaked, and the stench of mildew grew so strong that it made Tommy's nose wrinkle.

Tommy held his breath.

"Tommy?" The voice was faint, a hint of a whisper that he knew no one else would hear. "Tommy, can you help me? I'm very cold. I can't see."

The Gray Man was speaking to him. Tommy's skin crawled and he bit his bottom lip to make sure he didn't make a sound. The Gray Man's hand moved closer, reaching for him. Tommy had stayed in the same spot for most of the time they'd been in the building, except when Mr. Lee took him to go pee outside. Now he was back at his seat at the desk, and perched on the rolling chair. He slid off the seat as quietly as he could, avoiding the clammy hand that reached for him.

He wanted to wake Aunt Jean. She would know what to do. All he had to do was remember where she was, because it was too dark to see her anywhere. He wanted to call out for her, but ever since he'd seen the...

...his mind refused to let him remember what had happened to Becca and the others. He could remember them and that they were dead, but beyond that, he could manage nothing...

...well, ever since he'd been lost in the woods, he couldn't make himself talk.

Tommy took exactly two steps backward and tripped over his own foot in the darkness. He fell, pin-wheeling his arms, and slammed the edge of his head into the desk with an audible crack.

He winced and closed his eyes as the pain lashed through his skull and made his eyes water. His hands moved up in a futile effort to protect the spot where he'd just done himself harm.

The Gray Man stopped moving, stopped whispering, and even the wet sounds from around his body ceased.

Tommy whimpered, his mind's eye showing him a small smile spreading on the Gray Man's face, his head tilted as he listened for another sound.

"Tommy, are you there?"

Tommy felt the bump on his head, half expecting to feel the moist heat of blood, like that time a year ago when he'd dropped the cookie jar and it broke against him. Instead he merely felt the sting of the growing lump. When he was certain he wasn't going to bleed all over himself, he tentatively tried standing. Aside from a brief dizziness, everything seemed to be working.

Tommy reached out with his hand and felt the edge of the desk. This time he'd be smarter and move slowly. Moving around without being able to see was harder than he would have expected, because at home he always had his nightlight.

The desk worked just fine for keeping him going in the right direction. He took a careful step and then another, feeling more confident about being able to avoid the Gray Man.

The hand that covered his was cold and wet. The skin felt like the flesh of a rotting peach, and leaked something obscene across his knuckles.

Tommy flinched back, but the Gray Man's fingers closed over his wrist with a damp squelch.

"There you are, Tommy..."

Oh, how he wished he could scream.

CHAPTER TWENTY-THREE

Mark finished with his backups and dropped the bundle of memory sticks into his pocket. The miracles of modern technology: four years' worth of research and notes, more man-hours than he even wanted to think about, and all of it fit easily into his pocket. Well, the autopsied ogre didn't, but all of the notes and pictures did.

He moved to the next door down the hallway just in time to see Hannah finishing up. She was in an office that did not, technically, belong to her, but they had to salvage everything they could. "Got it?" she asked.

Mark nodded. "Yeah. All of it."

"Good."

"What the hell happened? There've never been any problems in the past and all at once, everything that can go wrong does!"

Hannah shrugged her shoulders and looked out the window, though there was nothing new to see. "We've never gone this far into the forest, either. There's a reason we've got all the safety features on the trams, Mark. You know that better than anybody."

"I just have to believe that there's something more

going on than a really inconvenient systems failure. I mean, come on, Hannah, in four years not so much as a rabid squirrel has come out of that forest. Now we have ogres charging the building? It doesn't make sense!"

"Preaching to the choir, Mark."

"It's just crazy."

"Still preaching to the choir, Mark."

Mark sighed. "We better get back to the control room before someone figures out what we've been doing."

Hannah put a hand on his and chuckled. "I think we'll be okay. We're protecting H.F.E. assets."

"Yeah, but I don't want them suddenly deciding they have to do a security check when we leave."

"Hey, we could always tell them we were making out..."

Mark laughed off her comment, which was much easier than it would have been under normal circumstances. But he'd just watched giant ogres murder a bunch of heavily armed soldiers, which had something of a cold shower effect on his libido.

"Either way, the sooner we talk to Steve, the sooner he'll tell us to get the hell out of here," he said. "I'm dedicated to my work, but I'm not going to be one of those researchers who drives into a tornado."

Hannah nodded, and they headed back to the control room.

They got there at a quiet moment. No new insanity had ensued. Steve was already talking with Laurie Schaefer from the public relations arena and two men that Mark assumed were lawyers. *Thick as thieves*, he thought.

There were fewer people in the office than there had been earlier. Hopefully the others were someplace far from the forest by now, perhaps Rhode Island. Mark walked over to the east side of the control center and looked out at the parking lot. Mostly empty. In fact, there probably weren't many people left behind that weren't in this room. Good.

Hannah had stopped to talk with Steve and his cronies. She looked his way with an anxious expression on her face. He quickly moved over to where they were all standing. "So what's the latest joyful news, guys?"

Steve looked at the two lawyers and then over at Laurie, who was looking as stressed as a crippled mouse in a mountain lion's paws.

"Well, Mark, you saw what those ogres did. Gonna be hard to put a positive spin on that for the media, especially since they killed some members of the media. No news on the tourists that were in the forest. We have Mullins flying around the perimeter right now, to make sure that all of the critters are staying within the boundaries, because these two," Steve waved his hand to indicate the lawyers, "tell me that we could be held liable if anything gets out of there and attacks someone else."

"How can you be held liable? It's not like you invited them in. Booth just owns the land."

One of the lawyers, who looked like he sucked on extra-tart lemons every day, shook his head. "It isn't that easy. As the owners of the land, H.F. Enterprises is responsible for whatever happens on the property. Kind of like the owners of a pit bull that gets loose."

"But we don't own the ogres. We own the land."

"Sufficient safety precautions were not taken. Kind of like the owners of a supermarket where somebody slips and falls on a patch of mop water."

"We took every reasonable safety precaution."

"But they didn't work. Kind of like—"

"Okay, okay, I'm not even involved in this part of the company. I just study the monsters. Do what you need to do."

"I'm on *your* side," Lemon Sucker reminded him. "We'll find a way out of this, although right now we're presuming that the tourists inside the forest are all alive and well. If they aren't, that could cause, ah, additional concern."

"Y'think?"

The lawyer gave Mark a cold smile. "We should talk soon. Obviously, the person responsible for studying the creatures would have been responsible for predicting their potentially deadly behavior, right?"

Mark wanted to punch him in the face, but elected not to. Great. He could end up spending the rest of his life in prison for negligence.

"At this point, H.F. Enterprises still has a chance," said the lawyer. "Clearly, the security personnel were well aware of the possible danger, and the media placed themselves in harm's way. If the tourists are fine, we may be fine. Assuming that the remaining forest inhabitants stay put. The town of Dover's Point *is* only a few miles away, as you know."

Mark turned to Steve. "So, has Mullins seen anything yet?"

Steve shook his head. "Thankfully, no. It looks like they're still staying inside the perimeter of the forest for now."

"So what are we doing to get the tourists out?"

Steve opened his mouth to answer and then stared past Mark, his mouth hanging wide and his eyes bugging. "What the hell?"

Mark and Hannah and the cronies all turned to look where Steve was staring. Mark felt his mouth drop open and stared, petrified by what he saw.

Twenty-five feet from the edge of the forest, a tree was rising from the ground. It thrust into the air, spilling arid topsoil as branches grew from the thickening trunk.

"No way." Hannah's voice shook. "Just...no way."

"Oh, shit," Mark said. This was so very bad. The Haunted Forest hadn't had a single new tree pop up since it came into existence. Nothing grew to replace the trees they cleared out to make room for the tram path. The forest hadn't expanded by a single inch in four years.

Now there was a brand-new tree. Within thirty seconds, it had grown to the same height as the others, as if it had stood there for centuries.

But this one wasn't a pine tree. It had the shape of an oak, but it was black. Twisted.

Before anyone else could add their own "No way" or "Oh, shit" style of comments, the ground shook again. It was a slight tremor at best, but this time the vibrations were accompanied by another tree thrusting out of the ground.

And then another.

And then another.

Mark watched, his pulse pounding in his temples, as four more trees broke the ground and rose toward the heavens. No two were remotely alike and none of them were from a genus he knew.

Steve's cell phone rang. Without taking his eyes off the new trees, Steve answered. "No. I know. It's happening here, too. How far out do they go, so far?" Steve nodded his head and sighed. "Thanks, Mullins. Keep me posted."

Steve killed off the call and moved himself to the

closest available chair. He dropped into it as if all of his bones had suddenly turned to liquid.

Everybody stared at him expectantly. After about ten seconds, Steve spoke, calmly, almost resignedly. "Well, ladies and gentlemen, the forest is now growing in all directions. We're all nicely fucked."

* * *

Barbara's eyes opened wide in the darkness.
I've gone blind!
No, no, you were asleep. Your eyes just need to adjust to the gloom.

Instead of letting her eyes adjust, she clicked the switch on the halogen flashlight in her hands. Then she really went blind as the searing white light assaulted her retinas.

"Ow!" Tina's voice was shrill. "Careful with that damned thing." Tina's eyes were squinted nearly shut and her hand moved to block the beam that turned her pasty white. Barbara apologized under her breath as she moved the light away from Tina and into the room.

The light was still strong, for which she was thankful, despite the blue spots she was currently seeing.

Behind the blue spots, she could see Jean curled into a fetal position on the floor. Moving the light, she saw Brad holding Tommy in his hands, his mouth stretched to an impossible level as he prepared to bite the boy's face off.

But as the light shone directly on him, Brad flinched and the deep black pools of his eyes narrowed in a field of pale gray mold that had covered his skin and his clothing alike. The mold even covered his tongue, but it had taken his teeth away. Where his incisors should have been, there were wavering pink protrusions that had reached out to flicker along Tommy's face.

Tina cut loose with a scream loud enough to rattle the walls and promptly dropped the rifle Barbara had let her carry.

Barbara screamed too and almost dropped the flashlight. Considering the day's events, waking up to the sight of something trying to eat Tommy was not altogether unexpected. Waking up to the sight of *Brad* trying to eat Tommy...now that was something she wasn't quite ready for.

Tommy flailed around madly, his tiny face gone ghostly white and his eyes rolling in his head. He'd peed himself, and though his mouth was open for a scream, no sound came out of him.

Tina stepped toward the couple and shook her head, her eyes even wider than Tommy's. "Brad? Is that you?"

"Tina, honey, I feel a lot better now. Right as rain." Brad tried to smile, but the wiggling pink cilia that had replaced his teeth took a lot of the charm out of it.

The door flew open. Lee and Mindy burst inside the office.

Jean woke up and called for Tommy. She called a second time, a lot louder, when she saw where he was.

Mindy didn't hesitate. She yanked a large framed picture of President Bush off the wall, rushed forward, and drove the edge of it into Brad's head.

"*Get the hell away from him!*" Mindy's voice was almost a roar.

Brad dropped Tommy immediately and turned his head to face Mindy. To Barbara's knowledge, no one could turn their neck that far without doing themselves permanent injury, but Brad managed it just fine. She could see where the picture frame had creased his skull. Ol' George Junior's face was obscured by the darker gray, gelid crap that had exploded from the inside of Brad's head, but the president's smile was still in place as his photograph wobbled back and forth inside of the wound.

Mindy staggered back and tried to get away from Brad. She didn't get far before his fuzzy gray hands grabbed her shoulders.

Tina picked up the rifle and started toward her husband. "Brad, you put her down! Put her down right now!" Her voice was too high; her eyes were too wide.

"Busy right now, Hon. Give me a minute." Brad's voice sounded phlegmy and the words were distorted. The wobbly picture kept on bobbing along as the shape of his head changed. The small tendrils that had replaced his teeth spread out and lashed onto Mindy's head, catching in her hair and slapping against her face. Mindy screamed again.

Tina charged, swinging the rifle like a baseball bat. Either she realized that she would likely hurt Mindy if she fired, or she just didn't think to point and shoot. Either way, it worked well enough for Barbara.

The rifle slammed into George W. Bush's face and frame and shattered both before it broke open the back of Brad's skull. More of the darker gray matter splattered away from the wound, moving with a consistency not unlike moldy chocolate pudding. She was almost certain she could see things slithering around inside the brackish goo.

Brad let out a grunt, but otherwise made no effort to stop his endeavors to eat Mindy's face.

Tommy crawled away, grunting and whining as he

scrambled for cover.

Tina looked at the gaping wound in her husband's head and stepped back, horrified with what she'd done, even if she'd done it to a mold-covered, attempted-face-eating monster.

Mindy screamed once more, and that seemed to catalyze Tina a second time. She swung her makeshift club again, this time hitting Brad in his knee. His leg buckled and, despite his desire to stand still and keep on trying to feast, gravity got the better of him and he dropped to the ground. The tentacles that were wrapped around Mindy's face pulled back as he collapsed and the older woman fell to the ground next to him, panting, shivering, her face covered with red welts where he'd touched her.

Jean charged in, swinging with one tennis-shoe-clad foot and kicking Brad in the groin. Just as with the back of his head, the area she kicked collapsed in on itself. More of the foul slop from inside him splattered across her leg and the lower half of her body.

It hadn't been a mistake; there were definitely things moving in the black filth. Whatever they were, they perfectly matched the wriggling shapes that had filled his mouth, and as they landed on Jean, they immediately began burrowing under her skin.

Jean shrieked, not in fear, but in pain as the worm-things dug in deeper. She slapped frantically at them, but only managed to spread them across her hands where they once again began eating.

Brad tried to stand again, but Tina was on him, swinging the rifle up and down in a frenzy, driving the barrel into his soft gray skin and punching hole after hole through him.

Barbara kept the light on Brad, not because she was being brave but because she couldn't make herself look away, couldn't manage to move to help. She was too horrified. The writhing shapes that escaped from Brad's ruined form turned away from the light, trying to hide, and Barbara caught on quickly. She moved in closer, aiming the light at the creatures that had probably lived in darkness for as long as they had existed. *Maybe*, she thought, *they'll burn if I hit them with the light.*

The worms did not combust. They just tried to hide. Unfortunately, they tried to hide inside flesh and the closest available source was Tina. The newly widowed woman spun on one heel and then jumped up onto the desk to get away from them. It might have worked, too, but the things Barbara had originally thought were teeth seemed merely to be larger versions of the same creatures. They were thick and pink and wriggly and they could stretch, just like earthworms, but these were nowhere near as attractive. Earthworms at least had a certain symmetry, whereas these worms seemed almost more liquid, as if they were not yet completely formed.

Whatever they were, it was obvious that they liked to dine. Jean had stopped screaming and was now lying on the ground and shuddering violently. Barbara didn't dare keep the light on her for too long, for fear that the worms might find new hosts.

Tina had retreated to the center of the desk and was stomping savagely on any of them that got too close to her. She moved her feet so fast and hard that it almost looked like she'd taken up tap-dancing lessons. Back on the floor, the slimy creatures curled into the edges of what was left of Brad, hiding in the moist, dark environment he provided.

Lee stomped a particularly juicy worm. "We have to get the hell out of here," he said, realizing that it was a rather obvious announcement but not caring. "This place isn't shelter anymore."

Barbara nodded and started moving; she slipped past the desk with Tina on it and found Tommy trying to curl himself into a ball. There wasn't time to be kind and nurturing, so she grabbed his arm and hauled him to his feet. He responded automatically and settled on his legs. Mindy was up and moving with Lee, careful to dodge around the remains of Brad on the ground. Tina jumped from the desk without actually managing to kill herself in the near darkness, and moved for the door.

Jean wasn't coming with them. Whatever the worms were doing to her seemed to have paralyzed her body, and Barbara wasn't feeling quite bold enough to drag her from the room.

Lee held the door for her and then slammed it shut as Barbara and Tommy vacated their temporary haven.

Lee led the way, carefully looking out for whatever might be on the walls, the floor or even the ceiling before they moved on. Inside of three minutes they were back outside of the reclamation center, huddled together on the small exterior stairwell and looking out at the Haunted Forest.

Barbara turned off the flashlight and shivered. No reason to waste the battery before the sun set. They might need it later, if there was, in fact, a later to come. A small sob escaped her mouth before she bit it off.

Not three feet away from her, Tina was on her knees, sobbing as quietly as she could for the loss of her husband.

Not only did she lose him, she had to kill him, Barbara

thought. There was nothing left of Brad when Tina delivered the fatal blow, but still, Barbara wouldn't want to be in Tina's emotional space right now.

Tommy had now lost his aunt for good.

Mindy had lost her son.

Barbara felt guilty. The closest person she'd lost was a sleazy co-worker, and he was probably bringing help back at this very moment.

Or Eddie was dead. He could've died ten seconds after he and Tina parted ways.

Barbara would stick with the "probably bringing help back at this very moment" theory for now. She liked that one a lot better.

She'd thought they'd be safe for the night in their stone shelter. Turned out they hadn't even made it to nightfall. And that meant the nocturnal creatures were only just getting ready to wake up.

She almost asked out loud how much worse it could get, but in the end she stopped herself. She didn't want to know.

Let's hear it for blissful ignorance.

But she figured they'd find out, whether they liked it or not.

CHAPTER TWENTY-FOUR

Eddie had two choices, both of which sucked. But the idea of facing the lunatic with the gun sucked a lot less than the idea of facing the monsters outside, so he rushed back into the wrecked tram.

"I said, get out of here!" shouted the man.

"Look outside! There are things all over the place! If I go out there I'm dead!"

"Not my problem."

"It *will* be your problem after they eat me! You think I'm enough of a meal to satisfy all of those monsters out there? You're next, buddy. Trust me."

The man didn't lower his gun.

"Screw it," said Eddie. "I don't have time to argue. I'm here to save your ass. Shoot me if you want to kiss it goodbye."

Eddie walked past the man, trying to demonstrate a carefree attitude while inwardly cringing and expecting the man to fire a bullet into his skull. Though he'd like to believe that he was at least safe from his fellow human beings under these circumstances, the man was clearly insane, unpredictable, and quite possibly capable of making good on his threat.

Fortunately, Eddie made it to the back of the tram without getting shot. In the second-to-last seat, a rifle rested on the lap of somebody who had nothing left of their body *but* a lap. He picked up the weapon and faced the front of the tram again.

The first creature entered the wrecked vehicle. It looked very much like a werewolf, with glowing red eyes. It rushed down the aisle toward Eddie. He fired. The werewolf let out a squeal as its furry forehead burst open, and it dropped dead.

A giant beetle entered. It scurried across the wall, passing the man. The beetle leapt at Eddie, and he blew it away in mid-air.

Another creature entered the tram, this one a...well, Eddie didn't know *what* the hell it was. It sort of looked like a giant slug, except that it had legs. It moved past the man and headed straight for Eddie. He shot it in the chest, or what he thought was its chest, and ooze sprayed out as if being pumped from a fire hose. Another shot and the slug popped like a water balloon.

As the man wiped ooze out of his eyes, Eddie hurried to the front of the tram and pressed the barrel of his rifle against the back of the man's head.

"What are you doing?" the man cried.

Eddie scooted into the seat behind him. "I'll kill you!" Eddie shouted. "I swear it!"

Several more creatures gathered at the tram door, but none of them came inside.

"How come none of those things tried to kill you?" Eddie demanded. "Those fuckers try to kill everybody. Why not you?"

"I don't know!"

"Bullshit! What, have you got some kind of repellant

or something?"

"No!"

"I'll kill you!" Eddie shouted again, more for the benefit of the creatures outside than to threaten the man. Though he doubted that the Haunted Forest residents spoke English, they seemed to get the idea. None of them moved toward him, though those with visible eyes seemed to watch him, warily.

"Explain," Eddie said.

"There's nothing to explain."

"Explain," Eddie repeated, rapping the man on the back of the head with his gun.

"If you want to kill me, go ahead," said the man. "If you want to revert to savagery and become no better than that werewolf you just killed, be my guest. But I will *not* allow myself to be bullied by a common thug like yourself."

"Common thug? I'm trying to get answers, not steal your wallet!"

"I have no answers to give."

"Fine. I'll accept that. Either way, the monsters don't want you dead, and we're gonna use that to get us out of here. Stand up."

"I'm not going anywhere."

"Yes, actually, you are. Think of this as a hostage situation. Stand up."

"I already said that I'm not—"

Eddie stood up, grabbed the man by the back of his shirt collar, and yanked him to his feet. "I've been fighting these creepy bastards all day, so no offense, but I'm not worried about handling a little dipshit like you."

"You're making a terrible mistake."

"I'm sure I am. Walk. Slowly."

"My name is Martin Booth. I own H.F. Enterprises."

Eddie hesitated. He'd seen a picture of the guy in the company newsletter, but had never met him in person. "Did you shave your beard?"

"Yes. Quite some time ago."

"It looked good on you."

"It itched. And you are?"

"Eddie Turner, tram driver."

"Here's the deal, Edward—"

"Eddie."

"Here's the deal, *Eddie*. If I leave this tram, more people will die than you can possibly imagine. I'm talking about horror on an apocalyptic scale. There will be oceans of blood on your hands if you interfere with this. I encourage you not to interfere."

Eddie stared at him for a long moment.

"Bullshit."

"It's the truth."

"I disagree." Eddie shoved him forward, still keeping his hand on Booth's collar. "Let's go."

* * *

The trees kept on coming, rising from the desert floor in a growing tide that blotted out the previous boundaries of the Haunted Forest. Mullins kept them abreast of how things were going elsewhere along the perimeter, though unfortunately they were going about the same, complete with trees rising through the highway extension that led to the offices. The good news was that there were two side roads that would let them get around the new growth. Other good news seemed to be in short supply.

Most everybody else at H.F. Enterprises had left. Mark

thought that was a fine idea, but Steve had insisted that he and Hannah stay for the time being. "You two know what's out there, and we may need your expertise."

Mark's expertise at this moment was pretty much limited to the knowledge that they needed lots of big guns to kill monsters with, but he didn't protest.

Outside, another twisted, gnarled tree broke through the dirt and rose into the air. Mark watched for a moment until something caught his attention. From the corner of his eye he saw something sweep between the trees, close to the same height as the window he looked through. He only saw it for a moment, but it was enough to capture his full attention.

Mark had spent four years studying the denizens of the Haunted Forest for a living. He'd never seen anything like this. Never imagined that anything like this could exist in the forest. How could it possibly have been living in the forest for four years without offering up any evidence of its existence?

His heart pounded in his chest as he scrambled for his cell phone. The shape disappeared between two trees for a moment and he held his breath, praying it would show itself again.

He got lucky and the dark shape swooped up toward the sky just long enough for him to capture its silhouette on his cell phone's camera. The picture wasn't perfect, but it was clear enough to make his skin crawl and his testicles try to find a safe place to hide themselves. As he looked out the window, the thing that caused his amazement dropped down below the tree line and vanished from sight.

"Hannah! Hannah, we have a new one! A big one!" He ran toward their office and had to force himself to breathe. He tried swallowing a few times but there was no saliva left in his mouth.

There was little by way of a point of reference in the shot, just a couple of trees, but he hoped they would be enough.

On one hand, he was ecstatic: a find like this was the sort of thing that had started him down the long and often penniless path to being a cryptozoologist in the first place. On the other hand, he was terrified: a creature like the one he'd just seen could potentially change everything that they understood about the Haunted Forest, and had the potential to do a *lot* more damage than the ogres.

"Mark? What is it?" Hannah was frowning at him and her eyes were just a little wet. He realized that she'd probably been crying, and as much as he might have liked to comfort her, this was far more important.

"Hannah, just...just look at this, okay? Please tell me you still have your computer hooked up and then look at this."

"I do." She pointed to the monitor, and without another word he dropped down his knees in search of the USB port that would allow him to download the single image he'd managed to capture.

Hannah waited as patiently as she could and dabbed at her eyes until they were dry. He tactfully ignored the slight run of mascara at the corner of her left eye and then showed her the new image.

Hannah looked at the silhouette on the screen for several seconds in complete silence and then started fiddling with the keyboard, trying to clarify what she was looking at. She finally managed to zoom in enough to show a partial of the creature's head.

"Oh shit." Her voice was as weak as his knees.

"Yeah."

"You saw that outside?"

"Yeah."

"That's...okay, I've said that enough things aren't possible for one day, but give me one more: That's not possible."

"I know. But we've got a dragon."

* * *

Emery Mullins lived for flying his helicopter. Technically he didn't own the machine, but he thought of it as his own, and since he had no children, the 'copter functioned as a perfectly good surrogate. Better, actually, because Duchess never gave him any backtalk or attitude. Fill her up with fuel when she needed it, perform regularly scheduled maintenance, and their relationship was pure bliss.

He banked around what had been the edge of the forest and looked at the unsettling amount of new growth. He didn't like what he was seeing. The growth seemed to come in waves, and they weren't getting smaller, they were getting stronger. At a guess, the new trees had expanded the forest by close to a quarter mile in a few places. He also knew that the forest was almost perfectly circular, which meant that the ragged growth spikes going on right now would probably fill themselves in before it was all done. If it was ever all done.

That was a scary notion. He didn't know if much could stop a forest like this from growing if it wanted to. You could gather the world's lumberjacks en masse and put 'em to work, but if fully grown trees were sprouting faster than the most aggressive weeds known to man, a whole army of chainsaw-wielding laborers wasn't going to be able to stop them.

He'd had plenty of discussions with his buds at Ricky's Bar about whether the forest should be destroyed. He always stood on the side of keeping it, but only because he depended on the damned place for a living.

Still, he'd thought of different ways that the forest could be destroyed. Bulldozers might be able to do it, but again, there'd have to be tanks or something bigger to help. As for fires, well, he'd seen the footage of the fire pit. The trees around the area should have gone up in smoke a long time ago, but they hadn't. Far as Emery knew, trees didn't take well to lava, but none of the ones in the area had suffered even a little heat damage according to the people at the home office. So he had to doubt fire would work. What did that leave? Toxic chemicals? Napalm? His Aunt Helen, who'd killed a plant a day for twenty years?

Just thinking about it gave him a headache.

Below him another tree started rising toward the sky. This one was all by its lonesome so far, and further out than any of the others he'd seen, almost half a mile from the edge of the forest. He envisioned the entire planet completely engulfed by trees. The hippies would be ecstatic.

Far below him he spotted Duchess' shadow racing along the ground, made tiny by his range. He reached for the radio to call Steve and let him know about the new tree and the potential problems it signaled, but before he could speak, he saw a second shadow closing in fast on the 'copter.

Not wanting to take any chances, Emery dropped

down a few hundred feet and turned as quickly as he could to see what might be following behind him.

There was nothing to see. Nothing at all. Maybe it was a passing cloud he'd spotted. He scanned the sky one more time to be sure.

The dragon came into view.

It came barreling down from above him, massive leathery wings held out and back in a power dive, its mouth open wide and its teeth bared.

Emery didn't think; he just reacted. The helicopter cut hard to the left as the reptilian nightmare ripped through the air, just barely missing Emery and his flying machine.

Emery let out a long, loud scream of panic and fought hard to keep enough altitude to avoid the trees below.

"What the hell was that?"

The long serpentine body was curling around and coming back for another try.

A dragon. He and Duchess had not signed on to engage in aerial combat with a fucking dragon. This was way, way beyond the scope of his contract. He could handle funky trees, but not giant mythical flying creatures.

The dragon came closer, wings cutting the air as it approached.

Emery shook his head and called out a whirlwind of profanities as he tried to veer off a second time.

When he looked up again, the dragon was right on him. Emery was smart enough to know that he was officially Fucked Up Beyond All Repair.

Rather than try to make an impossible escape, Emery angled the rotors at the dragon and closed his eyes. The thick blades of the helicopter met up with the heavily armored body of the dragon.

In a perfect world, the blades would have cut the dragon into confetti, and Emery would have returned home with a great story to tell his buddies at Ricky's Bar. *The dragon was right above me! I thought I was a goner for sure, but at the last second, I angled the rotors and chopped that son of a bitch up into dragon steaks. Ate one myself for dinner that night. Tasted like salmon.*

This was not a perfect world. The blades broke off against the thick scales, though they managed to hack a trench into one of the massive wings.

The dragon let out a roar.

Emery let out a scream.

The dragon lifted away from the helicopter and began to angle around for another approach.

Rather unobligingly, the helicopter dropped like a rock toward the forest below.

Not one to let a helicopter get in the last word, the dragon breathed out a massive plume of flames that completely engulfed Emery and the helicopter alike.

Though he took some small comfort in the fact that he and Duchess were dying together, Emery screamed all the way down to the ground.

CHAPTER TWENTY-FIVE

Lee saw a bright flash of light and watched for the two seconds it was visible above the trees. Whatever it had been, wherever it had been, it was gone almost as quickly as it showed itself.

Didn't look like a shooting star.

Looked like something on fire.

Either way, as long as it wasn't a meteorite bearing alien blobs, it had been a nice distraction for a moment.

They were still together, but as a group they'd moved away from the reclamation plant. Much as the desire to be near a real building or even in one was strong, after a brief discussion everyone agreed it was best to leave behind the worms and other dangers. They didn't need anybody else in their group to get taken over by possessive mold.

At least out in the open they could get a little more ambient light. Until sundown. Which wasn't far away.

They walked slowly, headed the same way Eddie had gone, back toward the tracks. It seemed like a much better idea than heading blindly through unexplored territory. Though Barbara clearly wanted to pick up the pace, she was stuck with a pair of old folks, a distraught widow, and a nearly comatose young boy who she carried piggy-back style.

The woods were almost quiet. Almost, because Lee had heard several things moving nearby. Big things, little things, wet-sounding squishy things and at least one thing that was big enough he could see the silhouette moving through the trees at a height of at least thirty feet. The good news, so far, was that none of them had come looking for dinner.

The bad news was that sooner or later one of them would.

They had no real weapons. Lee had broken a four-foot-long branch off a tree with a ridiculous amount of effort and used it as a walking stick. The wood was dense and the stick weighed in at close to ten pounds. Not bad, but he'd have preferred a really big gun with a few thousand rounds of ammunition.

The Proof Demon slithered up beside him.

He didn't see it or hear it first…he felt it. One second there was just the night and the next the odd collection of serpentine limbs was next to him, its eyes faintly glowing inside the hood that surrounded its face.

The thing contemplated him from just out of range of his trusty stick.

Nobody else acknowledged it. They continued their slow, half-dead walking pace.

Lee contemplated the demon right back. Somehow he doubted that its tentacles or multiple tails were knocking anywhere as hard as his knees wanted to.

"You seem to be in something of a predicament." He heard the cold voice very clearly in his head. His ears remained unaffected.

"What do you want?" Lee spoke out loud, having no sort of telepathic abilities that he knew of.

Not only had they not heard the demon, the others didn't seem to have heard Lee, either. Even Mindy, who was only a couple of feet away, didn't react to his question.

"You amuse me. You who spent your life waiting for miracles and instead found us."

"With all due respect, you can shove your amusement where the sun don't shine, mister." If he ever did write a book about his adventures in the forest, he'd give himself a better response. It wasn't like Mindy, Barbara, Tina, or Tommy could hear him.

"And that is why you amuse me, Lee Burgundy. You are decrepit, your heart is weak, and your body is frail, and yet you stand here ready to fight me to protect the others. Why?"

"It's the right thing to do."

"There is no right or wrong, old man. There is only what brings us pleasure."

"What do you really want?" Lee tightened his hands on the staff as the Proof Demon slid a few inches closer. He wondered if the others could see him at all.

"I have decided that I can help you. I can give you much, if you desire it."

"Like what?"

"You sound dubious."

"I'm not in the habit of trusting snake tails and freaky eyes in a cloak. Sorry."

The demon slithered closer and rose in height, stretching its body until it towered two feet above him. The eyes within the hood glittered brightly and pulsed with an odd rhythm. Lee caught the pattern immediately, because he could feel the rhythm inside his head. He'd spent his life debunking every kind of supernatural claim and that included telepathy. He'd have bet good money that what he felt was the equivalent of fingers rifling through the paperwork of his mind.

"*You would be correct, Lee Burgundy. I am reading you.*"

"Why?"

"*To gain an unfair advantage.*"

"I'm surrounded by five miles of hungry monsters. I think you already have that."

"*More than five by now, I think. Still, it helps to know what one has to bargain with.*" The thing had no shoulders, not in the traditional sense, but it shrugged them anyway.

"What makes you think I would bargain with you?"

"*You want to live through this event, don't you?*"

"I suppose." Maybe if he listened, he could work out a way out of his current mess. There was nothing to bargain with, really, but he could at least buy some time. "So what can you do about getting me out of here in one piece?"

"*More than you know. I can ensure your safety through what you call the Haunted Forest.*"

"You a bigwig?"

"*I am not in charge here, but I have connections, if you will.*"

"I don't know if I will or not until I hear what you're offering and what it will cost." Lee shook his head. "Somehow I doubt you take American Express."

"*I seldom take credit.*" It settled back a bit, and he watched as one of its arms came out from the folds of the tattered cloak. "*I offer you three things, Lee Burgundy. First, I offer you safe passage from this place. Second, I offer you your youth again.*"

"You're lying. Old is old and it doesn't change." The words were out of his mouth without his even thinking about them.

The Proof Demon let out a low hissing noise, and the bared collection of serpentine fingers reached out and grabbed Lee's wrist in a grip as cold as the grave. Lee tried to pull back, but his arm was firmly caught. He raised the stick he held in his other hand, and one of the creature's many tails lifted into the air and whipped around it, holding it still.

"*Watch and learn, Lee Burgundy.*" The hand on his wrist squeezed. Lee bit back a yelp and looked closely as the fingers opened tiny mouths and bit into his flesh. He felt the venom enter his body. It wasn't painful at all, but he wanted to scream anyway. As soon as the writhing digits had done their damage, they pulled away from him and the tail on his trusty stick did the exact same thing.

Lee pulled his arm closer to his face and looked at the wounds, wondering how long he had to live. The tiny bite marks vanished almost instantly, but a tingling sensation spread.

"What did you do to me, you nasty little fuck?" His ears were ringing and his heart felt like it was going triple-time in his chest. The muscles in his arm spasmed and the tremors started moving, sliding through his body in jolts that still didn't hurt but were scary as hell.

The seizure spread through him like lightning and Lee fell back on his ass before it was over, dropping his only weapon in the process.

He tried to cry out for Mindy, Barbara, anyone, but they continued walking, completely unaware of what was happening to him.

Anger lashed through him. Anger he hadn't felt since the day several years ago when he saw some teenagers run over a dog in the street, get out of their car to poke at the dying animal, and then return to their vehicle and drive off, laughing. His anger was both intoxicating and frightening in its intensity.

Lee climbed back to his feet and practically snarled at the Proof Demon, which remained—not surprisingly—unafraid of him.

Lee took two steps forward, his hands clenched into fists that felt like wrecking balls.

"Stop, Lee Burgundy, and look at yourself." Lee caught sight of his arm from the corner of his eye and stopped as he took a closer look. The fine gray hairs that had been on his arm for as long as he could remember were gone, replaced by thicker, darker hairs. The veins that had been so prominent in the last five years were still there, but partially submerged in heavy, corded muscle. Lee looked carefully at his hands, which were stronger than they had any right to be. He moved his hands up to his face and felt the geography of his flesh. The wrinkles were gone, filled in with soft flesh. The bones were the same but also partially obscured by muscular tone he hadn't felt in over two decades.

"You made me young again?"

"Oh yes. A sample before we conclude our business, Lee Burgundy."

"Just Lee."

"Lee then. Your freedom and your youth, Lee. I can offer you both of those, as well as the woman of your choice, from the ones before you or any others that live in this world of yours."

Lee looked again at his hands, at his arms, the muscles that had rebuilt themselves, the bones that felt stronger than he could ever recall. His head swam with the proof that miracles could happen.

Miracles. That was the rub. Miracles were the province

of the divine, not the infernal. Oh, the stories of demons and devils offering bargains were endless, but they always came with a price.

"I don't have much, I grant you that." Even his voice was young and strong again! "But I have no desire to sell my soul for fleeting youth and a free ride out of this dump."

"Don't forget the women, Lee..."

He looked again at Mindy and the others, who were now literally moving in slow motion. He'd had more interaction with the fairer sex in the last few hours than he had in the past year, and all of that had been here, in the craziest place he had ever walked. While purely primal, a part of him longed to hold a woman again, to kiss a beautiful girl's lips.

"I don't want your soul, Lee. That would hardly make a worthwhile bargain for you, would it?"

"Then what do you want?"

The Proof Demon sidled closer, the multiple lights of its eyes staring at him again.

"Give me the boy. Give me young Tommy and you shall have all that I promised you."

Lee turned his head to look at Tommy. He opened his mouth to speak, but no words would come.

CHAPTER TWENTY-SIX

Dover's Point was hardly a booming metropolis, but the last four years had seen something of a population explosion in the dusty little town. First, there was the claim to fame as the town closest to the Haunted Forest. That brought a lot of weirdoes and freaks into the area, to say nothing of religious fanatics.

Then came the people who actually bought all the land around the Haunted Forest and decided to make the unholy spot into a tourist attraction. Most of the residents in the area were a little taken aback at first, but the money came rolling in along with the construction crews, scientists, and hucksters that filled that place. After that, all was forgiven, or at least forgotten by a lot of the locals.

The rest of the country might be going through a recession, but things were looking up economically for most of Dover's Point and the population that called it home.

Aloysius Mortimer Gantry — Al to his friends, Allie to his mistress, and the honorable Mayor Al Gantry to everyone else — thought the Haunted Forest Tour was one mighty fine addition to the area, really. It was a nice diversion from the billion or so miles of sand and tumbleweeds that made up the rest of New Mexico. Of course, he'd made a damn fine lump of scratch when everything started, so he wasn't in much of a position to bitch about it, either.

Mayor Al was perfectly fine having monsters as neighbors just as long as they decided to keep to themselves.

Jake Steiner, the head of the police force in Dover's Point, was fine with that notion too. He wasn't so fine with the idea of sending his men out to the Haunted Forest Tour headquarters. He'd made that perfectly clear to Al only fifteen minutes earlier. One squad car stayed in town. The other nine went to check on what was going on. Why? Because the people running the tour paid good money to make sure the police force in Dover's Point was both sizeable and well armed. They were a cautious lot and since they were being nice enough to pay for easily half the salaries in town, Al felt he could be magnanimous about the whole thing.

It was good to have the right connections, even if now and then you had to do a little something in return for the favors.

Little Amy, his fourth granddaughter and just possibly the cutest child ever to walk the earth, in Al's heartfelt opinion, came over and climbed up in his lap. At all of five years old he could barely even feel her weight in his lap.

"Well, what are you doin', button?" He smiled at the girl, and she smiled back, clearly showing the lack of her two front teeth. They'd fallen out within three days of each other.

"Grampa, can you take me to see the new trees?"

"What new trees, button?" She was always asking him to go on adventures with her, and he was always more than happy to oblige. Like he told Candi during their "business trips," he was a family man.

Amy pointed down the road leading out of town, and Al looked where her finger indicated.

The smile that was on his face suddenly grew very heavy. He stared long and hard at the tree that was growing at the edge of Dover's Point, his heart thudding heavily in his chest. The tree hadn't been there an hour earlier. Hell with that, not even ten minutes ago. He was getting on in years, but Al didn't make mistakes like that. He'd have remembered a giant, ugly tree with fruit on it big enough that he could see them from his front porch. He licked his now-dry lips.

"Honey girl, you want to do your granddaddy a really big favor?" She nodded excitedly. Normally favors meant running inside to get him something. Said favors were often rewarded by a glass of soda and ice. "You go inside and ask your daddy to come out here. Ask him to bring the binoculars, okay, baby girl?"

"Okay!" She hopped off his lap and ran for the front door. Al stood up and stretched, feeling the twinges that ran across most of his back in the process. Getting old sucked.

He felt the boards under his feet creak and groan for a moment and frowned, wondering if he'd finally put on enough weight to make him fall through the old porch.

As it turned out, he had not. The tree that came out of the ground five feet to his left was the culprit. He hurried toward the front door just in time to run into his son.

Bernard gaped at the tree. "Oh, sweet Jesus in a

minivan, it's happening again!"

"Go get the chainsaw and be fast about it!" Al had to yell to be heard because the sound of splintering wood was loud.

Bernard nodded, jumped off the porch, and ran back around the house.

Al reached for the cell phone on his hip and dialed the police station on the speed dial. No reason for worrying with emergency numbers when he already had fast access to Steiner anytime he needed to talk to him. Sometimes it's good to be the boss.

And sometimes, not so much. "Jake, pick up the damned phone!"

The tree continued to grow and sprouted a thick branch that just missed taking out the front window. He'd have felt better about it if the growing length of wood didn't then catch the siding and start pushing against it hard enough to crack more boards.

"Answer the damned phone, Jake! Now!" Jake did not respond, which, to be honest, was to be expected as he was halfway to the H.F. Enterprises offices, along with most of the police force.

The tree limb pushed through the wall and cut into the roof as it rose higher, taking half the shingles along for the ride.

Al stepped back again and into the house. Enough was enough. He disconnected from his call and then moved, as quickly as his girth would allow, over to his office at the back of his home. He needed to make a call for back-up that wasn't on his speed dial.

A few frantic seconds to find the number and he was dialing again.

When somebody finally answered he breathed a silent

sigh of relief. "Yes, Bea? I need to speak to the governor right now please. It's most definitely an emergency." He waited a few moments and cringed as the tree kept rising. His grandkids and his son and daughter-in-law all looked at him where he sat on the phone. He waved them to silence as the governor picked up.

"Tom? It's Al Gantry. Yes, that's right, from Dover's Point. Remember a couple of years ago when we talked about what might happen if things should suddenly change out this way? Well, it's happening." He paused for a moment. "Tom, I think it's growing again. Fast."

He listened and nodded his head, as if the governor could see him on the other end.

"Yes, Tom. I'd say now would be the best possible time to call in the reserves." He shook his head. "Tom, I have a fucking tree growing into my house, pardon my French. I don't think we can afford to wait any longer. I'm ten goddamn miles away from the edge of the Haunted Forest! Yes, I thought you might see it my way. Thank you. Thank you very kindly."

Al hung up the phone and looked at his family. "Get your things. We're leaving town, right now."

As he moved, he made one more call, this one to Albert over at the fire hall. "Al? It's Al. No, the other Al. Mayor Al. Notice the trees, did you? Yes. Set 'em off. We're evacuating right now."

Forty-five seconds later, the air raid sirens cut through the October heat and sent a chill through most of the citizens of Dover's Point.

They'd lived next to the Haunted Forest for four years; they'd long since been prepared for the chance that things might go very, very wrong.

Another tree came out of the ground like a gigantic

fist, shattering the concrete walkway that led to the driveway where the cars were parked. This one was covered with thorns that were easily as wide as Al's finger when they first showed up and quickly grew to be as thick as his wrist. Al shook his head and cursed, looking back over his shoulder to call for his son.

The words never escaped his mouth. The thorns hooked into his broad back and sank deeply through layers of meat and bone before sliding almost gracefully through his face, neck, and chest.

The last thing he heard were his granddaughter's screams.

CHAPTER TWENTY-SEVEN

Though his situation had presumably improved, Eddie was terrified. He and Booth walked along the tracks, moving as quickly as they could while still allowing Eddie to keep control of his hostage. He never took his hand off the back of Booth's collar, and the gun stayed firmly in place against the back of his head. Booth stumbled every couple of minutes, but Eddie kept him from falling.

Monsters were everywhere.

On each side of them, behind them, in front of them, above them...everywhere. Things that crawled. Things that slithered. Things that growled. Things that hissed. They never came close enough to touch Eddie or Booth, but the two men only had a few feet of personal space, if that.

If his hostage got away from him, the creatures would rip Eddie apart within seconds. He was sure of it. He'd be strewn all over the forest floor, and shortly after that he'd be in the bellies of eighty different monsters.

Not a fun way to go.

But he had to think positive. They were making excellent time. Since they were following the tracks, he knew for certain that they were headed in the right direction.

He might just make it out of here alive.

Hopefully the others were doing well. It would take some of the joy out of his survival if he found out that the others were all dead. Not *all* of the joy, but some of it.

"You're making a mistake," Booth informed him.

"You've already said that."

"I'll keep saying it until you realize what you've done."

"And I'll keep saying that you're full of shit. Most likely you're the asshole responsible for this whole mess."

"Suppose I am?"

"Then I'm right. Cookie for me."

Booth stopped walking. "Suppose this is all my doing, and I make you an offer you can't refuse."

Eddie shoved him forward. "Talk while you walk."

"I had nothing to do with the forest's appearance," Booth explained. "But after it did, I made a deal with the Devil. Or at least a demon. It spoke in my head, called me to the edge of the forest one month after it sprouted, and said that it would make me the most powerful human on the planet."

"Eh, it probably tells that to everybody."

"It explained that nothing in the forest would leave, and none of the creatures would harm anybody who went inside, and I could profit from it as I wished, as long as I was willing to keep my end of the bargain at a time of the demon's choosing."

"Gotta watch out for those demon bargains," said Eddie, flinching as a two-foot-long mosquito came inches from his arm. "Why'd he pick you?"

"I owned the land."

"Good reason."

"So I got countless investors involved, and set up the Haunted Forest Tour. Let other people run it. At their insistence, spent a huge amount of money on safety precautions that we didn't really need."

Well, that would explain how the track was built without the loss of a single human life, Eddie thought.

"The tour was wildly successful. Life was wonderful. Until..."

"There's always an 'until'."

"Yes, indeed," said Booth. "The demon returned. Said it was very pleased. And now it was time to fulfill my end of the bargain. Said that I was to provide it with three-score sacrifices to the forest creatures."

"How many is that?"

"Sixty."

"Oh."

"Twenty times three."

"Gotcha."

"It worked out very conveniently, since two tram cars filled with people provided the three-score sacrifices with twenty-four to spare, in case anybody escaped. That would provide the demon with the power necessary to 'transfer dimensional space' or something like that."

"You didn't ask for clarification?" Eddie asked. "This seems like a situation where you'd ask for a shitload of clarification."

Booth ignored him. "The demon needed two more things for the transference. A willing human sacrifice, and a willing human host. It said it would take care of the sacrifice. I would be the host."

"Let me guess: The demon said you'd rule by its side."

Booth shook his head. "No, but he promised me

power beyond compare."

"And you believed him?"

"Whether I believed him or not is not the issue. The issue is whether he would rip my intestines out and strangle me with them if I refused. The answer to that issue is 'yes'. Maybe he plans to kill his willing human host. Maybe he plans to grant him power beyond compare. I'm willing to take the risk."

"And kill all of those innocent people?"

"I was not the demon's only option for a host. Somebody else would have done it, and those people would have died anyway."

"Whatever helps you not feel like a complete scumbag asshole." Eddie wanted to kick the son of a bitch to the ground, but of course that would be unwise. "Another question for you. Let's say I was attacked by a bunch of alien-looking things, and when I blew one of their heads off, all of the other heads blew up, too. What would cause that?"

"No idea."

"Doesn't that sound weird to you, though? I was thinking that there was some sort of deal going on where they were all part of the same organism, but then they all should've died when I killed the first couple of them, right?"

"I have no answers for you."

"Fine. Just keep walking then."

* * *

Tommy's just a little boy. Lee focused on that thought. It was hard to do when his body was almost singing with vitality and his heartbeat was thudding strong and solid in the chest where it normally liked to flutter. *Damned* hard to do, actually.

He looked over at Tommy, hanging on to Barbara's back as they continued to walk in slow motion, blissfully unaware of the Proof Demon's bargain.

He'd lost his aunt and uncle. Quite possibly he'd already lost his parents, which might explain why they hadn't taken him on the tour. He'd seen so much death and horror today, felt so much pain, that he might never be able to function like a normal child ever again.

Youth, safety, and the girl of my choice, all in exchange for one broken little boy's life...

Lee took in a deep breath and looked back at the Proof Demon.

"Fuck you."

The branch swept up in a savage arc that caught the creature squarely in its chest and shoved it back, stumbling on its multiple tails. A powerful hiss erupted from inside the cowl, and the demon reared up again, growing almost a foot in height.

Good. When it was bigger it made an easier target. This time he didn't bother with swinging the stout club. Instead he just lanced the end of it into the hood and felt the impact as it hit whatever was hidden inside there.

He didn't let himself think. Lee had been in combat several times, yes, but seldom in hand-to-hand and never with a demon from one hell or another. He trusted his instincts to save him, instead of trying to rationalize or dwell on the fact that he was trying to beat an otherworldly monster to death with what amounted to an unpolished broom handle.

The demon screamed as the stick plucked out one of its eyes. Then it lashed out in fury. Serpentine limbs seethed out from under the tattered cloak and wove around madly as it sought the best way to strike back.

Lee stepped back and swung his makeshift staff in a lazy figure eight, holding it close to the center. Each time the demon tried to strike he used his free hand to balance and direct the branch, letting him block the blows.

"*You could have had everything!*" The voice came not from the nominal head inside the cowl, but from the whipping limbs themselves, each of which had a mouth. "*You could have had your youth and your safety and all it would have cost you was one little boy.*"

"Again: Fuck you."

The demon slid back, seeming to expand again as the shapes within its cloak stretched further away from the center. Lee doubted there was any real solid body in there at all. Whatever it was that hid away seemed to be made of nothing but an endless knot of snake bodies.

Why did it need Lee to give up Tommy anyway? If the demon needed Tommy, why not just take him? Pluck him right off Barbara's back. It didn't make sense.

The Proof Demon stayed where it was, weaving slightly, maintaining its new size as the eyes underneath the hood glimmered like stars. "*Very well, Lee Burgundy. You will not sacrifice the life of a small child to save yourself and the others. But will you sacrifice yourself? Offer yourself willingly, and I will spare them. All of them. On this, you have my word.*"

"What good is the word of a demon?" Lee spat the words, both amazed by how calm he felt and unsettled by his willingness to die.

"*Your soul in exchange for their lives, their health. Give yourself to me, a sacrifice, an offering to me, and they are all spared.*"

It hadn't answered the question, but then he hadn't really expected it to. There was a different sibilance to its voice, one that seemed to border on the desperate. For whatever reason it needed him to lie down and die of his own volition.

Lee had no desire to accommodate the damned thing.

"Gonna pass on that, asshole. We're just fine without you."

"*I'll see you dead, Lee Burgundy. I'll see you dead and all those who stand by you as well.*" The eyes blazed, and a thin drool spilled from the cowl. Where the spittle touched the ground, the soil blackened.

He had little to lose, really. Lee was old and even if his body felt young at the moment, he knew it couldn't possibly last. Whatever the demon had done, it had to be temporary, either because he had denied it or because the youth was a lie.

In the long run, that was the deciding factor. He'd studied every religion known to man in his quest for proof of the impossible, and one fact never changed from belief system to belief system: Demons lie. Whatever promises they make always come with too high a price.

Lee charged forward and rammed his stick into the center of the body underneath that cloak, striking air at first and then finally hitting something more solid. The thing hissed again and Lee pushed forward, driving the tip of his club into that solid spot and feeling it start to yield.

"*Lee!*" Mindy shouted.

Lee's body no longer had its youth, but adrenaline rushed through his veins. It let him push on when all he wanted to do was run away. The tip of the stick splintered, he could hear it as well as feel it, but it also pushed in deeper at the same time, sliding past whatever sort of scaly hide the demon had and striking the meat underneath.

The limbs that had been waving in the air moved down fast and struck hard. Teeth punched into Lee's right calf, left thigh, both hips, and just below his left shoulder blade. The pain was incredible.

Lee screamed and pushed forward again, as one of the thicker snake bodies coiled around his waist and began to tighten. He caught one more breath and then did his best not to let it out as the constriction continued with bruising force. Another tentacle of muscle caught him at the ankle and slithered up his leg.

The mouth at the end opened wide and started snapping.

Lee opened his mouth wide and started screaming.

Barbara grabbed the thing just below its jaw and pulled back with all of her weight. She was screaming too, and had never looked lovelier to Lee than at that moment.

He shoved forward one more time, throwing all of the weight he could into it, and heard the Proof Demon scream. The contractions around his waist slackened a bit and he lunged, sucking in another breath and driving his stick even deeper into the center of the thing. Every muscle in his arms and across his back wanted to twist and tear, but he kept pushing, grunting with the effort.

Barbara let out a yelp as the serpent she'd been fighting with tried to take a bite out of her arm. A second of the powerful limbs had wrapped around her as well now, and she fought hard to keep from being trapped.

Lee felt something hard give, and the serpentine extremities around his body convulsed before letting him go.

Barbara let out a sound of pure disgust and kicked at

the twitching limb that had almost managed to wrap around her throat. The teeth that had been snapping for a chance to bite her flesh finally quieted, and she let the thing drop from her hands as she scrambled away from the dying demon.

Lee felt the sudden weight that gripped his branch as the thing finally died. The multiple limbs stopped moving, and the shape towering above him fell to the ground in a heap. He stared long and hard down at the shadowed face and saw the light fade from the eyes that had only seconds before seemed like beacons in the night. Dead.

At least he hoped with all of his heart that it was dead. He didn't think he could do much more to the damned thing.

Lee stepped back and promptly tripped on one of the snake bodies. He barely even had time to notice before he was falling and landing on his ass in the dirt.

He looked down at his hands again. His temporary youth was gone. But he still had his soul.

CHAPTER TWENTY-EIGHT

Christopher lay against the ice wall, covered with blood. The wounds thus far were all superficial, but there were a *lot* of them. Pestilence had spared his face—mostly—but the rest of his body bore countless red streaks.

Pestilence crouched down in front of him and smiled. "Does it hurt?"

Christopher spat some blood at him. It was from where Pestilence had slashed his tongue. "Go to hell."

"I bet it does. I bet you're just wishing you could die, huh? Look in my eyes and tell me that you want the pain to go away."

Christopher stared directly into the demon's eyes. "I thought I told you to go to hell."

Pestilence clapped his hands together in delight. "Just what I wanted to hear! What fun would it be if you gave up this easily? I still have body parts to sever. Organs to puncture. Eyes to devour. Eye sockets to lick clean. You would be quite the party pooper if you succumbed this early, don't you think?"

"You'll never get me to kill myself."

"I might. You never know. Tell me, Christopher,

would you sacrifice an innocent young boy to save yourself?"

Christopher shook his head.

"Neither would your friend Lee. He's a good man. Better than most. A lot of people his age would've said, sure, kill the little brat, he'll probably just be a vegetable for the rest of his life anyway, I want my youth back, but not Lee." Pestilence grinned. "You have no idea what I'm talking about, do you?"

"None."

"Then let me explain. While I've been slicing and dicing your poor body, Lee has withstood plenty of temptation provided by one of my alter-egos. If he'd caved, I would've killed you quickly and moved on with my little scheme. You see, my power here is growing. The forest is growing. But I still need my willing sacrifice for the *real* thrills to begin, and after that I've got a nice little human host waiting for me to set off the grand finale."

"Which human host?"

"Some guy. You don't know him. Anyway, Lee would've been a nice sacrifice. I would've liked to see him offer up a helpless little kid to save his own ass. Alas, he was too strong. Hmmmm...who else do we know who's strong?" Pestilence tapped his forehead. "Let me think...let me think...oh, I know! Your *mother* is strong, isn't she?"

Christopher stiffened. "If you touch her, I'll kill you."

"Is that so? Then why not be proactive? Kill me now."

Christopher lunged forward. The demon easily moved out of the way and Christopher landed on his stomach on the ice.

"So close, and yet so pathetic. Yes, yes, yes, I think

there'll be plenty of entertainment value in seeing if your mother will sacrifice herself for her son. What do you think? Will she do it? Want to put a wager on it? Hmmmm...I'll say two-to-one odds that she goes for it. How much money do you have on you?"

"I'll kill you," Christopher repeated.

"Yes, I know, we've already established that. So do we have a bet? No? You sure? Pity." Pestilence whistled loudly. "I guess I'll pay Mommy a visit. I wish I could carry you along with me, but unfortunately I don't have the power to bring passengers. So you'll have to return to a slightly less comfortable mode of transportation."

The giant black bird flew down into the ice bowl and landed next to Christopher.

"Remember my friend here? Bet you didn't know it was a round-trip flight. See ya on the other side. Try not to drip too much blood onto the trees."

The bird rose into the air again, dug its talons into Christopher's shoulders, and carried him off.

*　*　*

Freedom.

Eddie could hardly believe it as the sun shone through the edge of the Haunted Forest. He'd made it.

Almost.

This was no time to get caught up in giddiness. He was still surrounded by monsters, and things could still go extremely wrong. But he couldn't help but feel a bit of optimism. Not a "dance around and sing show tunes" level of optimism, but a "Hey, I may just get out of this without being devoured!" level of optimism.

He almost wanted to simply make a break for it, but

no. Stay smart. Stay alive. Other people were counting on him.

Whoa. Where had *that* come from?

Booth glanced back at him. "You're making a—"

"I know, I know. Terrible mistake. Duly noted."

"What are you going to do with me once we've left the forest?"

"You're just my monster repellent. As soon as we're outta here, I'm done with you. You can run back in there or you can donate your soul to Jesus; I couldn't care less." That wasn't true. He had every intention of finding out exactly what Booth's role was in this whole little nightmare. But he was only a couple of minutes from freedom and didn't want Booth to try anything funny at the last moment.

"Do you really think they're going to let us just walk out of here?" Booth asked.

"Dunno. Would be nice."

"You're living in a fantasy world."

"Was that statement intentionally ironic?"

"No."

"Oh."

Almost out...almost out...not too many steps left to go to get out of here without dying...oh, God, it would suck beyond belief to die this close to the exit...

Something slithered past his foot. Eddie didn't even look down. He had to maintain his concentration. If Booth really was concerned about leaving the forest, he was going to make his move any second now.

He thought the various growling sounds from the monsters around him were starting to get louder, but it was probably just his imagination. Yep, definitely his imagination. They weren't planning to attack. Nope.

Everything was happy for Eddie Turner in the ol' Haunted Forest.

"By the way, try anything and I'll blow your fucking head off," Eddie told Booth, just as a reminder. "You won't get a chance to see your monster friends take me down."

"They're not my friends."

"Whatever they are, you'll be dead before they so much as lay a pincer on me. Got it?"

"You've made this point before."

"I'm re-making it. Don't mess up."

"I wouldn't dream of it."

They continued walking. Eddie tried to keep from letting out a happy squeal as they came into the wide-open area where the tour began. Still in the forest, still surrounded by a shitload of beasties, but close enough that they could see several men in military fatigues standing on the lawn outside.

They immediately raised their firearms—scary-looking ones—and pointed them at Eddie and his hostage.

Oh, shit...

"Sir! Lower your weapon!" shouted the one who was closest.

Shit...shit...shit...

"I can't do that quite yet!" Eddie shouted back. "Give me thirty seconds!"

The growling was definitely getting louder.

"Sir, put down the weapon *now*!"

"He's taken me hostage!" Booth shouted. "I'm Martin Booth! I own H.F. Enterprises! The man is deranged!"

Eddie would have really liked to pull the trigger and give the monsters a nice shower of brains to feed on, but that would only leave the question of whether he would perish via machine gun bullets or tooth and claw.

"Sir! You have five seconds!"

"Promise you'll shoot the monsters before they get me!"

"Sir—!"

"*Promise!*" Eddie shoved Booth as hard as he could. The bastard stumbled forward several steps then pitched over and fell on his face.

The creatures pounced.

Eddie dove to the ground as the loud *ratatatatatat* of automatic weapon fire filled the air. Something squealed right next to him and a generous gout of some sort of fluid hit his back. He lay there, covering his face, as some bullets whizzed past him and others struck the unseen horrors that were coming after him.

Something dead and heavy fell onto his legs.

He let out a yelp as teeth clamped down on his ankle. He rolled over and fired a shot into the face of a furry creature that would actually have been kind of cute if it weren't trying to dine on him.

The machine gun fire continued.

Dead and dying creatures fell to the ground on all sides of him. A giant dragonfly practically exploded inches above his face. A bullet tore through the tip of his shoe, but he wasn't sure if he'd actually been hit or not.

A boar with way-too-big tusks was running toward him. Eddie shot at it and missed. Shot again and hit it right in the snout, but it kept on running. A burst of rapid fire shredded the rest of its nose and eyes and it veered off course, head splattering against a tree.

Eddie rolled back over and scrambled forward, keeping his body as low as possible so that the military men wouldn't hit him (again?) with their fire.

Booth was still on the ground. No monsters were trying to eat him, the lucky bastard.

"Hold your fire!" the soldier in front shouted. He waved at Booth and Eddie. "Run for it! Go! Go! Go!"

Eddie got up and sprinted out of the forest. The man in front didn't hold his own fire, instead taking out one, then two, then three, then four different creatures that dove at Eddie as he ran. Eddie half-expected Booth to run back into the forest, but instead he fled as well.

Free...holy shit, I'm free...

Something huge leapt from a tree—a black, deformed tree, not like the ones he was used to—and tackled Eddie to the ground. As he struck the grass his teeth clacked together right on his tongue. He heard a loud *crack* that he was pretty sure came from his own body. And the breath squeezed out of his lungs as if...well, as if something really heavy had landed on him.

A claw ran down the back of his scalp.

Machine guns fired.

Eddie wanted to scream but couldn't breathe to do so.

He spat out some blood.

More machine gun fire.

The thing on top of him roared.

Gurgled.

And then slumped over, motionless.

Eddie pulled himself out from under it, wincing at the bolt of pain that rushed through his side. He got up and staggered forward, as the soldiers blew away several more creatures that were coming for him. He didn't even look back to see what had landed on him.

"Enough already, goddammit!" Eddie shouted as he rushed past the closest military man. He then lost his balance and landed on the lawn again, but spun around in time to see the soldier pull the pin out of a grenade.

Sweet...

The soldier hurled the grenade into the mouth of the forest. It exploded in a blast of white light that illuminated the entire area.

Another soldier pulled Eddie to his feet. "Are any other humans following you?"

Eddie shook his head. "No, but there are—"

"Then let's go."

Under cover of the soldiers, Eddie and Booth raced to safety.

* * *

"I want that man arrested," said Booth, pointing to Eddie as they approached H.F. Enterprises. "He held me at gunpoint and forced me to..." Booth trailed off, obviously unsure of how he was going to explain the recent chain of events.

"He was delusional," Eddie said. "He refused to leave the forest, and I couldn't very well let him die out there." He spat out some more blood. "I couldn't have lived with myself if I let those things get him when I could've saved him. So I had to resort to extreme measures. You would have done the same."

The soldiers nodded.

"He's lying! Arrest him immediately!" said Booth. "I pay your salaries!"

"The American taxpayers pay my salary," said the soldier who'd thrown the grenade. "And, sir, you've been through a very traumatic experience, I need you to calm down."

"He was like this the entire time," Eddie explained.

"He almost got me killed."

"What's going on here?" asked a man, walking toward them. There was a young woman with him, and Eddie was able to distract himself from his pain quite easily by admiring the way she looked in her blouse.

"Mark! Hannah!" said Booth. "I need you."

"What's wrong?" Mark asked. "Where've you been?"

"I've been...I've been trapped in the Haunted Forest."

"You've *what?*"

"I went on one of the trams. I barely survived. This—" Booth looked over at Eddie and sighed, "—this gentleman saved my life. He was one of the drivers."

"We're going to need all of you to clear out," said the grenade soldier. "It's not safe here."

Eddie started to make a sarcastic comment, but decided to show some respect to the men who'd saved him, and who still had machine guns and grenades.

"I need to go back in there," said Booth.

"I don't think so, sir," the grenade soldier told him.

"It's essential!"

"Sorry. You know we can't allow that. Come with us and we'll take you to safe quarters."

"No, I'll..." Booth looked over at Mark and Hannah. "I'll go with you two." For a split second Mark looked a bit unsure, but then nodded.

"Wait, wait, I need to talk to him," Eddie said.

"I have nothing to say to you."

"He knows something."

"He owns the company," said Mark. "He knows lots of things. We'll take care of him."

"But—"

Mark took out a business card and handed it to Eddie. "You can call us with questions. For now, go with these men and get to safety."

Eddie snatched the card and shoved it into his pocket. "Fine. Drive safe."

"We will."

As the three of them left, Eddie returned his attention to the soldiers. "There are still survivors in the forest."

"How many?"

"Just a few. But I know where they are."

"I have news for you. They're either dead or will be dead. Nothing official yet, but I'll be damn surprised if the President doesn't authorize dropping a bomb on this place."

"You mean nuclear?"

"Big enough that you won't want to be anywhere near this forest, that's all I can say. You made it out alive. Count your blessings. You're lucky as hell."

Eddie nodded and spat out some blood. "Yeah. I think you shot my little toe off, by the way."

"I apologize for that sir. We'll take you to safety."

"Question for you. I got attacked by a bunch of things that looked like aliens, and I shoved a grenade in one of their mouths and blew its head off, and then all of the other alien heads blew up, too. Why do you think that happened?"

The soldier shrugged. "Hallucination brought on by trauma."

"That can't be it."

"Misinterpretation of events brought on by the stress and confusion of the situation."

"I'll just stop worrying about it."

"Thank you, sir."

CHAPTER TWENTY-NINE

Hannah stared at her car with a wide-open mouth. Her little Subaru was currently perched between two very thick branches that creaked and swayed a good twenty feet off of the ground.

"Maybe we better take my car." Mark started fishing for his keys.

"Oh, you *think?*" She shot him a withering look.

"That was a joke."

"Excuse me if I'm not in the mood to laugh."

Mark stared at her. He certainly couldn't pretend that he was a completely selfless individual. But to watch people get torn apart—*eaten*—and then get pissy about her car was cold. Damn cold.

"I'm just thinking it might get us the hell out of here a little faster at this point," Mark explained.

"I realize that."

"She doesn't appreciate the joke," Booth said.

Mark came *this* close to telling Booth to mind his own business before he caught himself. H.F. Enterprises wasn't finished yet. And he needed to be on Booth's good side as much as possible, in case they decided to find a scapegoat during the inevitable finger-pointing in the weeks to come.

In case? Oh, there would be a scapegoat. No doubt about it. And Mark didn't want that unlucky bastard to be him.

"Look," he told Hannah, "if you really want to take your car we can, but I don't think it's gonna go well. I'm just sayin'." Now he was just nervously babbling, stretching out a joke that wasn't funny in the first place to an unappreciative audience. Time to shut off the mike.

God, he was a lot more freaked out than he'd realized.

He didn't want to go to jail.

Without further comment, Mark, Hannah, and Booth headed over to his Saturn. "I'll ride in the back," Booth offered.

Hannah nodded, opened the passenger-side door, and got in.

"Do you think your car will be safe here?" Mark asked. "For all we know, the building might not even survive, if more trees keep popping up."

"My limo dropped me off this morning. Very inconvenient."

"Ah." Mark opened his own door and got into the car. He fastened his seat belt, then realized that Booth was still standing outside, staring back at the forest.

Mark rolled his window down. "Sir? Are you okay?"

Booth sighed. "I wasn't supposed to leave."

"What?"

"I wasn't supposed to leave the forest. I should've shot that asshole, but I couldn't do it."

"Sir, you should get in. We'll get you to safety."

"I don't think I can go back now." Booth looked down at the ground. "I couldn't shoot him. If I'd shot him, everything would be fine."

Great. Booth's cracked. Mark unfastened his seat belt, but Booth sighed once more and got in the back seat, shutting the door.

A moment later they were off, heading for the paved road that led back to the interstate and Dover's Point.

They drove in silence. Booth stared out the window, blankly. Mark wanted to ask him what he'd seen while in the forest, and more importantly, what the fuck he was doing in the tour tram in the first place, but he left the man to his thoughts. He had to be respectful. Stay on his good side.

Hannah also stared out the window. Under other circumstances, there would've been a delightful electricity in the air, with Mark desperately wanting to flirt with the woman of his dreams (second to Chloe, of course) but unable to do so with their boss in the back seat, like teenagers in the same room as their parents. But this time he didn't even care that the top button of her blouse had popped open.

Okay, he cared a little. Just not as much as he normally would have.

The road started cracking and buckling.

He let out a soft yelp and so did Hannah. He just barely managed to swerve into the other lane and avoid being flipped through the air as the tree came up.

Mark gunned the Saturn's engine and they broke the speed limit. The sooner they were away from the area, the better chance they had of surviving.

A mile away from the offices, new trees were still growing.

"Is it me, or are they coming up faster?" Hannah's voice shook a bit.

"Oh, they're definitely growing faster." He could see the ground starting to bulge just to the right of the road, and swerved before the asphalt could crack open and spit out a new hyperactive sapling. "Lots faster."

Mark managed to swing back to his own lane just in time to avoid the oncoming rush of police cars, complete with flashing lights and wailing sirens. They came on fast, and he honked his horn to warn them of the up coming obstacles. If they noticed, they didn't bother with a thank you.

Hannah's head was now moving around almost constantly, her eyes seeking any possible dangers. "Oh shit! Look!"

She pointed to the west, where they could finally see the end of the trees.

Well, sort of.

The tree line mostly ended, except for one string of new growth that pointed like an accusatory finger straight toward Dover's Point.

Mark slowed down as he looked at the town in the distance. He could see the trees punching out of the ground, one after another, and even from here it looked like some of the trees were already in town and doing damage.

"Jesus Christ!" Mark's hands hit the steering wheel. He'd known that the situation was dire, but getting a couple of miles away from the forest should've been the solution. This...this was like the trees were *attacking* Dover's Point.

He took out his cell phone and speed-dialed Chloe's number.

No answer.

Hannah leaned forward for a moment to get a better

view of something up ahead, and then leaned back just as the ground shook underneath them. Not a mild tremor like they'd felt previously, but the sort of vibrations that had Mark clutching the wheel and screaming like Speed Racer in an old cartoon. The Saturn skimmed across the surface of the road like an ice cube on a hot skillet and with about as much control. The asphalt disappeared from under them and was replaced by hard-baked soil and a few rocks.

Mark pumped the brakes carefully and fought the bucking wheel under his hands. Booth remained silent and eerily calm in the back seat. Hannah screamed her encouragement regarding the way Mark was handling the situation in the form of ear splitting shrieks and held onto the dashboard and the handle above her door until, finally, Mark managed to stop the car.

Both of them looked slowly back toward the road and the rising swell of dirt and ruptured pavement.

"What now?" Mark's voice was strained enough that he could barely recognize it.

"Just start the car, Mark. Get us out of here before we find out, please." Hannah made perfect sense, so he listened to her.

The car moved like it was supposed to, and he headed back for the road a good distance ahead of the swelling area.

They rode over the terrain until they caught the smooth road again and then he accelerated, casting a cautious eye toward the mounded spot behind them.

The road broke open, vomiting earth and gravel along the way. Then the source of the indigestion became apparent as the giant wyrm came out of the ground.

He couldn't quite justify calling it a worm, but the

archaic English word seemed to fit. It moved and pulsed as it rose into the air. The head of the beast was a line of hungry articulated feelers that grabbed the air and sought anything to stuff into the mouth just below them.

Mark sucked in a deep breath and gunned the engine again, forcing himself to look out the windshield as he headed for Dover's Point.

Sure enough, just as he feared, the wyrm turned in their direction and began to follow, shoving its unholy bulk out onto the road and heaving itself forward with unsettling speed.

Booth finally spoke: "That's a big one."

CHAPTER THIRTY

Christopher made no attempt to struggle. He silently willed the bird to fly faster, even though he knew it was ridiculous to think that Pestilence would allow the bird to drop him off in time to warn his mother.

But he wasn't going to let his mother die. Absolutely not. No matter what it took, even if he had to rip that demon's smirking head right off its shoulders, he wasn't going to let his mother die.

Just don't bleed to death, and you'll be fine. Mom will be fine. Everybody will be fine.

He cried out in pain as his legs crashed through some branches. The bird wasn't being quite as attentive to his personal safety this flight.

And then the bird swooped down through the trees, into a small clearing. It didn't set him down but instead hovered about ten feet above the ground, wings flapping. Birds weren't supposed to be able to hover like that, but they also weren't supposed to be able to do the bidding of demon masters.

Lee, Barbara, Tina, and Tommy were below. So was his mother. They all stood close together, staring at

Pestilence.

"Ah, our guest of honor has arrived," said Pestilence, looking up and winking at Christopher. Christopher tried to shout out a warning, but no words came out, just complete silence. He kicked and struggled and continued to scream silently.

"Mindy, step forward," said Pestilence. Christopher watched in horror as his mother took a hesitant step forward. Lee put his arm out, blocking her from going further.

"What do you want from her?" Lee demanded.

"You've already proven yourself, skeptic. This is Mindy's chance. This is her chance to save all of you, most especially her son."

Christopher shouted with such force that his lungs burned, but he still had no voice.

"You'll have to come through us to get her," said Lee.

Pestilence nodded. "If that's how it must be. I'll happily scatter your body parts for miles. You've all survived a lot this fine day. It seems a bit foolish to let yourselves die a ghastly death when you're so close to sweet freedom."

Mindy pushed past Lee. "What do you want?"

"Oh, nothing substantial. I just want you to sacrifice yourself. Give your life for the others. That's not such a big deal, is it?"

"You're not going to touch her," said Lee.

"Enough out of you." Pestilence smiled. "You've had a good, long life, haven't you, Mindy? Is it worth giving up your own life to save a young boy, a hero, and a widow? Perhaps not. But what about your son? Is it worth giving up your life to save your son?"

"How do I know you'll let them go?" his mother

asked.

No!

"Well, you could trust me, but I'll be the first to admit that I don't have trustworthy features. So we'll go with something a bit more over-the-top."

Pestilence gestured, and the bird flew toward one of the trees, bashing Christopher into it.

"Sacrifice yourself, and the trees will part like the Red Sea, revealing the path to freedom. Be a selfish old hag, and your son gets beaten to death by a giant bird, and I kill all of you anyway. When you stop to think about it, there's really only one good choice."

"He's lying," said Lee. "Don't listen to him."

Pestilence's smile vanished. "Skeptic, you are in grave danger of losing all of the good will I feel towards you. If you say one more word, or so much as utter a syllable that sounds like it might be in the process of forming a word, I will kill you where you stand. It won't be a heroic death. It will be a senseless and embarrassing one. I'm offering Mindy the opportunity to save all of you, so please stay out of it. Nod if you understand me."

Lee stood motionless for a moment, and then gave an almost imperceptible nod.

"Good. Now..."

Pestilence stared at Lee, who stared back. The two almost seemed like they had some sort of...*connection*. Like they were communicating without words. Christopher had no idea what they might be saying, but there was definitely something going on.

The demon blinked in surprise, as if suddenly realizing where he was. "Mindy, step forward."

Mindy stepped past Lee and the others. Even from his vantage point, Christopher could see that she was trembling.

"No need to be afraid," said Pestilence, his smile returning. "I guarantee that this will be painless. Much less painless than this." He gestured, and the bird slammed Christopher against another tree. This time he thought he might have broken a rib.

"Leave him alone!" Mindy wailed.

"Well, now, that's an option. Another option is for my feathered friend to bash your son against that tree until there's nothing left to hold on to. It's all up to you, Mindy."

"I'll do anything."

"I like that attitude. Unfortunately, it's a lot easier to say you'll give yourself up as a sacrifice than to actually do it and mean it. Come closer."

Mindy looked up at Christopher. He shook his head wildly and mouthed, *"Don't do it!"*

She took another step towards Pestilence.

"That's the way to do it," said Pestilence. "One small step at a time. That said, I can't keep the forest creatures away forever, so you might want to pick up the pace a bit."

Mindy took another step. Now less than five feet separated her from the demon.

"I need proof that you'll keep your side of the bargain," Mindy said.

"What sort of proof would you like?" Pestilence asked, stepping forward and closing the gap between them to three feet.

"Let them go."

"All of them?"

Mindy nodded.

"I'm not sure I see the logic there. If I'm asking you to

sacrifice yourself to save the others, why would I let them go before you've made the sacrifice?"

"I'm an old woman. Where the hell am I going to go? Do you think I'm going to kick you in the balls and run away?"

Pestilence walked forward and put his scaly hand on her shoulder. "So if I let them go free, you'll willingly sacrifice yourself to me?"

Mindy nodded, her face glistening with tears.

No! Please no! Don't do it!

"That's very selfless of you, Mindy. Are you sure?"

"You have to let them leave the entire forest."

"Of course."

"All of them. Including my son."

"That can be arranged. So if I do that, you'll offer yourself up as my sacrifice?"

"Yes."

"Look me in the eyes."

Mindy looked into Pestilence's eyes. Christopher thought his lungs were going to rip free of his chest from his silent screaming.

"I need to believe that you're telling the truth."

"I am."

Pestilence's grin widened. "You are. And unfortunately for you, that's all I need."

The blow caught her underneath the chin. Her head was not merely ripped from her body, but it seemed to *explode* in a shower of blood and gore that drenched Lee and the others.

Christopher's screams were no longer silent.

The bird dropped him and he fell to the ground, crying out in both pain and anguish.

Pestilence shook some of the blood off his hand and

let out a loud, cackling laugh. "Now the real fun begins, ladies and gentlemen. Enjoy the show."

CHAPTER THIRTY-ONE

Jake Steiner spit a stream of tobacco juice into his coffee cup. It was either spit or swallow and he didn't much feel like gagging that shit down. He'd given it up for a while on numerous occasions, but every now and then he just needed a fix.

Since he was on his way to the place that had given him more nightmares than he ever wanted to think about, he was pretty sure this counted as "every now and then." It was that or pop open a few beers, and he guessed that would go against the three years sober he'd managed so far in AA.

Two damned trees had eaten most of the road, and he slowed down the cruiser and carefully eased between them, cursing under his breath when he scraped up the left rear of his vehicle.

Something big and black jumped from one tree to the other and looked down on him as he passed under its territory. Whatever the hell it was, it made both trees shake.

He picked up the radio handset and called to the other cars behind him. "Got company, boys. Something up in the trees. Keep your wits and turn off your safeties, because we ain't here to interrogate any of the things living out this way."

"Amen, chief! Let's get ready to rumble!" That was Wilcox answering. The boy was enthusiastic about his law enforcement and almost as crazy about his side career as a professional wrestler. Would have worked better for Jake if Wilcox looked like he could wrestle more than a Twinkie.

"Save the battle cries," Jake said. "You might need 'em before we're done. Don't take this shit lightly. We're here to see if we can stop whatever's happening."

Wilcox didn't answer. He was too busy dying.

The black thing had dropped out of the tree and landed on the third cruiser, the one that carried Wilcox and his partner O'Brien. Jake couldn't make out too many details but near as he could tell, the thing looked like it was covered in scabs and had too many arms.

He pulled over to the side and called out on the radio for everyone to stop and render aid.

By the time he was done talking, Sheila Hannigan was out of the car. Sheila was his second in command, and more than capable of handling herself in a nasty situation. They didn't get a lot of murders in Dover's Point, but they got more than their fair share of drunks on the weekends.

Sheila pulled her .38, sighted carefully, and put a bullet into the thing on top of Wilcox's car. Whatever the hell it was, it fell down and stayed there.

"What in the name of *shit?*" Sheila ran over to the squad car and looked at the caved-in roof. Wilcox was dead and so was his partner.

Jake made it back to where she was standing and

looked at the mangled bodies. "Poor bastards." He spit out the tobacco in his mouth in honor of his fallen comrades. Wilcox had a fine little wife at home, along with two boys—the twins—and a baby girl on the way. He might have been a clown, but he was a good cop and a better man.

O'Brien was engaged. No kids. But his folks were long-time friends and now he had to tell them he'd let their only son get himself killed.

He rubbed at the back of his neck and felt a shiver that had nothing to do with the weather, especially since it was still hot as sin and the sun was just going down.

"Guys, I don't much like saying this, but Tony and Micah here are gonna call an ambulance and wait for it to show up. The rest of us have to go forward."

The other cops protested, as Jake knew they would. No one liked to leave a fellow cop behind, even if they were already dead. It wasn't respectful.

Of course, neither was the laughter.

Jake looked around, trying to decide which ex-employee of his had decided that two deaths were funny. All of them were looking around too. No one was laughing.

The first of the things landed on the car directly behind him, cackling away as it hunched down and bared some nasty-looking teeth. It was furry, dark with spots, and it seemed to be hunched over but standing on two feet. Both of the front arms were too long and almost scraped the paint off the black and white.

"What the hell?" That was Sheila again. She moved up next to him and started to aim. The laughing thing jumped into the air. It barely even seemed to flex its legs, just sort of shot skyward like it was on a springboard.

Sheila and Jake both watched it, and then tried to get out of the way. Jake made it, Sheila did not. The powerful hind legs of the thing landed on her chest and drove her backward and into the ground. Before she even finished bouncing, the front paws took two swipes and peeled her neck away.

Jake pissed himself right then and there. There wasn't much he could do about it, and he didn't have enough time to feel embarrassed before the thing crouched low and laughed in his face.

Big, golden eyes stared at him with slitted pupils that were as wide as his cat's at home when it was angry or hunting.

The laughter started up again, coming from in front of him. It was immediately answered from several other locations.

Jake didn't dare take his eyes off the thing. He'd seen how fast it was.

Teeth grinned at him in the dark furry face and the eyes almost seemed to shimmer. Not far away, he heard a gunshot and Sheila's leg exploded. The obvious target stayed on her chest and laughed.

"Son of a diseased whore!" That was Peters. He always had the most colorful curse words.

"Goddamn it!" shouted Jake, taking out his revolver. "Be careful where you're aiming!"

He saw them coming and shook his head, trying to focus on the one in front of him. There had to be fifteen more of the things laughing and giggling as they came closer, like the idea of taking on a group of armed cops was just as funny as all get out. They didn't move like people. They moved like something between a kangaroo and a mountain lion. Muscles shifted and the damned things hopped a good ten feet closer every time they moved at all. Jake brought his Smith & Wesson up and aimed for the thing still crouched over Sheila.

It moved, vaulting straight at him and laughing louder than ever. A millisecond after it passed him, Jake felt the fire spread up his arm. Five red slices cut through his sleeve and bled across the blue fabric. That part didn't bother him as much as the same red slices starting at his wrist and moving up to the sleeve on his bicep.

"Oh fu—" He never finished the word. The claws came at him again before he could, and this time they caught his throat, tearing out his larynx in the process.

Jake fell back and gurgled, blood flowing freely from the wound in his neck. He was alive long enough to see the other laughing things attack the rest of the squad. He died before they were finished with the task.

Mark and Hannah could have told him that the Gigglers always liked to play with their food before they ate.

* * *

Hannah was taking the giant wyrm chasing them remarkably well. She was screaming obscenities and looking over her shoulder approximately fifteen times a second. Mark felt he was holding up pretty well himself, because he was only looking into the rearview about twice a second.

"That is one big damned wyrm."

"No shit, Mark! Now could you possibly go a little faster?"

"I'm doing ninety!"

The wyrm lunged forward and Mark swerved hard

enough to put the car up on two wheels for a moment. The result was Hannah letting out another scream as they managed to avoid getting swallowed by the freaky thing.

Yes, *swallowed*. It was that big.

The ground where the car had been obligingly shattered when the wyrm hit it. The car went back on all four wheels and Mark stomped on the gas, almost stalling the car out before it leaped forward.

"We've got to lose that thing, Mark!"

"I believe he's trying," said Booth from the back seat.

"Well, tell him to try harder, damn it!"

"Tree," said Booth.

Mark swerved to avoid the enormous tree in the center of the road. The car slid off the pavement and onto the hard soil, spitting plumes of dust into the air. The rearview mirror showed that the oversized leviathan was gaining speed, undeterred by the cloud of arid soil.

Mark looked at the numerous trees ahead of him and the town now off to the right and swerved toward his left, aiming for a spot between two of the monolithic and completely alien plants.

"Mark? What are you doing? There are trees in the way."

"Yeah, I know." He urged the car to go a little faster as the segmented body thrust and lurched forward, tearing up the distance between them.

"Mark, I'm sorry for yelling earlier, I didn't mean a word of it. This is not the best time to consider suicide, okay?"

"Calm down, Hannah, I know what I'm doing."

"No, you don't. You really don't." Her voice rose with each word as they got closer to the trees.

Mark looked at the two black shapes ahead of him and

tried to calculate if he could really squeeze the Saturn between them. No. Probably not.

"I promise not to kill us," he said, figuring that he wouldn't get called out on his failure to keep the promise if he was dead.

Mark made one last careful adjustment with the steering wheel and then closed his eyes as they reached the base of the two trees.

The car shot through the gap, losing the paint on both doors as well as the side-view mirrors. The sound almost managed to drown out Hannah's screams.

Mark looked back at the receding trees and pumped the air with his right hand. "*Sweet!* We did it!"

The wyrm kept coming, ignoring the trees, and Mark almost wished he had enough time to watch as it smashed itself into a pulp.

Hannah watched for him, giving a blow by blow. "It's still coming...it's still coming...it's almost there...*splat!*"

Mark risked a look back, as there were no new trees in the immediate vicinity. The wyrm had indeed smashed into the trees, cutting its body along two points and spilling an enormous amount of what passed for its blood, a thick pale mess that painted the bark of both the barriers it faced.

For one brief second, Mark thought that was the end of the wyrm, but then it pushed forward again and uprooted both of the trees with a seemingly casual shrug. The trees flipped into the air, clots of soil falling from their roots.

And sailed in the same direction that Mark was currently driving.

No. Fuckin'. Way.

Mark opened his mouth to say something out loud to

that effect, but nothing would come.

The trees were still rising into the air and he couldn't decide where they were going to fall.

Mark slammed his foot against the gas pedal again, and Hannah pulled into a fetal position and screamed bloody murder. He really wanted to join her, but there just wasn't time.

The first tree landed ten feet to the left with a thunderous crash and snapped in two upon impact. Mark twisted the wheel to the right and kept it turned that way, spinning the vehicle almost a full half circle. The second tree rolled across the ground where they'd been a moment ago, shedding limbs and thick bark as it went.

Mark glanced up at the rearview mirror long enough to see that they had, indeed, avoided death by tree.

Then he looked forward and saw the wyrm recovering from the beating it had given itself. Bloodied and pulped or not, it was moving again, heading directly toward them.

The only good news was that it was moving slower now and looked like it might bleed to death before it could eat them alive.

He breathed a sigh of relief when the wyrm started pushing itself into the ground, the heavy feelers at the front of its mouth slicing the hard-packed earth apart and letting the gigantic beast disappear in a matter of two minutes, tops. During that time, Mark hyperventilated and said his thanks to God above, Hannah slowly recovered from her panic attack, and Booth sat silently in the back seat.

Finally Mark drove back toward the road as another tree started rising behind him, making up for the two that had been dislodged from the ground.

Up ahead, he could see Dover's Point a little clearer as the sun started to set. He could also see the fires burning at several of the houses.

He drove faster, worried not just for himself and for Hannah, but also for Chloe.

He tried to call again. No answer.

The ground shook and rumbled beneath the car as the wyrm burrowed deeper, but the beast was no longer his concern. Now he had to worry about what he would find when he got home.

* * *

The closest military installation was just over thirty miles from the Haunted Forest. The first of the military forces to make it to the area were in helicopters loaded with as many soldiers as they could manage while still carrying emergency medical supplies and firepower.

Four personnel transports landed at Dover's Point after hearing from the recon helicopter that there was simply no room to actually land at the H.F. Enterprises headquarters. The entire area surrounding the building was engulfed in trees or would be within the next few minutes.

The recon pilot also made a point of calling for more backup, because from what he could see they were flying into a massive clusterfuck.

Dover's Point was under siege, there was no other way to put it. The trees were rising from people's yards, from the street, and through most of the structures in the small town, including the Baptist church and what had been the town hall.

Colonel William Tyson did not like what he saw. What

was happening made about as much sense as a barbed-wire raft and looked almost as painful.

They didn't try to set up a proper command post, because they couldn't guarantee that any part of the ground would be safe from another tree coming up.

Tyson assessed the situation and called for more troops. He was promised that they were on the way.

In the meantime, he found out who owned the construction site at the edge of Whittaker Street and immediately got their people to start moving the bulldozers, forklifts of varying sizes, and the excavator on hand for serious digging. After a very brief argument about local regulations regarding the dispersal of explosives, Tyson had his men break down the door to the explosives shed and confiscate all of the dynamite.

The battle for Dover's Point was loud, to be sure. Trees rose up and fell down almost as quickly, but like weeds, more rose to take their places. Still, the soldiers made slow progress toward removing the worst of the invading plant life.

Then things took a turn for the worse. With the sun lowering on the western horizon and most of its light blocked by the unexpected plant life, the soldiers didn't see their attackers at first. They were looking at trees, and somehow the idea of searching the sky never crossed anyone's mind.

That changed quickly enough when the flying creature dropped out of the sky and attacked, sinking powerful talons into Private Hugo Lee's back as it captured him. Lee screamed for all he was worth but dropped his weapon.

The sleek, feathered beast lifted Lee high into the air and began feasting on him even as he struggled. It dropped the soldier around the same time that the bullets tore it and its meal nearly in half.

But there were other creatures in the air. Plenty of them.

The soldiers gave up trying to take out the trees when the black oak came out of the ground and crushed Colonel Tyson against the side of the Huey he was using as a mobile command. It kept pinning him until his chest caved in and smeared across the protesting metal side of the helicopter. A moment later, the whole machine slid sideways and toppled onto its side. The tree kept growing, not the least bit concerned about the colonel or the five-million-dollar flying machine it turned into scrap metal.

After the colonel died, the soldiers concentrated on rounding up the remaining citizens and getting them on their way to a safer place. Flying creatures plucked residents of Dover's End off the ground as if they were choosing treats from a box of chocolates.

The trees kept coming, and by the time most of the locals had been pulled from their homes, the road leading into and out of town had been overgrown.

Countless beasts leapt from the trees, seeking prey. There was prey galore at first. But the food supply dwindled quickly and new trees brought new mouths to feed.

Chloe Harper dragged herself across the floor of her kitchen, which was difficult to do with only one arm. Three different animals tore chunks of flesh out of her legs as she frantically tried to get to the phone.

Her final thoughts were of her husband.

CHAPTER THIRTY-TWO

No...

Christopher's mother was not dead. That was not acceptable. She was a kind, sweet woman who found joy in the smallest things and had an unparalleled zest for life. People like that did not meet their end in this manner. She was destined to pass away quietly in her sleep, not be decapitated by a fucking demon while mistakenly believing that she'd saved them all, instead of dooming them.

Not acceptable.

Christopher stood there silently, dripping blood from the seemingly infinite number of cuts he'd sustained during Pestilence's extended torture session. He stared into the eyes of Lee, Barbara, and Tina. Their expressions conveyed sympathy, horror, and an intense desire to get the hell away from there.

Her blood had splashed all over the bottom half of Lee's face. He looked as if he wanted to wipe it off, but wasn't quite sure if Christopher would take offense to the gesture.

At this moment, the only thing Christopher wanted to

do was throw his head back, let out an ear-exploding wail of misery, and rip out his hair in large handfuls.

He did not do this. His mother would not have approved of her son creating a ruckus and causing the death of the few remaining Haunted Forest Tour survivors.

So he remained silent.

Everybody continued to stare at him.

"Forgive me for stating the obvious," said Lee, finally, "but the trees aren't parting like the Red Sea."

Christopher shook his head. "No. No, they aren't."

Barbara stepped forward. "Oh, Christopher, I'm so sorry. But she didn't die in vain."

Christopher couldn't help but let out an incredulous laugh. "Actually, she died to fulfill part of a demon spell that, from what I understand, may signal the end of humanity. I may be exaggerating—I didn't get all the details. So, no, her death wasn't in vain, but it wasn't one of those deaths that's going to cause people to erect a statue."

Barbara seemed unsure how to respond to that. "Oh."

Christopher nodded. "Yeah."

Lee looked down. "Uh, Tina? You've got...you've got something on your foot."

Tina glanced at her foot. There was a small chunk of Mindy's skull on it, with an eyeball attached. She gasped and kicked it away.

"Okay, so, so, so, so I don't completely understand what has just happened here," Barbara admitted. "How exactly have we signaled the end of humanity?"

"The demon that rules this forest needed a sacrifice," said Lee. "He tried to get me to offer up Tommy, and then myself. After I refused I guess he went after, uh,

Mindy."

"He went after me before that," Christopher said, turning around in a circle so they could all get a good look at his cut-ridden chest and back. "Oh, I had a jolly fucking time after the bird snatched me. Time of my life. Cut, cut, cut, slice, slice, slice. Do I sound like I've gone insane? I feel like I sound like I've gone insane. Stop me if I sound that way."

"We really should get out of here," said Lee.

Christopher nodded his agreement. "Don't let the insane guy stop you. Did I just pass out?"

Barbara gave him a strange look. "No."

"Oh, good. Thought I passed out for a second. Listen to me, all of you. For all of us, there comes a time in every man's life—woman's too—when he has to take matters into his own hands. We can't rely on Eddie coming back with the Justice League of America to save us. Eddie didn't come back, right?"

"Right."

"Good. I mean, bad. I mean, I didn't think so. So it's up to us to save ourselves. I'm tired of letting this forest push me around. I'm tired of the bugs and the tooth-bearing things and the blood and the fur and the claws and the...the stuff. I'm tired of the forest stuff. Lee, could you hold me up for a second? I think I'm going to pass out for real."

Lee rushed forward and placed his hand on Christopher's shoulder. Christopher winced in pain.

"Sorry," Lee said.

"It's okay. You won't find any uncut parts. Did I pass out?"

"No."

"Good. That's very good. This all goes way beyond a

bunch of tourists who were too stupid to go to Disneyland. There is a human host, and that motherfucker is going to make it possible for a nasty-ass dimension to completely overtake our own. I think. Again, still not one hundred percent clear on the details. But we can't let this happen."

"How do we stop it?" Tina asked.

"No clue."

"Find the host," said Lee.

"That works," Christopher agreed. "Are any of you the host?"

Nobody responded.

"The host isn't here," said Lee. "Look, I talked to the Proof Demon—"

"What's a Proof Demon?" Christopher asked.

"I think it's either part of the demon that killed your mother or a follower or whatever. I'm not sure."

"Why is it called a Proof Demon?"

"Because it's proof of the supernatural."

"Why would Pestilence need proof of the supernatural?"

"That's what I named it. Christopher, I know you've just lost the most important person in your life and you're losing a lot of blood, but stay with me."

Christopher nodded. "My elbow hurts."

"Anyway, I'm not saying that we did a Vulcan mind-meld or anything but—"

The trees shook, sending down a shower of pine needles, as a demonic voice howled: *"Wheeeere aaaaaaare yooooooooou?"* The force of the voice was enough to knock Lee and Christopher to their knees.

"What the hell was *that?*" Tina demanded.

"Pestilence is pissed," Christopher noted.

HAUNTED FOREST TOUR

Lee stood up and then pulled Christopher to his feet. "Maybe something went wrong. That has to be good for us, right?"

"Yeah, because we're not in any danger standing out here in the middle of the forest," said Tina.

"Look, we have to get out of here," said Christopher. "We can't count on anybody to do it for us. Did I already say that? Anyway, we have to assume that help is not on its way, that Eddie is lying dead somewhere without his nose. We are the last remaining survivors of the Haunted Forest Tour, unless any of the people who stayed behind in the tram made it, which I'm pretty sure they didn't. Lee, Barbara, Tina, Tommy...Tommy's still alive, right?"

The little boy opened his eyes, peeked over Barbara's shoulder, and nodded.

"Cool. Lee, Barbara, Tina, Tommy...we're it. We're the only people who are going to get ourselves out of this mess. And we're not going to get out of here by standing around talking. Lee, I'm feeling barely conscious again, could you prop me up?"

Lee put his hand back on Christopher's shoulder.

"I'm not good at big speeches, and I'm not good at inspiring people, and I'm not good at oral exams, but goddamn it, I know when I see four people who deserve to live. You all deserve to live. We all deserve to get out of here. And we're not going to let that scaly prick who murdered my mother win. We're going to get out of this, and we're going to do it ourselves, because *nobody is going to help us.*"

"Do you hear a helicopter?" Barbara asked.

Everybody listened.

A familiar voice boomed over a megaphone: *"Ladies and gentlemen, this is Eddie Turner, here to save your asses!"*

***

Booth squeezed his eyes shut and winced in pain. Mark stopped the car and looked back at him. "What's wrong?"

"Nothing, I'm—ow, *shit!*"

"Migraine?"

"Something like that." Booth rubbed his forehead with both hands. "Don't worry about me; just get me out of here."

Mark glanced over at Hannah. "Do you have any aspirin?"

"I don't need aspirin!" Booth shouted. "I need for you to start driving!"

"Yes, sir." Mark applied the accelerator again, hoping very much that it was Booth instead of himself who went to prison. The way things were going, they'd end up sharing a cell and have to alternate bitch duties.

"*It wasn't my fault!*" Booth shouted. "*They made me!*"

"Who made you?"

"*I swear, it wasn't my fault!*"

Mark glanced up in the rearview mirror. Was Booth actually *crying*? He and Hannah exchanged a concerned glance.

"It wasn't my fault," Booth repeated, although now Mark couldn't decide if he was speaking to some unseen presence or to himself. "Not my fault."

***

Eddie would've loved to fly over the forest in a military chopper, armed with missiles and tear gas and gallons of monster repellent made from Booth's blood. Swoop down, snatch up the survivors, then be the one to press the button that wiped this forest right the hell off the map. Then he'd fly over to the MapQuest offices and make them revise their online directions to the forest at gunpoint.

But he wasn't in a military chopper. He was, in fact, in the Eye in the Sky Traffic helicopter for Channel 8 news. The young pilot was not thrilled to be flying over the Haunted Forest after hearing that the last helicopter to do so had been torched by a dragon, but the traffic reporter was ecstatic about the idea of covering the potential rescue.

They did not have missiles or tear gas or monster repellent. They did have one hell of a nice rope ladder that the military let them borrow, and plenty of guns.

Eddie pointed down at the reclamation plant building. "Any chance we can land on that thing?" he asked, shouting to be heard above the noise of the aircraft.

"Are you kidding me? It has a rounded top!"

"Just asking. I drive a tour tram, for Christ's sake. Get down as low as you can."

The pilot shook his head. "I'm staying above the trees. Gotta watch for dragons."

"Okay, okay, whatever you need to do." Eddie leaned out of the open helicopter door as far as he could without vertigo setting in and peered down at the ground, two hundred feet below. No sign of anybody, but they were probably inside.

"You sure they're still alive?" asked the reporter.

"Of course not. If they are, I hope they stayed put."

* * *

"I told you we should've stayed put!" said Tina.

To be honest, Barbara couldn't remember if Tina had been in favor of leaving the reclamation plant or against it. Not that it mattered. All that mattered now was to get back to it before Eddie gave up and flew away.

They'd make it. They hadn't walked far, ten minutes tops, and they'd been going slowly. If they really picked up the pace they'd be okay.

Christopher stumbled and almost fell, but Lee held him up.

Tommy on her back felt like he weighed four hundred pounds.

"I'm going to run ahead," said Tina.

"No, we shouldn't split up," Lee told her.

"Why? Are you guys going to protect me?"

"She's right," said Barbara. "Run ahead; make sure Eddie knows we're on our way."

Tina nodded.

Then she screamed.

She pointed at something behind Barbara. Barbara spun around to see what it was. Nothing there. She spun back around to face Tina.

"What? What is it?"

"It's on Tommy!"

She twisted her neck around so quickly that it hurt. Tommy's eyes were closed, but she couldn't see anything on him.

"On his shoulder!"

"I still can't see it! Tommy, you have to let go!"

The little boy's arms were wrapped around her in a death-grip. She frantically tried to pry them off...how could a six-year-old be so strong?

"Tommy, please! Let go so I can help you!"

Something scraped the back of Barbara's neck.

Lee rushed forward. Christopher wobbled a bit but didn't fall over.

"It *hurts!*" Tommy squealed.

Barbara grabbed Tommy's wrists and pulled as hard as she could. "Tommy, I can't get it off you while you're on my back!"

"Don't worry, I've got it!" Lee assured her. She couldn't see what he was doing, but Tommy's squeal suddenly intensified.

Barbara counted three—no, four—sets of glowing eyes watching them through the trees.

Christopher stumbled over to help Lee.

Barbara finally pried Tommy's arms open. She gently but quickly knelt down and wiggled out of his grip.

"*It hurts it hurts it hurts!*"

Barbara turned around and saw what was on Tommy. A fish. A fish with translucent skin, allowing her to see the skeletal structure, and a head full of oversized teeth like those horrific fish that swam at the very bottom of the ocean and never saw light.

It also had tiny wings. A flying fish should've been a comical sight, but this one was about as funny as an infant's funeral.

Lee crouched down and jabbed his walking stick through the fish's side. It came out the other end, and he wrenched the fish away from Tommy's shoulder. Three teeth remained lodged in the little boy's flesh as Lee tossed his stick aside. Christopher plucked them out.

"*It hurts!*" Tommy wailed.

"I know it does, sweetie," said Barbara, wincing at the vicious bite marks on his shoulder. "But we'll be out of here soon, I promise."

"*It hurts it hurts my leg it hurts!*"

Barbara gasped as she saw that an identical fish was on Tommy's leg, biting through his jeans. Lee grabbed for it. The fish snapped at him, taking off Lee's index finger at the first knuckle.

The old man did not scream, though it looked like it took every ounce of self-control that he possessed to keep from doing so.

Eddie's voice boomed over the megaphone again. "*I repeat, this is Eddie! I'm hovering over the building where I left you! If you're still there, come out so I can see you!*"

"Run!" Lee shouted at Tina. "Go get help!"

Tina nodded and sprinted off.

"Help me roll him over," said Christopher. He and Barbara rolled Tommy onto his back, and then Christopher raised the boy's leg and smashed it onto the ground, hard, crushing the fish underneath it.

He raised Tommy's leg. The fish was still squirming, so he repeated the process. It stopped squirming.

"You okay, Lee?" he asked.

Lee cradled his injured hand to his chest. "Better than you still, but no."

Tommy was still screaming and sobbing. There wasn't much they could do about that. Christopher and Lee pulled him to his feet while Barbara got in position to give him another piggyback ride.

Up ahead, Tina had just about disappeared from sight. She was nothing more than a shadow.

Then another shadow with glowing eyes leapt at her, bringing her down.

CHAPTER THIRTY-THREE

Captain Charles Buchanan looked around the area and scowled. He was supposed to start clearing out what Colonel Tyson euphemistically called "the new growth." Sounded like a fucking rash. He braced himself as he saw a tree break through the roof of a house not thirty yards away.

New growth. Yeah, right.

"Henderson!"

"Sir!" Henderson was a smart boy. He didn't panic and he always answered.

"We need chainsaws, Henderson. Lots of chainsaws."

"Excuse me?"

"I said we need chainsaws! Are you deaf, soldier?"

"But where?"

Buchanan shook his head. "The proper fucking answer is sir, yes sir! Go hit that hardware store and take every last one of them! Send out two boys to start taking them from garages! Now move!"

Henderson screamed out a proper "Sir, yes sir!" and ran.

"New growth my ass! Time to clear a fucking forest."

* * *

There were trees ripping the world apart. Devlin Hopewell had watched his house torn asunder by the trees and nothing he could do would stop them. But he was smarter than any plant, any day of the week.

He found the perfect hiding place, in his tree fort. He sat up in the well-crafted fort his father had built for him and rocked back and forth, looking at the flaming wreckage that had been his house only ten minutes earlier. His parents both worked, and he was home alone. Well, if you didn't count Mr. Tom, the fat old cat his family had had since before he was born. Mr. Tom had gotten out of the house and gone somewhere else. He had to hope the old cat was alive, same as he did with his mother and father.

He was still shaken, but he was alive, safe from the new trees in the place where he'd had a billion adventures over the years. The one place in town where he figured the new trees would leave him alone.

The tree under him let out a scream of protest as it split from base to crown, making way for the new tree coming up from below. Devlin screamed too, as he held on to the wall of his fortress and braced for the impact. Gravity was kind, and the fort house slid slowly down, giving him a lot of time to scream and holler and pray on the way to the lawn below.

He waited until the house was almost completely on the ground before jumping clear of the wreckage. Alive! He was alive!

Devlin was still celebrating that little victory when the pincers lopped off his head.

***

Chainsaws roared and screamed in defiance of nature gone mad. Soldiers went to work, cutting savagely at the trees as quickly as they grew. Some of the trees actually fell; most did not. The things that came with the trees saw to that.

Chainsaws roared and screamed.

Monsters roared too.

And soldiers screamed almost as well as their tools.

***

"I did *not* sign up for this! I just wanted to kill some goddamned terrorists!" Corporal Everson wasn't really happy with the way his day was going. He held onto the chainsaw and groaned as it hacked into the dense wood of the black tree in front of him. The sap was thick and purple. No tree should have purple sap. It wasn't natural.

"Did I just hear you complaining, Everson?" Sarge was being a dick, as usual.

"Yes you did!" He spat out a plume of sawdust. He wasn't very good at chopping down trees, and the damned stuff was trying to get into his eyes like it already had his nose and mouth.

Sure, he was going to get in trouble, but he was a reservist. He was just the unlucky bastard who had to work the weekend everything went crazy. If he'd been back at home he would have never even heard of Dover's Point.

"Well, don't it just suck to be you!" Sarge came closer, snarling like a baboon. That was being kind, since his face bore a stronger resemblance to the less attractive end of the aforementioned ape.

The chainsaw chose that moment to jam inside of the tree. Everson pulled hard at the blade as the engine roared and sputtered.

The tree pulled back. It was slow, but it was much, much stronger. Everson flew through the air with the greatest of ease and broke his spine as he ran into his commander.

* * *

The soldiers moved as fast as they could, running from door to door and checking for civilians. Anyone found alive was ordered out of their houses and apartments, given time only to grab a pair of shoes, essential medication, and their personal identification.

The command had come down: everyone was to be evacuated, no exceptions. There were a lot of people who wanted to protest. The soldiers were under orders and didn't take no for an answer.

The civilians stopped arguing quite so vigorously when the monsters started showing up in force. It was one thing to think about the hideous things living in the forest down the interstate and another thing entirely to have the living nightmares come looking for fresh meat.

The term free-for-all was designed for exactly the sort of situations that arose in Dover's Point. Flying things swept down from the sky, some with claws and some with even stranger appendages, to pluck new meals from the ground.

The soldiers fought back, and the civilians did their best, but none of them were well prepared for what was happening. Military textbooks rarely included discussions of how one might avoid being stung to death by a human-faced scorpion that was the size of a Doberman.

To make matters worse, the sun was lowering, and the bright day had become twilight. Those creatures that preferred to avoid the daylight were more comfortable, and the people who lived in town were more vulnerable than ever before.

The Wellington family had just gathered together and found each other again when the ogre showed up to play. The Wellingtons lasted exactly seventeen seconds.

On Archer Street, where most of the municipal buildings were found, a giant wyrm sporting several nasty wounds came out of the ground and began knocking buildings aside with ease. It bled as it crushed the town hall, but it kept going, warbling out its distress as it thrashed and rolled over stone walls and the occasional vehicle.

It might have done better to leave the Dover's Point Gas and Power building alone. The electricity hurt, but the natural gas storage tanks did much worse when they ruptured and their fumes made it to a burning car half a block away.

The wyrm and the buildings around it went up in a fireball that could be seen from the edge of the original forest, or would have been if the trees weren't obstructing the view.

The trees that kept rising from the ground almost as fast as the eyes left in town could watch them.

* * *

They came from several bases, jets and helicopters that

cut across the twilight and sought to put a stop to the cancerous growth of a nightmare forest that shouldn't have existed.

The jets arrived first, moving over the forest and then to its growing edges, where incendiary missiles tried to remove the sickness. The missiles struck and exploded, igniting acres of fresh growth and lighting up the sky with fresh fires.

All for nothing. Like a phoenix, the trees came back, rising from the burning debris as if nothing had happened. Worse, in some cases they rose higher than before, as if the very fuel that should have destroyed them fed them instead. Hell's little super-fertilizer.

The jets banked around for another run, instructed to stop the new growth and not to fire into the heart of the Haunted Forest. There were still over eighty people unaccounted for and no one was quite willing to be the first to risk using the term "collateral damage" just yet.

As they turned in the skies over the unnatural woods, the forest returned the volley of fire. The first wave came in the form of insects. Not your usual swarm of bees or even plague of locusts, but all new flying things that had never been seen outside of the forest before. They were heavily armored and defied rational physics with their ability to lift off of the ground.

The people who worked at the Haunted Forest Tour called them "Harpies," a name granted by one of the early tourists who noticed that they had almost human faces and rather attractive ones at that. Their full, sensual lips did not move and their delicate noses seemed to serve no purpose, but their eyes—often a deep blue or green—were as complex as the ocular organs on any terrestrial insect. The fact that each of the bugs was almost five feet in length made it possible to see them very clearly.

The thick chitinous exoskeletons were sometimes found in the woods after molting season, and a few of the deeply adventurous types had managed to peel them off of trees and take them back for a careful examination. Said husks were not impervious, but a fair estimate was that they could withstand close range fire from a .22 caliber handgun using standard jacketed shells.

Two squadrons of ten jets each met up with several hundred harpies in the air. The first surprise for the pilots was that the harpies could keep up with them. The jets roared and the harpies screamed as they flew through the air, the movement of their wings giving off a sound "not unlike a young woman's shrieks as she was stabbed to death," at least according to Mark Harper, who many people said enjoyed his job just a bit too much.

The jet fighters were perfectly willing to fight anything that came their way. They were not prepared for the five-foot-long kamikazes that deliberately flew into their jet engine intakes.

Flaming metal and flesh rained down across the forest, scorching the trees and tinkling down to the mulch and dirt.

The remaining harpies flew back to their primary hive, annoyed by the death of one of their colonies, but only moderately so. They were not emotional creatures unless riled.

The Black Hawk helicopters that came in next were better suited for dealing with the harpies. Though the insects were actually faster, the seasoned combat crews on the Black Hawks were very capable with their .50 caliber machine guns, and despite their terrifying size and speed, the Harpies lacked any ranged method of attacking.

* * *

The fire spread, burning a hole in the center of the map of Dover's Point. The trees stopped growing where the worst of the fire was, and the scorched earth and ruined asphalt collapsed in on itself.

Sparks rose high into the air, and smoke soon followed. More of the earth gave way, revealing a new challenge for the remaining people in town. Where there had been a town center, there was now a lava pit, filled to overflowing with molten figures that slid from their plasmic waters and walked the face of the earth.

No one was foolish enough to try speaking with the shambling creatures. Well, one guy was. Briefly.

The figures lovingly touched whatever they could. Everything they caressed burned beneath their eager grasp, and they relished the sensation.

It had been so very long since they'd had new things to play with.

* * *

The H.F. Enterprises building was designed to last. Reinforced walls and shatterproof windows that could withstand mortar fire held off the forest for longer than Dover's Point managed to stay alive, but in the end, even the building designed to be as safe as Fort Knox gave way to the inevitable progression of the Haunted Forest.

The few people foolish enough to stay behind looked out through windows that should have survived anything short of a nuclear blast as the army of nightmares came their way. The first guards in their bunkers fought well, cutting down several ogres, a pack of Gigglers, and three heavily armored things that looked like bald mammoths with horns on the tops of their heads.

They never had a chance against the specters that floated through the air and shrieked out deafening cries of pain as they moved closer. Wavering, constantly shifting figures slid toward the guards through the air and ignored bullets and grenades alike.

What they touched died of fright or was frozen to death.

When the hail of heavy artillery stopped, the other creatures in the forest moved forward.

The doors of the H.F. Enterprises building were solidly reinforced. They were designed to sustain incredible damage and bounce back for more.

The big problem was simple enough, really. A minor oversight that, considering the situation, could be seen as forgivable: nobody locked the doors.

Walls that were meant to survive tremendous damage were left untouched. The reporters and remaining employees were not.

On the winning side of the argument, the William Partneau Construction Company had a ringing endorsement for how well they'd finished their contract. The windows were still unbroken and the floor did not let a single tree rise from below.

Sadly, no one directly involved in the contractual agreements between H.F. Enterprises and Partneau Construction was available to return the construction company's requests for a quote.

* * *

Fire from below, nightmares on the surface, and death from above, Dover's Point went into its final minutes with a series of screams that would have shamed the best heavy metal vocalists in history.

Dover's Point did not die without a fight, but it most definitely died.

CHAPTER THIRTY-FOUR

Pestilence was not happy.

He had picked the right human host. Ensured that none of the denizens of the forest would harm the host or allow him to come to harm. Watched him board the vehicle. The host was nervous, anxious, even terrified, but that was understandable. It did not matter. The host had no task to complete except to wait.

But as loath as he was to admit it, Pestilence's power was not infinite...yet. In fact, it was quite weak. He could send a small piece of himself out as what Lee Burgundy called a Proof Demon (*how adorable*) but he could not watch everything that happened within the forest.

The demon had grown cocky. Amused himself with childish games of torture and temptation. But that was what it was all about. He was weary of drawing blood and screams from those in his own realm of existence. His spell offered the potential for an entire world, a much larger world, filled with playthings to torment.

But the host was not supposed to leave the forest.

How could he have predicted that a human would interfere? Or that the host would hesitate to kill in order to preserve the integrity of the spell?

If the host had simply shot the one called Edward Turner when he had a chance, Pestilence would be relaxing in a boiling pool of blood right now, gazing upon the mangled bodies that hung above him like a baby's mobile.

All was not lost. He could persuade the host to return. When he did, Pestilence would complete the spell, and the trees would rise from the earth as one, consuming this entire realm.

If not...well, the sacrifices were enough. His dimension would still completely overtake this one.

It would just take longer.

* * *

Tina lay on her back and gazed into the glowing red eyes of the hellhound above her. This could be it. Sweet, merciful death. An end to the heartache and pain.

Or not.

She wasn't going to die in this forest. It could take Brad from her, transform him into some homicidal mold-man, but it wasn't going to get *her*. She might not get out in one piece, and tomorrow morning she might decide that a world without Brad was not worth living in, but for right now, she was getting out of this forest alive. That was all there was to it.

Now she simply had to prevent the hellhound from breathing fire on her head.

The hellhound raked her with its claws, but she barely felt it. She wasn't even scared...much. She was angry. *Pissed.* Tina Landry was too close to rescue to let some devil dog end her life. She clenched her fists, extended her thumbs, and thrust them up at the hellhound's eyes.

Back during her tree-climbing adventure, she'd blinded the panther that chased after Christopher. That was with a branch. This was a little more up-close and personal. Her right thumb missed the target, smacking against the side of the hellhound's muzzle, but her left thumb punctured the orb.

Thick fluid that felt like boiling grease spilled out onto her hand, making her flesh sizzle. She *did* feel this particular pain, but it didn't stop her from slamming her right thumb into the hellhound's other eye. This time the eyeball splattered onto her face and neck. She immediately wiped the burning goo off her cheek with her untainted fingers, smearing a sizzling path across her skin.

The hellhound yelped like a hurt dog. The yelp was accompanied by a burst of flames that struck Tina in the chest, igniting her shirt and quickly flame-broiling the skin beneath.

In a day that had been filled with pain, this was unquestionably the worst so far.

She could smell her flesh burning. Everything in her mind shut down except for the one piece of advice that had been drilled into her as a little girl.

Stop, drop, and roll.

The stopping and dropping was already taken care of, thanks to the hellhound. She rolled to the left, vaguely aware that the hellhound slashed at her with its huge claws, but not really caring. A small burn, such as accidentally pressing her finger against a hot stove, was bad enough. This was pure agony.

She rolled and rolled. She rolled over something living but took no satisfaction in the loud *crunch* its body made.

When she struck a tree, she rolled back the other way.

The hellhound staggered away from her, fluid still pouring from its punctured eyes. Fire sprayed from its mouth.

Though she didn't feel any better, Tina's shirt was no longer on fire. She stood up and kicked the hellhound in the head as hard as she possibly could, trying to break its neck.

It took four kicks before she succeeded.

She was still alive. That's all that mattered. Her shirt hung in charred scraps, and what was left of the bra beneath seemed to have fused to her skin. She didn't care. She was alive. She was getting out of this forest.

She ran.

* * *

"Why don't you give me the boy?" Lee asked Barbara. "You'll never get out of here with him on your back."

"I'll be fine."

"The hell you will."

"The monsters are well aware of our presence. And the helicopter isn't going to be able to get to us from here. So maybe now is a good time to leave behind the people who don't have much of a shot, huh?"

Barbara looked at him with shock and horror. "I'm not leaving you!"

"Okay. Just throwing that out there to ease my guilt. Grab the boy and let's go."

* * *

Christopher blinked some blood out of his eye. He

could handle the pain; he just wished the dizziness would fade. Part of him wanted to lie against a tree and bleed to death, while another part of him wanted to get onto that helicopter and fly away to a hospital.

The rest of him was determined not to let Pestilence win. He didn't know how such a feat might be accomplished, but it would kill two birds with one stone: save humanity, and get revenge. His years working at Novellon had taught him the importance of combining goals wherever possible.

Just don't keel over, he told himself. *Lee is a really nice guy, but he's not going to carry you. You keel over, you're fish food.*

"I think they're circling us," Lee said. "The way they did when the tram first stopped."

Barbara nodded. "I think you're right."

Christopher looked around. Glowing eyes on all sides of them. "Guys, I hate to be whiny, but I'm not sure we have any place to go."

* * *

"Let's get out of here," said the pilot. "Dragons, remember?"

The reporter ignored him and continued filming the ground below. "You should be brave. Everything you say is being recorded."

When Eddie proposed that the news crew, which was there to cover the Halloween tour, help him rescue the survivors, the cameraman had shoved his video camera into the reporter's hands and told him good luck.

"Yeah, well, you can record me saying we should get out of here, or you can record me screaming as the dragon knocks off our propeller. Nobody's down there."

"They would've come out of the building by now, if they were still in there," Eddie said. *Or at least if they were still alive in there.* "Can we just fly around and search?"

"What would we be able to see down there? Do they have a flare gun?"

"No."

"Then no, we cannot just fly around and search. I'm done." The pilot adjusted the controls, and the helicopter began to rise.

"No! No, no, no! I see somebody!" Eddie shouted, pointing at the ground. Somebody came out of the woods next to the building and waved her arms over her head. It looked like the lady with the hurt husband.

"You're right! Drop the ladder! Drop the ladder!" shouted the reporter.

Eddie kicked the rope ladder over the side. It fell to the ground and the lady, Tina, quickly rushed over to it and started to climb.

Something flew out of the woods and made a beeline for her.

It was a giant bat. These days, Eddie was not impressed by a giant bat. He took careful aim with the semi-automatic rifle and opened fire. It took a few shots, but he struck the bat's wing and sent it spiraling down to the ground.

Several dozen bats emerged from the woods to take its place.

* * *

"Oh yeah. This ain't good," Lee noted. He stopped walking, as did the others.

"They probably smell blood," said Christopher.

Lee held up his bloody half-finger. "Probably."

"Maybe...maybe I could distract them." Christopher bit his lip. "If I run the opposite direction, wave my arms and make a lot of noise and stuff, they might all go after me."

"And then they'll kill you," Barbara said.

"I'm not saying the plan is in my best interest. But my mom's sacrifice was for nothing. Mine wouldn't be. Unless you all got eaten seconds after me. You wouldn't, right?"

"Can't go for that idea, sorry," said Lee. "No more sacrifices."

"Not your call."

Christopher raised his hands over his head and turned to run. Then a wave of dizziness struck him and he promptly pitched forward, landing on his face.

* * *

Tina tried to climb faster as she saw the swarm of bats coming right at her. Above, Eddie was shooting at them, but she was pretty sure he wouldn't be wiping out a whole swarm of bats before they got her.

Which was going to be in three...two...one...

The bats struck her like baseballs. They weren't even trying to bite her; the damn things were just bashing into her at full speed. Her left hand slipped off the ladder. She was about halfway up, meaning she had a nice hundred-foot fall to look forward to if she lost her grip.

She slammed her left hand back on the rope and tried to pull herself up another rung, as the bats slammed into her again and again. Several of them struck her burnt flesh, sending almost unbearable bolts of pain through her body.

As she screamed, a bat pushed into her open mouth.

* * *

Christopher was in a wonderful dreamland, where elves danced and fairies flew and leprechauns spoke in charming accents about their pots of gold, and where old men nudged him very hard with their foot against his bloody—

He looked up.

"Get up!" Lee said, extending a hand.

Christopher couldn't possibly have been out of it for more than a second or two, but the glowing eyes and shadows were definitely getting closer.

* * *

"Up! Up! Up!" Eddie shouted.

"Why?"

"The bats may not follow us up! Go higher! Hurry!" He set down the gun and picked up the megaphone. *"Hold on!"*

* * *

Tina crushed her teeth down on the bat's head.

She spat it out as the helicopter did such an abrupt rise that she nearly lost her grip with both hands. But she held on. She vomited over the front of her shirt, a reaction sparked by both the sudden upward acceleration and the whole "biting off the head of a bat" incident from a couple of seconds ago.

More bats bashed into her. But fewer than before.

She resumed climbing as quickly as she could as the helicopter continued rising. A couple more bats hit her, but she could handle that, no problem.

Eddie reached down for her. Tina grabbed his hand and let him pull her up into the helicopter, letting out one last yelp from the pain in her burnt fingers.

"Anybody else alive down there?" Eddie asked, shoving her into a seat.

Tina nodded frantically.

"Bring her down," Eddie told the pilot, as he began to pull up the rope ladder.

"Why are you doing that?" Tina asked.

Eddie grinned. "I'm no longer out of grenades. I don't want to damage the ladder when I damage the bats."

Despite everything she'd been through, Tina managed to grin as well.

CHAPTER THIRTY-FIVE

"I could try again," Christopher offered.

Lee frowned at him. "Don't bother."

"You think Tina made it?" asked Barbara, adjusting Tommy's position on her back. He was getting heavier with every passing second.

"Do you want my honest answer or the answer meant to be comforting in our final moments?"

"Comfort."

"Oh, yeah, definitely," said Lee. "She's on that helicopter relaxing with a glass of champagne and a personal masseuse."

"Good for her."

"Is she really?" Christopher asked.

Lee and Barbara stared at him.

"I was kidding," said Christopher. "I'm not *that* far gone. So does anybody know any good death songs? We could sing our way to the grave."

"Are we going to die?" Tommy asked, his voice so small and scared that Barbara's heart immediately broke.

"No," she told him. "We're not. We're going to get out of here, and then people are going to come in and kill all of the bad monsters."

"Good."

There was a loud explosion coming from the direction of the water reclamation plant.

"What do you think?" Lee asked. "Good explosion or bad explosion?"

Barbara smiled. "Sounds like an Eddie explosion."

Another explosion followed. Some of the glowing eyes and shadows scurried away.

Moments later, gunfire. Lots of it.

Moments after that, Lee could see the flashes of gunfire as well as hear them.

"*Heads up, kids!*" Eddie said through the megaphone. "*Cover your ears!*"

The third explosion knocked Christopher off his feet, although that was not a particularly difficult task. Creatures of all sizes and shapes fled all around them.

Eddie came into view, lowering the megaphone. "Hi. Did you guys think I was going to leave you to die?"

"I did," said Barbara.

"Me too," said Christopher.

"The idea did occur to me," Lee agreed.

"Well, I've got guns, grenades, a helicopter, and a friend of yours. Let's get the fuck out of this shithole, shall we?"

"That is a *wonderful* idea," said Barbara, hurrying forward.

"You wouldn't happen to have the human host, would you?" Christopher asked.

Eddie frowned. "Say what?"

"Just wondering. You missed it, but there's a demon involved here. Spells and stuff."

"But what do you mean by human host?"

"Dunno, to be honest."

"Would this human host be protected? I mean, would the things living in the forest not want him to come to harm?"

"What are you talking about?" Lee asked.

"Let's chat while we walk," said Eddie, pulling revolvers out of his belt and handing them to everybody. He shot another hellhound and started walking back toward the water reclamation plant. "I got out of the forest because monsters weren't trying to eat the owner of this place."

"You mean Pestilence?" asked Christopher.

"No, Booth. Martin Booth. Owner of H.F. Enterprises."

"He sounds human."

"He is. He was in the other tram, and he didn't want to leave. Weird as hell."

"Well, I don't know about the rest of you," said Lee. "But that sounds like human host behavior to me. Do you know where he is?"

"I know who has him. Why?"

"I think we can use him to stop this."

"How? Kill him?"

Lee shook his head and fired at something he couldn't quite see. Since the trigger finger on his right hand was missing the piece that would actually pull a trigger, he had to use his left hand, and his aim was bad. Barbara made up for it. He actually questioned the wisdom of giving Christopher a firearm in his current condition, but didn't say anything.

"Killing him won't work. We need to mix up the spell. The demon got his tram full of sacrifices. He also got his willing sacrifice."

"Who the hell was that?" Eddie asked.

"Mindy."

"Mindy...?"

"My mom," said Christopher.

"Oh. I'm sorry."

"Now he just needs his human host. But if we fuck up the ritual, cross-wire it, if you will, I think we can stop this."

"And how exactly do you know this?"

"I don't know it exactly. But there was this, this—"

"Vulcan mind-meld?" Christopher asked.

"It wasn't a Vulcan mind-meld. I'm not sure what it was. But Pestilence isn't in complete control of his powers out here, and when he read my mind, it...I don't know, it's hard to explain, but I got a flash inside his mind right before he murdered Mindy. I think we can mix up the ritual. That's all I know."

Eddie held up a hand. "Hold that thought." He pulled a pin from another grenade and threw it out in front of them. They all ducked and covered their ears as the explosion cleared out the monsters ahead. "So how do we mix up the ritual?"

"Make the host sacrifice himself. But it has to be a *willing* sacrifice."

"Oh. Well, that's easy. We'll show him flash cards of the people who died and make him feel bad. C'mon, that's no solution. The guy is obviously a moral black hole. If he's willing to cause the deaths of all these people, how on Earth would you get him to sacrifice himself?"

Christopher gestured to his chest. "Do you all see what the demon did to me?"

"Hard to miss."

"A willing sacrifice doesn't have to be selfless. If the host wants the pain to go away badly enough, maybe he'll kill himself."

Eddie gaped at him. "You mean torture him until he commits suicide?"

"Pretty much, yeah."

"That's fucked up."

"Pretty much, yeah."

"He's right, though," said Lee. "Cross-wire the ritual. Kill the host, and things will keep on going the way they are. Turn the host into a sacrifice, and the spell collapses upon itself."

"You're sure?" asked Eddie.

"No."

"Good enough for me." He patted his pocket. "I've got the phone number of the host's babysitter. Now let's get into the air so I can make a call and...*aw, shit.*"

As they stepped into the clearing outside of the water reclamation plant, they looked into the air and saw that the helicopter was gone.

* * *

"Where are you going?" Tina demanded.

"I'm done with this," said the pilot. "Dragons. There are dragons out here. I don't mess with dragons."

"You can't just *leave* them!"

"Turn around," said the reporter. "There are innocent people on the ground."

"Do you know how to fly a helicopter? No? I do. Are we in a helicopter right now? Yes. That puts me in charge. And I say, we get the hell out of here."

"*Turn this fucking helicopter around!*" Tina shouted. "*If you don't go right the fuck back to where the fuck we left my fucking friends I'll rip your fucking throat out and drink your fucking blood!"*

The pilot looked back at her.

"Okay," he said.

* * *

The helicopter came back into view, returning to its original hovering spot. The rope ladder dropped in front of Eddie. He reached for Barbara.

"Here, sweetie, I'll take the kid."

"I hate when you call me sweetie," Barbara told him, lowering Tommy to the ground.

"I'll keep doing it then. C'mon, kiddo, climb on to your Uncle Eddie."

Barbara thought it seemed like a cruel thing to say, since Tommy had lost his aunt and uncle today, but Tommy didn't react. He just climbed onto Eddie's back.

"Watch out!" Lee shouted, pointing to a double-sized wolf as it rushed out from the trees. Lee, Eddie, Christopher, and Barbara opened fire, bringing the wolf down several feet before it could maul them to death.

"I'll save the kid first," said Eddie. "The rest of you follow close, okay? Watch out for the bats. They suck."

Eddie grunted at the strain of his new passenger, but quickly began to scale the rope ladder. Up above, Tina waved her encouragement.

Barbara followed right behind him.

"You first," Lee told Christopher. "You're bleeding more."

Christopher grabbed the first rung. "Thanks."

Eddie was making excellent time, even with Tommy

on his back. The bats made him their first target, bashing into him again and again, but he kept climbing.

Christopher's dizziness had faded, replaced by the excitement of finally being saved. Every single cut on his body felt like it was splitting even wider as he frantically climbed the ladder, but that was okay. Chicks loved scars.

Barbara cried out as a bat bashed against her kidneys, and for one horrifying second Christopher thought she was going to lose her grip. Though her ass would be a pleasant final sight as it plummeted toward him, he preferred that she *not* fall.

As he made it halfway up the ladder, he glanced down to check on Lee. The old man wasn't doing very well. He'd only made it a quarter of the way up the ladder, and had stopped for breath.

"Come on, Lee!" Christopher shouted down at him. "Rest inside the helicopter!"

Lee looked up as if he wanted to say something but merely nodded and reached for the next rung.

Christopher heard a whoop of joy up ahead as Eddie made it to the helicopter. Moments later, Barbara joined him.

Three saved. Two to go.

"Aw, crap," Christopher whispered as an entire flurry of bats zoomed at him. The creatures bashed into him, reminding him of all of the dodgeball horrors he'd endured in elementary school.

His right hand, slick with blood, popped free of the rope ladder.

A bat struck him right in the ear. The dizziness returned.

"Come on, Christopher!" Barbara shouted above him. "You're almost there!"

He wasn't. He was only halfway. But her encouragement was appreciated. He grabbed the ladder again with both hands and pulled himself up one more rung.

A hundred more feet. No big deal. Then he could take a bath in hydrogen peroxide so that he didn't become an infected, pus-dripping freak from all of these exposed wounds.

He climbed another rung, gritting his teeth as more bats struck him. At least they weren't vampire bats trying to suck his blood at the same time. Thank God for little favors.

He glanced back down at Lee, who was now having similar bat problems. He was still at the fifty-foot mark and no longer climbing.

"Keep going!" Christopher shouted.

Three bats struck the old man at once. He lost his grip on the ladder, waved his arms frantically in mid-air for a split second, and then fell to the ground.

He didn't make a sound as he hit.

Before Christopher could even react, the helicopter rose into the air. In seconds, Christopher was dangling over the tops of the trees, holding on for dear life.

"No!" he shouted. "We can't leave yet!"

What the hell were they doing? Hadn't they seen what happened to Lee? Lee had steadfastly refused to leave anybody behind, and now they were going to leave *him* behind?

Something was flying toward the helicopter.

Something huge.

Something that was breathing fire.

CHAPTER THIRTY-SIX

"I told you!" the pilot shouted. "I told you! I told you! Dragon!"

"I see the goddamn dragon," said Eddie. "Get us away from it!" He flipped open the cell phone he'd borrowed from the reporter and punched in the number on the card.

* * *

Mark's phone rang. Unknown number. He hoped to God it was Chloe calling from somebody else's phone. "Hello?" he answered.

"Mark Harper?"

"Yeah." *Please don't be a lawyer or reporter...*

"Eddie Turner. We met earlier. You gave me your...*oh, shit! Pull up! Pull up!*"

Mark heard somebody on the other end shout at Eddie to shut the fuck up and let him fly.

"What's going on?" Mark asked.

"You're a biologist, right?"

"Cryptozoologist."

"Well, forget that. Forget everything you think you know about the forest. You still got Booth with you?"

"Yeah."

"Don't let on what we're talking about. You think it's strange that our boss was on the tour, and wanted to run back into the forest even though just about everybody else got slaughtered? *Pull down! Pull down!*"

"More than a little, yeah."

"Okay, you're going to have to give me some big-time trust on this one, but when you hear what I have to say, keep in mind that trees are popping up everywhere. This ain't science or technology. It's magic. Really bad magic. Wanna save the world?"

"Uh...sure."

"Booth is the key to all of this. He's the host. If you don't want this forest to keep growing forever, you need to take care of Booth."

"Kill him?"

Hannah glanced over at him and raised an eyebrow.

"No! That would be bad."

"Okay, good."

"You have to torture him until he kills himself."

"I beg your pardon?"

"*Swerve left! No, right! No, left! Fuck!*"

Mark almost asked what was going on, but decided that he didn't want to know.

Really bad magic. Yeah, he was a man of science, but he also was not a complete idiot. Though they studied the forest and its inhabitants as scientific phenomena, it was understood by all that a forest did not sprout up fully formed in a matter of hours without *something* else going on.

There were ghosts, for Christ's sake.

It was haunted.

It was magic.

"You still there?" asked Eddie.

"Yeah."

"You need to stop whatever you're doing, and make our boss want to kill himself. You need to do it fast. The entire town of Dover's Point has been consumed—"

And Chloe along with it...

"—and more are gonna follow. Make him want to die. Make the host want to kill himself. You can't just kill him, he has to *want* it. Understand?"

"I'm not—"

"*Oh shit, don't let it—!*"

The phone went dead.

Mark pulled over to the side and turned off the car's engine. "Who was that?" Booth asked.

Mark looked at his boss in the rearview mirror. His boss who'd been on the tram for no reason, on the very tour where everything went to hell. His boss who had to be forced out of the forest at gunpoint. His boss who'd been talking to somebody who wasn't there.

He'd never met Eddie before today. The guy could be a complete whack-job. Or he could be the one responsible for all of this.

Mark turned around to face Booth. "Are you the host?"

There was a flash of concern on Booth's face, and then he frowned. "What are you talking about?"

The flash was all Mark needed. He leaned over and punched his ex-boss in the face, as hard as he could.

* * *

Tears streamed down Lee's face as he lay on the ground in a crumpled heap. He'd landed feet-first, and if the bones weren't shattered into a million pieces, it was at least a thousand.

They'd left him behind to die.

Not that he could blame them. You couldn't get an old man with two broken legs up a two-hundred-foot rope ladder.

So this was how he died. Alone in the forest, easy pickings for the ravenous inhabitants.

Well, not *that* easy. Eddie had given him a pistol and some clips of ammunition. He could fend off the monsters for a little while longer, anyway. He'd shoot them until he had no bullets left, and then he'd throw his empty gun at them, and then he'd throw goddamn leaves at them until they finally got the better of him. It might be a pathetic fight, but Lee was going down fighting.

His legs didn't even hurt all that much. He wondered if that was because he was dying.

* * *

The helicopter veered sharply to the left. The rope ladder trailed behind it like a flapping tail on a kite. Christopher clenched the rope so tightly that he thought his knuckles might burst. There was no way he could climb right now, so he just had to hold on.

And do a lot of screaming.

The dragon missed the helicopter by less than ten feet. It was moving so quickly that it sailed past its target and kept going.

Above, he could see Barbara and Tina struggling to pull up the rope ladder. They didn't seem to be making much progress, but every inch helped, assuming that the dragon were to miss him by a single inch, which seemed unlikely.

The dragon, which was hundreds of feet away, flew in a half-circle and then headed toward them again, wings flapping vigorously. Huge bursts of fire jettisoned from its mouth.

It was going to be upon them in a matter of seconds.

The helicopter abruptly veered upward, and the dragon sailed underneath Christopher's feet, missing by quite a bit more than an inch but not by nearly enough to keep him from wetting himself.

He screamed some more.

* * *

"What did you do?" Hannah screamed, as Booth slumped over onto his side. "Why the hell did you punch Booth?"

"Do you trust me?" Mark asked.

"Well not *now*!"

"I need you to trust me, because things are going to get more fucked up than you can imagine." Mark got out of the car, opened the passenger seat and dragged Booth out.

"Have you gone mad?" Booth asked.

Mark punched him again, knocking him against the car. One more punch to the face and Booth dropped to the ground, stunned.

"Mark! What's going on?" Hannah had gotten out of the car, and she rushed over as if to stop him.

"Don't come near me, Hannah," Mark warned. "Not until you hear me out."

He told her, quietly so that Booth couldn't hear.

Her reaction was predictable: "What the *fuck*?"

"It all makes sense," Mark said. "Well, no, no, it doesn't make sense at all, but there's *something* going on, and this is the only solution that makes any sense whatsoever, even if it makes no sense. Am I making sense?"

"No!"

Booth rubbed some blood from the side of his mouth. "He's gone insane, Hannah. You'd better run."

"Tell her that you're the host," Mark said. "Tell her what's going on."

"Nothing's going on."

"Then why were you on the tram?"

"I wanted to see the tour."

"Why did you want to go back into the forest?"

Booth was silent.

"Listen to me, Hannah, I realize this is one big-ass leap of faith, but we don't have anything else except a forest that's growing and that probably—" his voice cracked "—killed Chloe."

"I'm sure she's fine."

"I'm sure she's *not* fine!" Mark pointed to Booth. "And it's his fucking fault!"

"I did nothing! Hannah, don't listen to this madman. Get away from him. For your own safety, get away from him."

Hannah looked at Booth, and then she looked at Mark.

"Okay, Mark, what do you need me to do?"

"Get me some things out of the trunk."

* * *

The helicopter dove down to avoid another dragon attack. The lower half of the rope ladder slapped against the treetops, and Christopher sincerely hoped that one of the rungs wouldn't get caught on a branch and snap the whole thing off.

Above, Barbara and Tina were still trying to pull him to safety. Now only fifty feet separated him from his ridiculously precarious position and a "still not particularly safe considering that there's a fire-breathing dragon in hot pursuit but still substantially better than what he had going on at the moment" position.

The helicopter dipped lower, and Christopher's legs bashed against the treetops. It hurt a lot worse than when the bird had made this happen. He focused every bit of his attention on maintaining his grip on the rope.

Then he lost it.

* * *

Mark looked at the man in front of him, now tied up with nylon rope, and contemplated how to proceed. He'd never tortured anyone before. Once, as a child, he pulled the legs off a grasshopper, but got so upset over what he'd done that he'd ran inside and tearfully confessed everything to his mother.

He looked in the toolbox again and pulled out a socket wrench. Really not what he was looking for.

Tire gauge? No.

Tape measure? No.

X-ACTO knife? That had potential.

Hannah paced nearby. Now and then she'd stop and look at him for a moment and then she'd go back to pacing. She didn't seem particularly cool with this whole idea, but that was okay, because he wasn't particularly cool with it, either.

But it had to be done.

God, how he hoped that it truly had to be done, and that he wasn't just about to commit the worst atrocity of his life for no reason.

He picked up the X-ACTO knife, walked over, and crouched down next to Booth.

Then he threw up.

* * *

Lee shot something that looked like an emaciated child—but with fangs—between the eyes. His best shot so far of the two clips of ammunition that he'd used up.

Too bad there wasn't a photographer around. If he survived this, the image of him on the ground, legs twisted and mangled, a gun in his hand, would make quite the author photo for the back of his next book.

The helicopter flew overhead, and for a split second he thought they'd returned to save him. Maybe they'd gone to get a stretcher.

Nope. It flew past, moving too quickly for him to believe that they'd even considered making a stop to pick up ol' Lee.

A moment later, he realized that a dragon was in pursuit.

Okay.

Hmmmmmm.

Maybe the broken old man lying on the ground and using up all of his ammunition was going to be the final survivor of the Haunted Forest Tour after all.

* * *

The first incision he made simply cut open Booth's pant leg. The second drew a line of blood down Booth's actual leg, from his knee to his ankle.

Booth let out yowl of pain.

"Oh, God, I'm sorry!" said Mark before he could stop himself. Pretty hard to project the image of a cold-hearted torturer if he apologized to his victims for hurting them.

Hannah stepped back away and gagged.

Mark didn't figure there was much chance that Booth was ready to end his own suffering yet, so he grabbed the ridiculously expensive shoe off his left foot and then sat down on both of the man's legs to keep struggling to a minimum.

"What are you doing?" Booth sounded justifiably worried.

"Saving the world. I hope."

"Don't do this, Mark! I can make you a very powerful man!"

"I'll pass." Mark pulled off the sock on Booth's left foot and noticed that every toe was perfectly manicured. That was a little annoying, because he was still suffering from two ingrown toenails, himself. Considering the current state of his employment, he'd probably have to live with them for a while.

"You killed my wife, Booth. This is going to hurt."

"I didn't kill anybody!"

Mark ran the blade into the bottom of Booth's foot and held on tight as the man tried to kick and escape. Just to make sure he'd gotten his point across, he carved a second line into the sole, closing his eyes so he wouldn't have to look at the blood.

Ironically, Mark was completely against the idea of the United States using torture to gain information from its enemies. But he wasn't trying to gain information here. He was trying to counteract a spell that spawned a haunted forest and released giant wyrms. When magic and wyrms were involved, he had to switch to a slightly different set of core values regarding the subject of torture.

Booth kicked like a fish desperate to get off the hook and back into the water, but Mark held on. He moved the blade down again and drove it deep into the fleshy pad of the heel as Booth cursed God several times.

"I don't think calling Him names is gonna help you right now."

Booth flailed around some more.

Mark opened his eyes and saw the damage he'd done. The bottom of the man's foot looked like he'd gone skating on razor blades.

He threw up again.

He looked away and saw Hannah staring at him.

"I don't know if I can keep doing this."

"It's either you or me, Mark, and I *know* I can't do it."

Mark returned his attention to Booth. "So what if I offered you a way to make all of the pain go away, forever?" *Until you end up in hell, you son of a bitch.*

"Fuck you!"

"I was afraid of that." He started sawing away at the big toe. *Just think of it as an autopsy. An autopsy on somebody who isn't dead yet. But a "save the world" kind of autopsy.*

He worked the meat most of the way off the bone, but there was no way in hell the thin little blade was going to cut through the remaining digit. Booth was screaming so loud that it was literally painful to be next to him, although certainly not as painful as to *be* him.

Hannah reached into the tool chest and pulled out a pair of pliers and a large set of toenail clippers he'd been looking for since last July.

"Would these help?"

Mark looked them over and finally nodded. "Yeah."

Her hand shook a bit as she handed them over. His hand shook, too.

"You're doing fine," she said. "All things considered."

He opened the pliers and placed them against the bloodied ruin of a big toe.

Booth screamed.

* * *

Tina had to admit that she felt kind guilty about forcing the pilot to stay in the air despite his dragon-related concerns.

Still, until the beast let loose with a blast of flame that instantly melted the helicopter's propeller, he'd been doing a pretty good job of keeping them out of harm's way.

The helicopter went down, leaving a trail of black smoke.

CHAPTER THIRTY-SEVEN

A wave of revulsion and self-loathing struck Mark with such intensity that he dropped the pliers.

"Suddenly decide to become human?" asked Booth, the sarcasm obvious even though his voice was barely a croak.

"Shut up. Just shut up."

"Mark, you have to see this through," Hannah insisted.

"I can't. It's not worth it."

He wiped the perspiration from his forehead. That was it. He couldn't do this anymore. Let Eddie hire a professional if he was so damned sure that this was the way to go. Mark didn't have it in him.

Nevertheless, he went to his trunk, opened the gun case, and took out a pistol. Then he returned to where Booth sat and crouched down next to him.

"Open up."

"No."

"I said, open up."

"Just gonna kill me now? Hide the evidence of what you've done?"

"No, Booth. I'm going to let you in on a little secret.

By taking your own life, you can save the lives of thousands, maybe millions of people. You can stop this forest infestation and the killing machines that come with it. One life for a million. Your life. I think it's worth it."

"Why don't you blow your own brains out, Mark? Put yourself out of your misery."

"I'll find it in myself to keep going. I'll slice your leg until there's nothing left of it. I'll find ways to create pain so excruciating that you'll *beg* me to let you put this gun into your mouth. Why go through that, Booth?"

Mark pressed the barrel of the gun against Booth's closed lips.

"This is your last chance to make the pain go away."

Behind him, Hannah screamed.

Mark had wanted Hannah since the day he met her. Chloe was his wife, but Hannah was his love. Only cowardice, and the self-delusion that he was an honorable, devoted husband, is what kept him from leaving his wife for his co-worker.

So when she screamed, he reacted.

He spun around.

A Giggler had leapt onto her shoulder, knocking her to her knees.

Before Mark could make a move to save her, Booth twisted the gun around in his hands.

There was a white-hot burst of pain as the bullet tore through his right ear.

The soft cartilage was not enough to slow its velocity, and the bullet punched into Hannah's forehead.

She dropped face-forward onto the ground.

And then, in what seemed like a conscious attempt by the Haunted Forest to mock him, a tree burst through the ground directly underneath her, carrying Hannah and the Giggler that feasted upon her away from him.

* * *

Christopher broke through branch after branch, hoping one of them would slow his fall without impaling him. He struck an especially large one, and his blood rained down upon the forest floor.

He lay in the branches and wondered what kind of creature would get him first. Maybe another panther.

"Christopher!"

He looked down. Nope. Not a panther. Pestilence.

The demon was not grinning.

* * *

One clip left.

Lee had no plans to save a final bullet for himself. If he had to get eaten, he'd get eaten.

* * *

The helicopter smashed through the treetops, coming to a sudden stop as it wedged between two trees. All of the glass shattered on impact, spraying everybody on board.

The passengers remained silent for a long moment.

"I *told* you there was a dragon!" the pilot shouted.

Eddie looked around. "Is everybody alive?"

Barbara plucked some glass out of her arm. "I think so."

Tina, Tommy, and the reporter all acknowledged that they, too, were still alive.

One of the trees couldn't handle the weight and began to bend. The helicopter popped free and fell the remaining distance to the ground with a crash that completely crumpled the underside of the vehicle.

"What now?" Eddie asked.

* * *

Getting the gun away from Booth was easy. So was breaking his arm to make sure it didn't happen again.

Hearing Booth's screams was not, since the gunshot had deafened Mark, most likely for good.

Tears streamed down his face as he returned to the trunk of his car. Tears for Hannah, not for what he was about to do.

He grabbed the jumper cables.

Raised the front hood of the car.

Hooked them up.

Used the X-ACTO knife to cut away Booth's pants while the man screamed silently.

Cut away his underwear.

Hooked up the other end of the jumper cables.

And then turned on the engine.

* * *

"I see that you didn't get out of the forest, Christopher," said Pestilence. "Pity for you. I think I'll make you my own personal toy. Doesn't that sound like fun?" Despite the demon's words, there was no trace of the playful nature from before.

"Is that supposed to scare me?"

"Yes, actually. Doesn't it?"

"What I've seen of you is that you can kill an old lady. But, of course, you have to catch her off guard and make sure she *wants* you to kill her. Tough demon, huh?"

"So what is this, Christopher? The part where your words anger me to the point where I make a foolish mistake?"

"Nah. Just making conversation."

"Babble all you want. The forest continues to grow. Things did not work out exactly the way I planned, but they worked out well enough. You'll get to swim upstream in vast rivers of blood, Christopher."

"Why would I swim upstream? Is that just part of your effort to make things sound scary?"

Now Pestilence grinned. "I like you. I like Lee, too. Both of you would've made excellent hosts. Oh well. Instead I'll have to kill you. Why don't you come down from that tree and fight?"

Without hesitation, Christopher leapt upon him.

* * *

"I'm alive," said Tina.

"Me too," Barbara added.

The pilot gave Eddie the finger, which he interpreted as another negative comment about the fact that they hadn't heeded the dragon warning.

"So am I," said the reporter, seconds before clawed hands dragged him out of the aircraft and turned that statement into a lie. His blood splashed into the open door as Eddie shot the multi-mouthed creature that had taken him.

Tina fired a shot through what had been the windshield.

More and more forest monsters approached, seeking a feast.

* * *

Lee had two bullets left. Should he shoot the spider, the Medusa-looking thing, the imp, or the giant ant?

He shot the Medusa-looking thing, but missed the imp.

* * *

Booth shrieked and sobbed and begged for mercy, but as Mark crouched next to him again, Booth's eyes widened in realization that no mercy was coming.

Except in the form of the gun that Mark gently placed in his mouth.

Booth allowed him to push it in.

Mark kept a firm grip on the weapon so there could be no further issues, but Booth curled his finger around the trigger and squeezed, spraying blood and brain matter all over Mark's car.

Mark Harper tossed the gun aside, buried his face in his hands, and wept.

* * *

Pestilence did not let out a grunt as Christopher smashed into him, but the demon was clearly surprised. Christopher attacked like a rabid animal. He had nothing to lose. Might as well fuck up this demon as much as he could.

He threw blow after blow against the demon's chest,

until Pestilence favored him with a punch to the face that knocked Christopher back at least ten feet and onto his ass, though it thankfully did not take off his head.

"What are you trying to accomplish, Christopher? You think you can beat me in a *fistfight?*"

It took every ounce of strength he had, but Christopher stood up. "Maybe. Or maybe I'm just trying to piss you off."

He could imagine how pathetic he looked. Beat-up, covered with blood from head to toe, legs wobbling as he tried to keep from falling back on his ass. But he had determination. The demon killed his mother. It was going to pay. Maybe not pay a *lot*, but it was going to pay.

"I admire your spirit, Christopher," said Pestilence. "Unfortunately, I think it's time to end this little comparison of penis sizes and..."

The demon trailed off.

The tree next to him sunk into the ground.

"Oh, no..."

The tree next to that one did the same thing.

"Oh, no...*no!*"

All around them, trees began sinking into the forest floor. Pestilence let out a howl of fury and then wrapped his arms around one of them, as if he could keep it upright through brute strength. It slipped through his arms and vanished.

"NOOOOOOOOOOOO!"

* * *

The giant ant sunk into the ground as if it were quicksand, followed immediately by the imp and the spider.

Lee watched the trees around him sink into the ground and decided that maybe he wasn't quite so screwed after all.

* * *

Eddie and the others scrambled out of the helicopter, only to be greeted by the sight of the dragon hurtling down directly toward them. The pilot screamed and covered his face, while Eddie fired a couple of useless shots into the air.

The dragon slammed into the ground next to them and disappeared, leaving an enormous hole.

"What the hell...?" Eddie asked, as the trees around him began to sink.

* * *

Mark watched the tree in front of him sink into the ground, bringing Hannah down with it. The Giggler took one last bite out of her neck before it disappeared with the tree.

Hannah's corpse did not disappear.

Mark crawled over to her. "I'm sorry," he whispered. "Oh, God, I'm sorry."

He'd saved the world, maybe. But right now, he didn't give a shit.

* * *

Pestilence roared as his foot sank into the forest floor. Most of the trees were already gone, but the demon yanked frantically as his other foot began to sink as well.

Christopher walked toward him. For a moment he thought he was going to lose his balance, but he managed to keep going.

"You know who this is for," he said, punching the demon so hard that the bones in his hand broke with an audible *snap*. Christopher didn't care. What was one more injury?

The demon sunk to his waist and grabbed for Christopher's leg. Christopher stepped back out of the way, and this time he did lose his balance. He fell, and then watched the shrieking demon disappear from sight.

Christopher hurt everywhere, but he felt good.

* * *

And even more quickly than it had sprouted, the Haunted Forest disappeared.

EPILOGUE

Christopher walked down the hallway, ignoring the stares.

Under his clothes, he was covered in gauze from his neck down to his feet, making it look like he'd gone on an eating binge and put on a shitload of weight.

The process of cleaning out the cuts sucked almost as much as receiving them in the first place, but they'd heal. His body would be Scar City, but they'd heal.

Lee wasn't going to get out of the hospital anytime soon. He talked excitedly about the new book he was going to write, and had even asked Christopher to proofread the first few pages. Christopher suggested that he wait to write the book until he was no longer on morphine. Lee promised to consider that advice.

Barbara was doing fine. Milking the publicity. She'd probably become an actress or a model after all this. He was pretty sure that "tour guide" was off her list of career aspirations.

Eddie was milking it even more than Barbara. Christopher was genuinely grateful to the ex tram driver for saving his life and stuff, but he was also a bit sick of seeing him on every freakin' channel. There was word that he was in talks to endorse the same brand of grenade that had saved their lives. Christopher didn't even know that grenade brands *had* endorsements. Still, he couldn't begrudge the guy his fifteen minutes of fame.

Tina...well, she'd thanked him for coming to Brad's funeral, and she cried when he told her how proud Brad would've been of the way she handled herself, and they never really spoke after that.

Tommy was with his parents. Christopher had talked to the little boy on the phone, and Tommy had told him all about the new Transformers action figure they'd bought him. His mother confided that Tommy screamed in his sleep, and he didn't much like his counselor because she "smelled funny," and he clearly wasn't the same little boy they'd sent on a fun tour with his aunt and uncle, but he'd be okay. They hoped.

H.F. Enterprises was in complete disaster-recovery mode. The last Christopher heard, they were trying to blame the entire thing on an employee named Mark Harper. He'd apparently tortured and shot Martin Booth, the owner of H.F. Enterprises, and also shot his co-worker Hannah Chambers. Nobody had found him yet.

Christopher had told the authorities, the government, and everybody else who questioned him the entire story, leaving nothing out. He didn't know what would happen to Mark if they did catch him, but he'd stated everything he knew about Pestilence for the record. If things had really happened the way Christopher suspected they did, the man was a hero, even if he'd achieved it in a rather stomach-churning fashion.

They'd recovered his mother's body and buried it next to his father. Her tombstone said "Happy Halloween."

Christopher knocked.

"Come in," said Mr. Tylerson.

Christopher stepped into his boss's office. Mr. Tylerson looked surprised to see him. "Christopher! I didn't expect to see you anytime soon!"

"Sorry I missed our Monday meeting. I've been kind of busy for the last week."

Mr. Tylerson didn't seem quite sure how to respond to that, so he merely fidgeted with his tie.

Christopher leaned across the desk and spoke very clearly. "Mr. Tylerson, thank you for allowing me to slave away at Novellon for all these years, but as of now, I quit. Oh, and fuck you."

He walked out of the office, feeling good.

Damned good.

- The End -

OTHER BOOKS BY JEFF STRAND

Stranger Things Have Happened
An Apocalypse Of Our Own
Cyclops Road
Blister
The Greatest Zombie Movie Ever
Kumquat
Facial
I Have a Bad Feeling About This
Pressure
Dweller
A Bad Day For Voodoo
Dead Clown Barbecue
Dead Clown Barbecue Expansion Pack
Wolf Hunt
Wolf Hunt 2
The Sinister Mr. Corpse
Benjamin's Parasite
Kutter
Faint of Heart
Graverobbers Wanted (No Experience Necessary)
Single White Psychopath Seeks Same
Casket For Sale (Only Used Once)
Lost Homicidal Maniac (Answers to "Shirley")
Suckers (with JA Konrath)
Gleefully Macabre Tales

JAMES A. MOORE & JEFF STRAND

The Severed Nose
Disposal
Elrod McBugle on the Loose
Out of Whack
How to Rescue a Dead Princess
Draculas (with JA Konrath, F. Paul Wilson, and Blake Crouch)

For information on all of these books, visit Jeff Strand's more-or-less official website at http://www.jeffstrand.com

Subscribe to Jeff Strand's free monthly newsletter at http://eepurl.com/bpv5br

OTHER BOOKS BY JAMES A. MOORE

Under the Overtree
Serenity Falls: Writ in Blood
Serenity Falls: The Pack
Serenity Falls: Dark Carnival
Little Boy Blue
Vendetta
Cherry Hill
Smile No More
Seven Forges
The Blasted Lands
City of Wonders
The Silent Army
The Last Sacrifice (Tides of War)
Blind Shadows (with Charles R. Rutledge)
Congregations of the Dead (with Charles R. Rutledge)
Subject Seven
RUN!
Possessions
Newbies
Rabid Growth
Vampire: The Eternal Struggle: House of Secrets (with Kevin Andrew Murphy)
Werewolf: Hell-Storm
Buffy the Vampire Slayer: Chaos Bleeds
Fireworks

Blood Red
Bloodstained Oz (with Christopher Golden)
Bloodstained Wonderland (with Christopher Golden)
Deeper
Slices
Harvest Moon
The Wild Hunt
Homestead
Alien: Sea of Sorrows

For information on these books, visit James A. Moore's website at http://jamesamoorebooks.com

.

Printed in Great Britain
by Amazon